WHALEBONE

THE THIRD DOCTOR SIX NOVEL

James Rozhon

Gotham Books

30 N Gould St.
Ste. 20820, Sheridan, WY 82801
https://gothambooksinc.com/

Phone: 1 (307) 464-7800

© 2023 James Rozhon. All rights reserved.

No part of this book may be reproduced, stored in a retrieval system, or transmitted by any means without the written permission of the author.

Published by Gotham Books (March 3, 2023)

ISBN: 979-8-88775-193-1 (sc)
ISBN: 979-8-88775-194-8 (e)

Because of the dynamic nature of the Internet, any web addresses or links contained in this book may have changed since publication and may no longer be valid.

The views expressed in this work are solely those of the author and do not necessarily reflect the views of the publisher, and the publisher hereby disclaims any responsibility for them.

TABLE OF CONTENTS

Chapter 1 6
Chapter 2 12
Chapter 3 19
Chapter 4 25
Chapter 5 30
Chapter 6 35
Chapter 7 41
Chapter 8 49
Chapter 9 54
Chapter 10 61
Chapter 11 67
Chapter 12 74
Chapter 13 81
Chapter 14 88
Chapter 15 93
Chapter 16 98
Chapter 17 104
Chapter 18 109
Chapter 19 117
Chapter 20 122
Chapter 21 127

Chapter 22	132
Chapter 23	138
Chapter 24	145
Chapter 25	151
Chapter 26	157
Chapter 27	163
Chapter 28	169
Chapter 29	174
Chapter 30	180
Chapter 31	185
Chapter 32	192
Chapter 33	199
Chapter 34	204
Chapter 35	209
Chapter 36	213
Chapter 37	217
Chapter 38	222
Chapter 39	230
Chapter 40	235
Chapter 41	239
Chapter 42	244

CHAPTER 1

I rolled onto my back and the voices were still there. *Doctor? The pain starts to the left of my stomach and lasts all day.* Or. *My knees are so weak that I can't stand unless I use my arms.* Or. *I see odd things floating in the air. Then they change position when I blink.* Or. *I can't feel my left toe.* Or. *My left shoulder hurts when I sleep on it. It wakes me up.* There seemed to be nothing I could do to make them go away either. Who do the voices belong to? Patients. Who am I? Doctor Evangeline Monica Sixkiller-Collins Collins. Doctor Six for short.

The voices were why I was two miles north of Kevin, Montana, in an RV park that Mario, my husband, arranged to be empty of everyone except mine and Wanda Lansing's family. Seventy-six spaces, all empty, but us. It cost a smuggler's fortune to arrange, but he knew I needed it. I hadn't allowed myself a vacation in fourteen months. Exhaustion didn't begin to cover how I felt. Complete exhaustion didn't either.

I sighed. I needed to go jogging but I wanted to stay in bed because Mario crawled into it and I curled under his arm. He's a safe harbor, mine. "I'm a mess," I whined.

He held me tighter and said the one thing that started the whole chain reaction. "Hey. I love your new attempt to grow fat and lazy." I didn't hear the next sentence. He smiled, held me tighter and said, "Don't worry. Just relax. You deserve it." No, I didn't hear his unconditional support of me. I heard "fat and lazy". I love him immensely and I know he loves me. But as a prod, it didn't get much more pointed or sharp than that.

Exasperation and exhaustion don't make good companions. I know because his words pushed me off the bed, out from under his comforting arm and to my knees where I actually pulled my hair and growled at him. "I'm going jogging with Wanda," I managed to say with as much grace as I thought the situation required.

"Does she know?" he asked, smiling from his position on the bed.

My answer was another growl.

Our RV is a motor home. No, I don't know who made it, what year it is or any of those technical details. That's Mario's function. I know less about Wanda's. Hers is a trailer because she pulls it with a pickup that has a big hitch in it. I've heard the term "fifth wheel" to describe it but that's as far I can push the subject of "RV vacationing" and how it relates to her rig.

Since I knew Maddy, my daughter, and Becky, Wanda's daughter, were in her trailer playing with their generation's latest attempt to rip off Barbie, I didn't bother to knock. I opened the door and yelled inside, "Hey, Lansing! Get your running shoes on because we're going!"

She was sitting cross-legged on the floor with Maddy on one side of her and Becky on the other side. Maddy screamed that," It isn't fair! You're short and I'm the green giant!"

Becky screamed back, "And I'm Tinkerbell and you're cute! It isn't fair!"

Wanda put her arms around them and said, "How about Maddy staying here with me and Becky going with Evie?"

Well, naturally. Maddy jumped toward me and Becky sprang toward Wanda. Travis, my son, picked that moment to walk past the trailer and say to his best friend, Woody, "And that is what stupid sisters look like."

All Woody said was, "Dude." As near as I can tell, all males are born with a one-word vocabulary and that's it. The females in their lives add more as they age. As his mother, it was my job to add a few more. "Travis?" I smiled at him. "C'mere." He sighed, hung his head as though the gallows were summoning him and came to where I sat in the door. "And this is what a mother looks like." I hugged him and tousled his hair.

His response was like every boy before him. "Mom!"

They ran off and I leaned into the coach and said to Wanda, "I'll wait outside."

It took only a few moments before we were jogging toward the park exit. Leave it to her. "Why do you jiggle and I don't?"

"Genetics," I said grumpily.

"Ah, the good senator gave you all her best ones?"

My mother, Melodie Chang, is the junior US Senator from Maine. "Yep," I said a bit harshly holding my hands over my breasts. "And good old Mom could have kept some of her genes to herself." She won the election last year and her rack is better than mine. Yes, she's fifty-seven years old and hers is *still* better than mine.

"I should be so lucky," she scolded me.

Kevin Road can be unbearably boring. While there are hills off to the left and badlands in the distance, the road is nothing but a dirt trail running north toward nowhere and south toward the town that gave the road its name. Perfect for jogging, in other words. Wanda is my best friend, but she can be a pain, too. For example, as we jogged – and she can pace me step-for-step – she put her hands to her chest and said, "At least mine aren't in danger of falling off when we do stuff like this."

My response was sharp, incisive and rational. "Shut up."

That's when my life began to swerve off-road a little. We saw a group of men in the distance off to our left. What colored them as a *bit* different were their uniforms. They were the color of the uniforms the cavalry guys wear in movie westerns. You know, hard dark blue with the yellow shoulder patches. Those uniforms. The guns were modern, though. Rifles. That's all I knew about them. I stopped and said, "Let's go back the other way." I don't like guns. The fact that there were thirty or so of them added to my decision to turn around.

My life would have continued normally but for one reason. The damned Hummer one of them drove. As soon as the guy standing in the sunroof saw me, binoculars went to his face, trained on us and then the guy standing there barked an order. The Hummer came to life like a great beast, headed toward us and my life went from being mildly stressful to outright scary.

Trust me. We tried to run. We went from jogging to running and still the Hummer paced us, passed us and brought us to a stop in the middle of the dirt road when it crossed our path completely. The guy in the top of the Hummer, ducked down through the door and stood facing us as though we were in boot camp and he wore the biggest boot. With crisp precision, he pulled something that I assumed to be a photograph, held it next to my face and announced, "Sixkiller."

"Collins," I corrected him, my hands on my hips.

He had a gun in a holster on his hip. He put his hand on it just as the driver's door opened and a young man got out and held his rifle level to the ground at both Wanda and me. Trust Wanda.

"Oh, for pity sakes," she said and turned her back on them. "Of all the idiots in Montana I have to get the two top-ranked ones on the same day in the same place."

"You both have children," the first, as yet unnamed, man said.

Wanda threw her hands into the air and said with her back still to them, "And you figure that by killing and/or threatening our kids that we'll help you. There's an old Anglo-Saxon word that applies here. If I need to tell you what that word is, then you've made it to the top of yet another list."

Hmmm. I looked at the first guy and asked, "You got a name or a title or a favorite odor?" I asked. "Because I smell garlic. Pizza, I figure."

The first guy's jaw went wobbly and the second guy deferred to him. Still, he pulled himself fully erect and announced his name as, "Colonel Daniel Freeman of the First Citizen's Militia of Montana." Then he grunted toward the goon with the rifle and said, "Private Donor."

Wanda sputtered into laughter and said to him, "Dude? With a name like that, you really need another job."

Donor grew agitated but Freeman turned and barked, "At ease, private!"

That settled Donor. Well, except for the hatred in his eyes toward Wanda. I figured I had a place on his list only because I knew Wanda.

Freeman walked directly between Wanda and me and said lowly, "Please accompany me," as he passed us.

I shrugged to Wanda and said, "Babysit the jerk with the gun. I'll be back."

Freeman walked maybe twenty feet up the road and I followed him. He stood with his back to both the Hummer and to Private Donor. He stood with his hands clutched tightly behind his back. I'd put his age at around thirty-five. Militarily short brown hair and clean-shaven, Freeman was making an enormous attempt to appear disciplined. His race up that road in a Hummer canceled it out, however. I thought his actions portrayed him as desperate. The corollary was that desperate people with guns are a bad combination. I decided to listen and drop my antagonisms. "So?" I said. "What's so important that it took thirty armed men to talk to me?" Okay. Maybe I hadn't dropped my antagonisms. I still heard "fat and lazy" in my mind.

As an aside? I noticed the slightly yellowish tinge to his face and hands. I immediately thought, "he has liver issues," but kept it to myself. As another aside? The pigmentation problem I saw in him was slight enough that it was possible no one else knew about it. It was conceivable that he hadn't recognized it either.

His face became troubled and I counted that as another problem. He took a deep breath and said quietly, "I need a doctor." Then he looked at me down the length of his once-broken nose and said, "Quietly. I need to see someone off the record and you have an excellent reputation."

Possibly, everything started right there on that dusty road. Quite possibly. But the real catharsis was still ahead of us. But you remember my exhaustion? You remember how

I said that *complete* exhaustion didn't cover it? Well, damn. This vacation was Mario's idea. He planned and executed it. This? Standing in the middle of nowhere with a gun nut next to me? I reverted to form and became a doctor. I might have been mentally unprepared for what happened, but my basic nature is that of a healer. I hope I succeeded because my life was about to become frantically hectic. And considering that my husband thought I was "fat and lazy", I wasn't really focused.

Except medically.

Always on.

CHAPTER 2

I suppose I shouldn't have been surprised. When the Hummer got us back to the RV park, Mario was gone. Yes, I know. There were four children in the park and, being the only adult, they should have been under his supervision. I knew better when we got to our RV and the four kids were watching the latest DVD. Each of them had a bowl of microwave popcorn, too. No, Mario is a smart man and this had his fingerprints all over it. I wanted to smile but I kept it to myself. Wanda had it figured out, too. I knew that to be true when she winked at me.

I shouldn't have been surprised that Freeman knew it, too. He said as he stepped into the coach after us, "Where's your husband?"

"He was here when I left," I said truthfully.

Wanda rolled her eyes and said, "I wish I could say he was in my pants," she said.

That brought a stern, "Wanda!" from me.

"Hey, he asked," she shrugged. Then her smile became of the wicked variety when she added, "That is one fine man."

Freeman cut into our levity by asking the kids, "Where is your father?"

Travis, who I always figured got more of Mario's genes than Maddy did, just shrugged as he swallowed a huge handful of popcorn, "He said he was going to the moon. In case anyone asks. That's what he said. 'In case anyone asks, I'm going to the moon.' That's it."

Freeman looked angry and frustrated. Given what Becky said next, I don't think his mood improved. "Mister? You look funny."

It didn't matter that I agreed. What mattered is that I knew where Mario had gone. It settled my mind and I said a silent thank you to the smartest man I've ever known. *Mario? When this is over, you're going to get extra specially lucky.* Anyway. He was on the roof of the motor home. I knew that from the night last summer when Mario said to Travis, "Hey, pal. Let's go to the moon." He put his arm around his son and they crawled up onto the roof of the RV and spent an hour up there looking at the stars. When Maddy discovered they'd had more chocolate up there than any two people could eat, she started asking when she could go, too. All three them spent an hour on the roof the next night. It caused me to pout at them, "I like the stars, too." The third night? All four of us spent an hour on the roof of the RV looking at the stars. Travis pointed out the Big Dipper and Orion. Becky pointed out the Pleiades cluster and said, "It's a makeup brush." I thought the night up there was as close to heaven as I'm likely to get. Perfect, peaceful and placid. That described our night to a tee.

Freeman turned to Donor and said, "Go back to the unit and bring them here. We'll start a search for him."

"Yes, sir," Private Donor said, his eyes still angry at Wanda and me. Still, he left. We listened to the sound of the Hummer driving away.

"That's leaves me some time here," Freeman said to me. "Use it wisely, " he said, his hand on his gun.

I looked at Wanda and said, "Take care of stuff. I'll be in your place." Then I looked at Freeman and said, "Let me get my bag."

"Quickly," he said, his hand still on his gun.

I keep my medical bag in our bedroom. It's at the back of the coach, the air vent directly above the bed. If Mario was up there, he knew where I was going because he heard me say it. I went back there, grabbed my bag from the small chest of drawers back there and glanced at the vent. He smiled back. I mouthed, "I'm okay. Don't worry."

"Okay," he mouthed back.

Freeman and I exited the coach and headed next door to Wanda's. Her coach would be empty and that's all I wanted – time alone with a patient.

As soon as we got inside – and alone – he said, "I think I'm sick and I can't allow any of my men to become suspicious."

"Describe your symptoms."

He looked troubled. "I get tired easily. That hasn't happened before." Then he rolled up his left sleeve and revealed a series of bruises that extended from his forearm to his bicep. "I got these last night when I danced with my wife. The marks on my arm are almost exactly where she had her right hand. And she didn't do anything but hold me the same way she'd done many times before. What is this?"

"No other symptoms?" I asked.

"Well," he said thinking. "No. I don't believe so."

"Has your skin always been tinged yellow or is this new?" I said indicating his arm.

He held his arm toward the light coming from the door. Clearly, he'd never noticed it before. He frowned at his arm, then rolled back his other sleeve and held it to the light as well. As near as I could tell, both arms had the same yellowish tint. His frown got deeper. "Look, this is recent. I would have noticed it when I showered."

"It indicates something with your liver, Mr. Freeman."

"Colonel," he said sternly, like an officer to a private.

"I'm not in your army, Freeman. Don't pull rank on me." Then I asked him, "Has your skin always been that dark or is that another symptom as well?" Brown and yellow discoloration of the skin could mark a wider systemic problem. As I waited for an answer, I said, "I'm going to start with your kidneys. I can cut short my vacation and meet you in my office."

That's when I can honestly say that things started. He pulled out his gun and pointed it directly at my face, cocked it and said, "No. You will diagnose and treat me right here. We will be here for the next few days and your treatment of me will be complete in that time."

I don't believe he would have shot me. Call it stupidity on my part, but I actually leaned into the gun barrel until it rested against my forehead. "Go on," I said. "Shoot me." When he didn't, I said, "Look, you need me. I suspect at the very least liver damage to make your skin yellow. But brown? That throws a curve at me that I'm going to need tests to determine. Treat you here? Damn, pretty boy Colonel with your nice fancy gay uniform, but you could die out here unless you stop acting paranoid and let me do my job." Then I swiped the gun aside because his eyes went blank.

"Die?" he said.

"Dramatic effect," I said. "I don't even know what's wrong with you and you won't let me do my job."

Freeman had an interesting face. In another time and place I would have…told him to take two aspirins and call me in the morning. No, I think I've always wanted to be a doctor – and I've never met anyone who as patient with me as Mario has always been. Still, Daniel Freeman's face held equal amounts of courage and paranoia. He held his courage in his jaw line and the way it seemed set on its purpose. He held the paranoia in his eyes. It showed in the way he squinted at me, arrogant and fearful at the same time. But in some small measure, I saw intelligence there as well. He wouldn't shoot me as long as he needed me. However, that didn't stop him from putting the gun back into the middle of my forehead and spitting, "I am not gay!"

I rolled my eyes again and said, "Oh, yada yada. Either shoot me or let me do my job."

"What do you need?" he said, his jaw clenched.

"A sample of your blood and a courier to my office in Kalispell."

"Private Donor could be the courier," he said considering it. "But that's over a hundred miles. Won't the sample deteriorate?"

"That's the beauty of being intelligent and not paranoid. I can think of other things besides my imagined enemies." Then I leaned even closer and said, "I have a secret. It's called ice and our refrigerator can make as much as we want." Then I looked around and said, "But don't tell anyone."

"Funny," he said. "I can give the sample now."

"Back to my place," I said. "I can prepare the sample there and give it to the guy with the real stupid name for a soldier."

"He's a good man," Freeman snapped.

"He's a hothead with a gun," I replied pushing him toward the door.

He shrugged off my arm and pushed it away. "He's a patriot!"

"He's an idiot looking for easy answers just like you!"

Okay, okay. I know better than this. I'd never insulted clients like this before. Not once and my last job was in an ER in Compton, California, before I came to Montana. I worked there for a year and my personal record for seeing the same person more than once was five. I'zzak Jenkins came to the ER where I worked five times in the year I worked there. He may be dead now for all I know because on three of those five times, I'zzak saw me for gunshot wounds. The other two were overdoses. He turned nineteen just before his fourth trip to the ER. Despite my personal feelings toward what he was doing, I was sweet to him, almost motherly. If one of the ER nurses had not been able to translate what I'zzak said, I might never have known what he said to me. Thank you Honor Grant for being there. Thank you for not treating me the way I treated Daniel Freeman.

I sighed, squeezed shut my eyes and said with as much grace as I could muster, "I'm sorry, Mr. Freeman. Colonel Freeman. Let's go get that blood sample and get Private Donor on the road."

He nodded and allowed me to leave Wanda's trailer before he did.

Again, it didn't surprise me in the least that Mario was there when we got back. When Freeman stepped inside our RV, he yelled, "Sergeant Wheeler!"

A hard-faced man with a missing front tooth appeared and snapped off a soldierly, "Yes, sir?"

"Who found this man and where was he found?"

The man I assumed to be Wheeler looked hard at Mario and said, "We're still looking for her husband."

Freeman looked to me and said, "Is this him?"

I smiled at Mario and never doubted his ability to climb down from the roof of the RV and get inside it without being seen. I said, "Yes. This is my husband, Mario."

Mario wiggled his fingers at him.

Freeman asked as though commanding an answer, "Where were you?"

"Takin' a dump," he said sounding like a hick. I kept my smile to myself.

Freeman looked at Wheeler and said, "Get Private Donor to standby at the door and then secure the perimeter."

"Yes, sir," the pretend sergeant said.

Secure the perimeter. Maybe he'd been watching movies and picked up a buzz word. *Collins? Do your job and leave his personality out of it.* It never dawned on me that he caused the rest of his men to scurry to the park buildings, the exits and the property boundary for no other reason than to leave his blood sample without any of them knowing who gave it.

I drew his blood, then secured it inside a tube and put it in a small Styrofoam ice chest. Then I covered it with all the ice in our freezer. Freeman called Donor inside and told him that he'd given permission for me to have a blood sample taken from Mario and driven to my office in Kalispell. I wrote the address on the chest and gave it to Donor. "You know where this is?" I asked him.

He smiled and said, "The Flathead Braves lost the best wrestler in the state when I graduated."

I smiled at him and said, "Please hurry, but don't speed."

"Who's blood is it?" he asked.

"My husband's."

"What's wrong with him?"

"Liver trouble. I'm worried about him."

The last item on my list was a call to Liz Dempsey back in my office. She's the office manager and she's so good that there have been times I had to force her to go home. And take vacations. And take lunch. And have a social life. I grabbed my wallet and rummaged through it until I found her picture. And, yes. I have so many pictures in my purse that I have two wallets. One for money and one for family and friends. The one for family and friends is bigger than the one in which I keep money and credit cards.

I showed it to Donor and said, "Don't give that sample to anyone but her."

"Yes, ma'am," he said.

And that minor blood test became Step Two in what happened. Private Donor left with the sample and I called Liz, my phone on speaker while Freeman listened as patiently as a paranoid could. Liz knew what to do with it. Freeman's sample was marked "John Doe". I told her that and her reply was, "So you don't think I know enough to keep it professional."

"Thanks, Liz."

"Dinner. On me," she replied.

"Sure," I said because she wouldn't relent. She'd keep badgering me about dinner until my entire family sat down with hers. She has a husband and three kids.

Thankfully, none of this would land on them. Just me. Well, and Mario. I swear there are times I think his name is Clark Kent and that he's looking for a phone booth. But that would make me Lois Lane and I hate that bitch. Sorry. I guess I needed this vacation *a lot* more than I thought I did.

Step Three happened the next day.

I didn't have time to fear it.

CHAPTER 3

Despite the empty park, the office and store were still open. We were parked at the opposite end of it from them, so I had to walk past all those empty spaces as I headed for the story to buy batteries for my camera. Yes, yes, I have a battery pack for it, but it's at home on my nightstand *right where I left it*. It's probably fully charged by now and will be ready the next time Mario does something romantic like this. And yes, I count this as a terribly romantic vacation. I don't get to see my kids often enough and I see Wanda at the hospital where she's a an ER nurse more than I see her as a friend.

Travis and Woody were at the park lake. There were trout in it and they wanted to catch dinner. It sounded like fun, so I volunteered to walk to the store to buy batteries for my camera. I wanted more pictures for my wall at home. Wanda offered to come with me, but Becky and Maddy wanted to help with dinner, so she wound up in the kitchen with them. Mario went with the boys.

The building is a long, low white one near the park entrance. There are eight parking spaces in front of the twin doors. They were all empty as I entered. The offices were to the left and consisted of a suite of two that were fronted by a person at a desk. The person was a young man who was talking on the phone. I didn't noticed that he hung up as soon as he saw me. Then he grabbed his sweater and left via the back door. The people inside the offices left, too. Dimly, I heard cars start up and drive away. None of this registered. Behind the counter at the cash register was man that looked like he'd rather be fishing with my kids. He had a blustery red complexion and short red hair. All the signs were there, but because they weren't related to medicine, I missed them all. Worse, I never ever suspected. Anyway. "I need some AA batteries," I said to him.

There was a display of them on a shelf just over his left shoulder. "Sure," he said with a small smile. He turned and said, "Four pack or eight?"

"Four. Don't need more than two."

He took down a four-pack, stared at it and let out a long sigh. "Damn," he said at last. "Expired."

He smiled and it looked comfortable on him. His name tag betrayed it as Beryl. "This is embarrassing," he said. "I have to go into the store room to get more batteries."

"That's okay," I said. "I'm not going anywhere."

"Wait here?" he asked happily.

"Sure," I said.

"Be right back," he answered.

He exited to his left around a corner. Since there were no other people in the park, I was the only customer. I should have suspected something, but I didn't. I was eyeing a Three Musketeer candy bar and trying to paste another five pounds on my expanding butt. No, Mario says it's fine. Then he stares and drools. Okay. He loves me. He's *supposed* to do that sort of stuff. Me? I think my butt is the size of Siberia after a blizzard. That's another way of saying that I got distracted. Maybe what happened wouldn't have worked had I not been considering the caloric consequences of a candy bar.

Well, I'd never know because Beryl peeked from around the corner and whispered conspiratorially, "Psst. C'mere." He even wiggled his fingers at me. He looked at a camera that was above and behind the register and whispered, "No camera. I'd like to give you the batteries because I was such an ass and tried to sell your expired ones. C'mere and just take them."

Just for the record: no, he didn't try to sell them to me. He noticed they were expired and went to get some that weren't. Still, I suspected nothing. It never even dawned on me that they weren't expired and that it probably wouldn't have mattered. I raised my eyes to the camera but didn't turn my head toward it. Then, I smiled and went to where he stood just around the corner.

I ran into a fist. He punched me on the point of my chin and I folded up quicker than Mario did when my mother last played poker with us. Look, I know why you pass out when you get punched on the chin. Your brain hits your skull and out you go from shock. Sure, a punch to the nose will do it, too. Your chin is more muscular, though. It can take more punishment. If asked which I preferred, I wouldn't have been able to choose. Maybe he did me favor by not asking.

Dim flashes of consciousness accompanied me. For example, he groped me. I don't know what that word means to other women, but to me it means that he got a handful of my boobs and fondled me. That other thing? You know, when he put his hand between my thighs? Maybe that means I got groped in two different ways. I don't know. Things were too foggy for me to defend myself. And, no, I would not have been able to it had the opportunity presented itself. All the self-defense I learned from Alex Payne when I was sixteen were useless against someone that hit me like that. He had me. The only other thing he accomplished was silencing me. Otherwise, I would have screamed.

Again, dim flashes of memory suggested that someone carried me out of the building, his right hand cupped around my right breast. Then a car door slammed. Someone laid me on my stomach. Maybe we were in a pickup with a camper shell or some other sort of truck. It didn't matter. My hands were put behind me and I had the odd sensation of being tied. The same thing happened to my ankles. Then my knees were bent and my wrists were tied to my ankles. I think I was waking up. I shook my head and tried to push myself to my feet. I couldn't. Instead, I smelled dirt and dying leaves. If I'd been put in the bed of a pickup, it was dirty. I couldn't use my hands and that didn't compute. I tried again to push myself up and my hands wouldn't work.

A voice above me said, "She's waking."

Another said, "Put her down. We're not clear yet." *Put her down.* I was in the company of abandoned and diseased dogs.

I was pushed onto my side. A hand reached around and pinched my nostrils shut. Then a hand clamped my mouth shut as well. No breath, no way to breathe. Panic. I tried to scream but I couldn't. I tried to take a deep breath but found nothing worked. My struggles grew to be of the futile variety. I thought I was dying. There were sparkles in my eyes and I tried one last time to fight. My lungs felt as though they were going to burst, then I tried one last scream and found my effort wasted. I was dead. Or at least unconscious. In that moment, it didn't matter. All my panic, all my fear, all my frantic yearning to live were gone. If I never woke, I'd never know. But I did. I woke to bouncing.

I wanted water. I wanted to see. I saw nothing. I blinked and still saw no light at all. I got scared and tried to say something. I couldn't speak. I had a ball in my mouth. At least that's what it felt like. My hands were still immobile and my knees were flexed. I hurt. My hands tingled. I tried to move my feet and all I could manage were ineffective wiggles. My jaw hurt. That led to my first coherent thought. *He punched me.* I remembered his name. *Beryl.*

I needed to be able to think. I prized that ability above all others. Despite that, I came to realize I was blindfolded. I closed my eyes and tried to sense my surroundings. *You're tied hand-to-foot. That precludes escaping. But he didn't kill you when he put his hands over your mouth and nose. He wants me alive. Does that give me any bargaining room?* It was worth a dismissive laugh. *Are you kidding? You can't even wipe your nose.* I wiggled my fingers and they tingled. *The rope is too tight. It's cutting off the blood supply to my hands. How long have I have been tied? How much longer can I be tied before damage occurs?*

A hand slid across my butt as a voice – *Beryl's* – said, "I'm untying her feet. I'm not going to carry her again." *Of course not. I must weigh a metric ton.*

"Go ahead. But she stays blindfolded and her hands stay tied until we get inside."

"That's cool," *Beryl's* voice said.

My second worst fear is getting passed around like warm beer. Yeah, second worst. Oh, sure. There are millions of women who would put my present ordeal before just about anything else. Getting fondled and groped – and I *still* don't know if those are the same things – ranks up there, just not at the top. Not being able to think ranks higher, right at the top. I could be wrong, but keeping a cool head seems to be a survival trait among our species. That didn't mean I wasn't scared. I was terrified as he untied my ankles. I had no idea where we were and what their plans were for me. It notched up my anxiety. It notched up again when he pulled my ankles and I slid unceremoniously to a seat of some sort. *You're on the tailgate of a pickup.* A hand wrapped itself in my sweater and pulled me to my feet. "You're with me," he said.

I stumbled over and over, the ground being uneven. He pulled me to a series of steps, then up them. A porch. We were on a porch. A door opened and we were inside a chilly house, or at least a chilly room. I wiggled my hands and they were still securely tied. My hands still tingled.

From the way my shoes echoed across the floor when I walked, I'd say we were over a basement. That supposition proved accurate when I was led down a stairway into it. His hand wrapped tighter around my sweater as we walked down the steps. As my mind struggled to clear itself, I saw his grip as a positive thing; he did not want me to stumble and fall. I had value. Maybe as an appetizer for warm beer, but value. That fact alone made me feel a bit better.

That feeling went away when my hand were untied, I was pushed against a pillar and then my hands were tied again. Had that ball not been stuffed in my mouth, I would have asked them not to tie my hands so tightly. Still, I took those few moments to flex them, roll them and get the circulation flowing again. Once my hands were tied again, the knots were tighter than before. Tape went around the pillar and then around my neck. Then my ankles were fastened to pillar in the same manner. I was theirs to do with what they wanted.

I thought I had that part figured out when my sweater was ripped from me. Then my pants. My sweater dangled in shreds from my wrists and my pants were around my ankles. I thought I knew what they wanted from me at long last. I was that appetizer. A man – *Beryl* I assumed – unhooked my bra and then pinched my nipples. It hurts worse than you can imagine. Sure, there are worse pains, but that one humiliates a bit more than a lot of others. I expected anything except what happened.

"Leave her," the second voice said. "We have better things to do than mess with her."

"Yeah," Beryl said. "But she's nice."

There was a pause during which I imagined he leered at me. Maybe he did. Maybe he decided that his appetizer would be nice when he partook of it. Maybe anything. But his words were anything but those of a man who had plans for me *later*.

"We have things to do that don't include her. Let's go."

Beryl agreed. "Yeah." At least he sounded reluctant.

Yeah, score one for the broad with the fat ass.

CHAPTER 4

Time means nothing when you're blindfolded. A minute becomes an hour, an hour becomes a day. Conversely, an hour becomes a moment and a day becomes a memory. It's worse when you're tied to a post and forgotten.

My first sensations after the blunt savagery of being striped, was the chill in the air. Not cold, but enough to want my thin sweater back. I rolled my fists and discovered that the knots gave a bit. My hands were no longer tingling. Still, they were useless if someone found me and wanted to do things that *Beryl* found repulsive. Yeah, can you believe it? I felt insulted for a while that neither Beryl nor the faceless man found me attractive enough to rape. That passed, though. Thankfully, because I began to think about my situation.

First, I had no idea where I was. But. *You were taken by pickup, girl. If it was a four-wheel drive rig, then you could be anywhere off-road.* The most logical place might the hills directly west of the park. It's isolated and smack in the middle of nowhere. Of course, this *is* Montana. There's a lot of nothing here. That said, they could have taken me anywhere.

Second, I was still alive – in pain, with my jaw sore, but alive. My biggest fear after my location was my family. We're wealthy. The family money came from my grandparents, Jack and Nikki Collins. Well, grandma would have rolled her eyes and said, "*Sixkiller*-Collins." Maybe that's where I got my stubbornness about my name. *Grandma?* I said to her spirit. *I promise I'll wear those heels. I swear.* I have a closet full of them but haven't worn any of them since…*our last poker game.* And the last game was three months ago. And the last time I had time for Mario was before that. I began to cry.

There was a third point, but I couldn't think of it. In frustration, I tried to stamp my foot but the tape held me fast. I tried to shake my fist at the world but the rope held me in its grip. I tried to wipe the tears from my eyes and could only blink them away beneath the thick folds of the blindfold. I tried to talk but the ball muffled and garbled anything I tried to say. I tried to scream but little came of my effort. I would have hung my head in frustration, but the tape around my neck held my head stubbornly upright against the pillar.

Then one word invaded my mind again. *Think.* Then a flurry others that I was ashamed to admit came from my mind. Let's leave it at this: if one of kids said them, we'd sit down right then and they'd get a firm discussion on decorum and what wasn't. *Get a grip, you lousy dimwit.* I can remember countless times in my bedroom when I was a kid at home in Portland, Maine, when I studied the medicine my mother took. I didn't matter that she knew I did all that stuff, that I snuck a peek in her medicine cabinet and wrote down the names of all the stuff in it. And, no, it wasn't all that much. Dad never took anything. But all those times with a flashlight under my bedcovers led me down a path of studiousness that still clings stubbornly to me today. I can force obscure stuff from such sparse material. So, *think* came to mind.

It didn't matter that I stood mostly naked against that pillar either. If I was going to get out of this, it wouldn't be because I had better physical abilities than they did. Well, crap. The physical abilities I had – mostly boobs – would play against me anyway, so I had to be better than them mentally. *Be tough, kid – tough, but not confrontational.* That seemed to be a suicidal tack. I have no physical skills other than charm – and not much of that. Ask Mario. *Dammit. Stop. You want them back and the only way that's going to happen is if you can think your way out of this.*

The first thing that came to me was obscure at best. *They ripped my clothes, but not my bra.* It stopped me completely.

Why would they do that? Moreover, *you're still in your panties. They left them intact and didn't touch them.* Had I not been tied to a pillar, I would have paused in thought anyway. In that moment, I *wasn't* tied. I was under my covers back in Portland with a flashlight reading the fine print on prescription bottles. *It suggests that they assume I'm going to need my underwear, but not my clothes.* Why? Then another shoe dropped. I didn't know how many were going to drop, so I left the analogy alone. *What's wrong with my clothes?* Then. *They want me to conform to their norm.* Yeah, Freeman and his bunch. Despite my condition, I smiled because it felt like a victory.

I decided to listen to the house because I hadn't been. Were there signs that someone was in it? Noises? Bumps? Dim voices? Anything? Well, with little else to do, I took the time to listen. And nothing happened. Not a sound. I stood and listened for at least five minutes. Okay, that's entirely subjective, but it was longer than any time I'd taken to that point. But, still I waited and listened. Other than the soft sounds of the house settling, there were no sounds at all. No footsteps across the ceiling, no TV, no toilets flushing, no water running, no voices.

I rolled my hands inside the rope. It didn't yield. I tried to stamp my foot again, but the tape didn't give at all. I took a deep breath and made a conscious effort to think. My mind made an interesting connection. *Animals.* Okay, it was late August. Did that mean anything? Naturally, I had no idea. Were there bears around? Grizzlies? Snakes, possums, squirrels? Rats, cats, bats? Anything? Since anything in this area that I didn't know could kill me, I decided to think about that problem for a while. For example, it was chilly in the room. Aside from my nipples standing up erotically, did that mean a door was open somewhere? *Think, fool. Is there a draft?* No. As near as I could tell, the chill in the air wasn't due to a draft. *Does that mean that no animals can enter the house?* No. *Make an assumption.* I did. *The doors are closed. I'm alone in an empty house.* Why? *Me. Either of them could have raped me, but neither one did.* That left me with one conclusion again. *They want me alive for some reason.* Another thought hit me. *Ransom.* That was the one that hit pay dirt as far as I was concerned.

Yeah, I've already alluded to Jack and Nikki Collins. They're dead, murdered years ago. They left their wealth to their seven children, six of whom they adopted. Mario was one of them. Albert, their only naturally born son, lives in Portland. The others are scattered around the country like autumn leaves before a breeze. It left me with one thought. *Why me? Why would anyone kidnap me when there are so many of us around?* Our grandparents – Jack and Nikki – didn't shelter their wealth. That meant there were other people who amassed fortunes simply because they either knew them or worked for them. Mom's best friend, Paula, comes to mind. But literally, there are so many people that got touched by the Collins wealth that the list is lengthy. So, again. Why me? None of us employs a bodyguard, so any of us would be easy to snatch off a city street. Well, not Mario, but he's just one guy. It left me frustrated *again.*

I'm used to pacing when I think, my old bedroom antics notwithstanding. That's where the frustration entered. I couldn't pace. *Dammit. Think. Don't think about pacing.* I took a deep breath and calmed myself. Again, despite the blindfold, I closed my eyes and shook my tied hands in order to get a sense of looseness. Okay, I couldn't pace, but I could imagine myself being able to. I took another deep breath and started with the thoughts I had about ransom. *If it's ransom, then they're stupid.* That seemed obvious. Why? Because I use a lot of my wealth on my practice, the medical one. If they want to ransom me, then they made a huge blunder by not simply talking to me and telling me why they needed money. Therefore, if it was ransom, then they were stupid and would make other mistakes. The logical part of me said, *They're not kidnappers.* It left me to find another reason for snatching me like they had.

Damn. It brought me back to Freeman and his band of playtesters. This is how my mind put me here against a pillar: *if they wanted to play sexual games with me, then either of my two kidnappers would have done something en route to this house.* Well, they had. Beryl himself fondled me several times. *Yeah, and then he left your panties on. Not a wrinkle.* Hmm. Conflicting evidence. I wanted to convince myself that Beryl *et al* had no sexual motives toward me. But Beryl himself about a handful several times and then pinched my nipple. *Yeah, and given all that, he still didn't molest you in any other way.* Well, I decided that I was convinced.

Then I heard a car approach the house and park. One, two, three, four car doors slammed and I knew my day was about to get interesting. Or night. I had no way to know.

Suddenly, I felt naked. And my hands were tied behind my back. A thing that hadn't really bothered me until now.

I realized that one way or another, I was about to become their appetizer.

CHAPTER 5

Heavy footsteps crossed the floor above me. Men in combat boots. Heavy, gruff voices followed them. One of them was deeper, harder and easier to follow than the others. I pulled at the rope holding my wrists together and still nothing happened. Being in that condition was one thing; having others around to leer and fondle was quite another. The door at the top of the stairs opened and the same heavy footsteps came down the steps. Okay, this officially qualified as fear.

From the sound of the footsteps, I guessed that one of them stopped at the bottom of the stairs. He bellowed, "Freeman! Get your ass in here!"

More sounds, these quick and prompt sounded and a familiar voice said, "Yes, sir." It was Daniel Freeman. Should I have been afraid of him? At least wary?

"Cut that woman down and then report to me how she got that way! And I mean pronto, mister!" the first man bellowed.

"Yes, sir," Freeman replied.

The other feet tromped up the stairs and out. They continued across the floor above me and then became more muffled. Did that mean they went up another flight of stairs? Maybe. Freeman had my attention, though. The others became ancillary problems.

I expected him to say something, but he remained silent. A knife cut through the tape holding my head against the pillar. I could hear it slice through it. Then he cut the rope around my hands and they were free. My wrists were sore, but I said nothing. Then I felt him kneel and cut through the tape around my ankles. The first thing I did was spit out the ball. I heard it bounce away. Then I reached for the blindfold and expected to be stopped. I wasn't. I expected Freeman to have company. He didn't. I expected him to apologize. He didn't.

That left me to my physical condition. I slid down the pillar onto my butt, not caring that I was still mostly naked. I put my face in my hands and said, "Thanks, asshole."

"Get dressed," he said blandly. "We need to talk."

"A guy named Beryl," I said into my hands. "That's all I know. There was one guy with him. Other than those two? No one else."

He knelt beside me and said, "That's not what we need to talk about. Please. Get dressed."

Sarcastically, I said, "I'm fine, thanks."

He said it again, this time gruffer. "Get dressed." Then he spat, "Or do you think this counts as rape?"

"No," I replied the same way. "Abduction. Maybe kidnapping. Maybe being held against my will. Something along those lines."

"You can pursue any of those courses after you're freed," he said, his eyes hard and unyielding.

I dropped my hands and said, "You're going to let me go?"

His next growl showed his teeth. "Dammit. Get dressed. You're an attractive woman and I don't need this shit!"

I grumped, "You haven't seen my ass then."

He put his face in mine and spat, "Yes, I have! Get dressed!" Then his face melted and he said, "Please."

Mario is the most romantic man I've ever known. Period. He's done so many wonderful things for me and our family, that they are literally countless. Before we had children, his romance was directed at me. So, no. I don't hurt for it. Maybe he hurts for some sort of reciprocation. Maybe. I never think of it from his point of view. Take him for granted? Yes. I do. I regret it every time it crosses my mind, but it doesn't stop me from my monomaniacal intent on medicine. But this? Freeman? Lord, no. Something flashed against my heart, something I had to shield from myself. Turn to stone? Turn cold? Ignore him? No. None of those things became necessary because he turned toward the stairs and walked away from me.

I've heard it compared to falling from a great height. It's worse than that. It's free fall through endless clouds. It never ends and you never quite remember where it started. What is it? I can't call it love and lust is far too common. So, whatever passed from him to me, struck a chord of light inside me and left me speechless, dumb and smitten. Totally.

But he never turned around to look at me. I stood and made no move to cover myself. To move otherwise was to risk everything I'd ever worked toward. To speak was to throw away my family, my life and everything that went with it. I closed my eyes and began reciting to myself the steps involved in taking a blood sample for an arterial blood gas test. I saw a patient extend his left arm, palm up. I dabbed alcohol on the site and considered whether or not to apply a local anesthetic. *No. It's not...* and my mind wandered. *I saw him.* I turned toward a blank wall and said, "Damn."

"Are you okay?" he asked, his back still turned.

Are you kidding? I'm sixteen again. I fumbled with my bra. "Um, yes," I finally said. "Um, my clothes are…"

"You'll be issued a uniform," he said coldly.

Please, touch me. Then I squeezed shut my eyes and berated myself as I hooked my bra back together and then surveyed the damage to my pants and blouse. I could hold my pants together, but my blouse was in tatters. "I'll need one," I said softly.

"Are you okay now?"

No. You screwed up my entire life. "Yes," I said instead.

"Wait here," he said and disappeared up the stairs. He went through the door at the top of the stairs, then closed and locked it.

My heart was hammering and my palms were damp. What the hell happened to me? Is this what an affair feels like? Is this what guilty women do? Do they push aside everything that is important to them and decide that the moist feeling in her heart means more than the tangible things of her life? *You were taught better than this.* Hell. *You know better than this.* I took a deep breath, clutched my blouse and pants as best that I could and decided to see where I was.

Okay, a basement. Maybe twenty feet square, no more than that. No furniture, nothing had been done to it at all. Rough timbers made up the ceiling, roughly laid concrete made up the floor. There were a row of narrow windows at the top of the walls where they met the ceiling. All of them had been painted black. A second pillar stood at the other end of the room. Other than a ceiling light, that was it.

I headed up the stairs and rattled the doorknob. "You damn backwater jerks!" I yelled. "Let me out of here!" I heard a noise. Then something softer, maybe boots scuffing across a floor. Among them were lowered voices. I wanted to say they sounded neutral, but they didn't. They were full of vicious intent. At least, that's the way my mind interpreted them.

I beat on the door and noticed the red, raw marks on my wrists. They took my mind off Freeman's eyes. I rubbed them, but the effort failed. I saw his eyes again. *He's your captor. He's been cruel and dismissive of you ever since he caught you on that road.* Then, the argument. *See reason.* It always worked before. Always. Reason always won out. Without it, I couldn't practice medicine. Without it, I'd be a shaman summoning the gods to help me. Reason has been my constant companion since I was seven. It began when I implored my mother to see it, to see *reason.* It began with childish outbursts like, "Mom? Those aspirins can kill you!" Or, "Mom? Jogging like that can cause heart failure!" Reason grew with me, grew into a weapon I used on myself. It pushed me through medical school, through a courtship with Mario and was always there like a smiling friend. Now, reason seemed to be turning on me, seemed to be deflecting my best efforts to use it. But. *No. It isn't reasonable. Freeman is responsible for this, for you being here.* The argument in my head was going to have to wait. Footsteps were approaching.

I backed down the steps and stood at their bottom staring up at the door. It opened and Freeman tossed a handful of clothes down at me. "Put these on. Come upstairs when you're dressed." Then he closed the door, but didn't lock it.

I was thirty-four years old that day. I'd seen my share of challenges and dealt with them in the best and most *reasonable* way I could. This? As my heart fluttered, I tried my best to see what was happening around me and failed completely. For example, the basement that was empty of everything except matching pillars? Well, something else was there, something Freeman knew about. It was why he wanted me to get dressed and follow him upstairs.

The last thing that happened to me before I got dressed and went upstairs was entirely too typical of me. I forgot about Mario. I forgot that I have always considered him to be the most competent man I have ever known. Had he not been, I can't say where my life might have gone. As it was, things were going to get dicey for me in more ways than just one.

And the first chance I took was waiting for me at the top of the stairs.

Um, no. Not him.

CHAPTER 6

Naturally, the pants were too tight. Not tight enough to split the seams when I sat down, but tight enough that I felt immense gratitude that the uniform blouse was long enough to cover my butt. I sighed and that became the first clue that Mom's genes were going to pop a button if I did that again. Well, okay. The uniform blouse was just a bit tight. I sighed again, berated myself one more time, and decided my fate was at the top of the stairs.

I expected to see Freeman, but instead I got a pasty-faced kid with an acne problem. I wondered if he was Wally or the Beaver. *The Beave.* There were two men behind him and all of them had guns. The two that flanked the Beave carried rifles. The Beave carried a pistol on his hip. I took it as a sign of progress that none of them had their gun pointed at me.

The Beave said, "Were either of these two men the one that assaulted you?"

The guy on the left looked old enough to be my father. The guy on the right looked old enough to be Travis's best friend. "That's easy," I replied. "No."

"Dismissed," the Beaver said, his voice breaking a bit. I'd say he was eighteen but that would mean he might have graduated high school and I didn't think he had. The two men exited through a door to their left. Then I heard them go up the stairs. That left the Beaver.

"I'm Sergeant Custer," he said.

I couldn't help it. I laughed. "Kid? With a name like that? You should go home and pull the covers over your head."

"Real funny," he said. "I've heard it a million times and it still ain't funny." He nodded toward the door that opened out from the kitchen. "That way."

"And if I don't?" I said stubbornly.

He smiled. "Oh, please. Resist, lady. Give me an excuse."

"Asshole," I sneered.

"Just go," he said again.

I did. I headed toward what would have been the back door in my home. The Beaver – um, Custer – followed me. I opened the door and saw Freeman standing under an oak tree that stood maybe twenty-five yards from the door. There were no fences, no efforts at domesticity, nothing to show any interest in making the house into a home.

Custer pushed me out of the door and said, "He's waiting."

I shook off his arm and wanted to tell him that his parents weren't married, but kept quiet. Instead, I focused on Freeman and tried to get my head straight. I didn't want to see him as long as my feet weren't on the ground – and they weren't. I took a few hesitant steps toward him and decided to keep my jangled emotions to myself. In other words, I decided to be a doctor.

I've never gotten used to it. Being stared at, I mean. That way, I mean. He wasn't. Standing with his back to me, he appeared to be looking at the mountains in front of him. He probably knows their name. Me? No idea. I mean, they have nothing to do with medicine, so why should I bother to learn their name?

As he heard me approach, he turned and my heart fluttered again. *Control yourself, girl. You're married and this is a problem you don't need.* Worse for me, he didn't even notice the tight buttons over my bosom. Or the pants or the look of consternation I brought with me. His face remained neutral in every respect.

"Okay," I said to him, my voice bringing with it a tinge of nastiness I did not feel. "What now?"

His jaw seemed set on something. "I assume that neither of the men Sergeant Custer showed you were one of the men who abducted you?"

"Correct," I said. "Neither of them was Beryl."

His eyebrows did something funny and he said, "I apologize, Mrs. Collins. Your presence here is not necessary. You will be escorted back to the RV park."

Well, no. And not just no, but…well, never mind. I don't like that word. But I wasn't going. "Look, asshole," I said choosing a word I had no problem saying. "Do you mind telling me what your damned paranoia has to do with me? Even if *you* don't need me, someone thought it important enough to bring me here!" Then I threw my arms wide and said, "And dress me in clothes tight enough to prove my natural hair color is black! I'd like to know what I was dragged into!"

He glanced toward the house and stared intently for a few moments. My emotions were so scattered that they rendered me helpless. It allowed him to continue to stare at the house. Finally, he said, "I cannot disclose our purpose here." His voice was soft as a waterfall and as tight as a vise.

Doctor time. I took a deep breath and a button actually popped from my tunic. I closed my eyes and never saw his small smile. When I opened them, I said, "And you came to me, Freeman. Specifically to me. You even had my photograph. I'm involved. Whether you like it or not, I'm involved until I find out what's wrong with you."

He wiggled his fingers between us. "Can you keep this between us?"

"Doctor-patient confidentiality. Yes."

"I sought you out, actually brought our troop to its location because I knew you were going to be here."

"How?" I said. "I didn't even know where we were going."

"Your husband did and so did the people who own and operate that RV park. Can we leave it at this? When I heard you were going to be there, I took our troop to the area just north of the park. My issues with you – namely my health –

have nothing to do with why we're in the area anyway. All it means is that we were infiltrated."

Paranoia. That's what my mind threw back at me after his short speech, especially the part about their group being infiltrated. It never dawned on me that it was true. However, while true, it did not mean that the object of their being out there in the first place had any merit at all. I looked down, then back at him and said, "Donor should be here. Is here?"

"No. I got a call from him. He's on his way."

"My office would not have told him anything. They'll tell me directly."

"So, you need a phone."

"Yes. I was carrying mine and now it's gone."

"Anything in it that might compromise you?"

"Nude pictures, you mean?"

Anger spread across his face like an oil slick. "No. Personal information, patient files. That sort of stuff."

So, I said it. "Do I look like an idiot?" Then immediately wished I hadn't said it because he looked at me. Briefly, but he did. The part that unnerved me just a little were when his eyes settled on my bosom at its missing button. I came *that close* to putting my hands over them. Then I stubbornly held them at my side. "No," he answered. You do not look like an idiot. But my question stands. Did your phone hold any information that might compromise you?"

No. It didn't. A few phone numbers, friends mostly. There were a few professional contacts. There were some family pictures. My mother….*Shit.* Frustrated, I said, "My mother is…"

"….Senator Chang, yes. That's fairly common knowledge."

"I have contact numbers for her in that phone. A complete set."

He smiled and my heart raced. I clenched my hands into fists. "She's a former private investigator. Then you have her personal assistant, Paula Watkins. Together? No one is going to take them down. Throw in her baggage train and anyone wanting to do her harm would be dead before the attempt started." Then he asked, "I meant if there were any documents on your phone or anything else that might cause trouble if they fell into the wrong hands."

Still thinking, I said, "No. I still believe the best way to talk to someone is with actual speech. Words, you know."

"Good," he said ignoring my intended sarcasm.

I smiled, my sarcasm still intact. "I could call my phone company and cancel my service to that phone." I pushed my smile wider and said, "My purse. I was also carrying my purse that had everything important to me in it as well as my stinking phone. Are you going to replace the pictures of all my nieces, nephews, uncles, aunts and parents? Are you going to cancel all my credit cards? Damn, Freeman. You could at least tell me what's happening here. It seems I have a vested interest in your paranoid fantasy."

Paranoid fantasy. Okay, I'd been dismissive of his being here, being *here*. I dismissed his "troop" as being little more than an adult fantasy and his rank as being little more than an echo of reality. But what happened to me was a crime and not a sorority stunt. All that, however, seemed moot. He was willing to send me home and that should have been enough. But, no. I had to find out about Daniel Freeman and why he came to this particular piece of Montana. Maybe he'd tell me something. Maybe he'd show himself to be an ill-disciplined wannabe. Maybe he'd just admit that they were here for no other reason than it was summer and this was how they spent summer vacation.

No. His face closed up tighter than a vestal virgin's. "No, Mrs. Collins. You will be sent home."

Be a doctor. "And if your blood test comes back positive for something for which you should be quarantined?"

"We cross that bridge when we get to it."

"Oh, really," I said still dismissing him and his troop. "Think of what you just said. You'd risk contaminating every member of your fraternity. Think hard, Freeman, because there is something wrong with you and I will find out what it is and then cure it."

He looked at me – and really for the first time. His stare put me into a pit that I found increasingly uncomfortable, too. I played the role of a thirty-something housewife who found her butt too big, her beauty fading and a man all too willing to shower me with attention. In short, I'd do whatever he said. I figured that I'd read him correctly when his gaze settled on my bust. Then he frowned and said, "This won't end well." He stared hard at me again – and at the same place – then said, "Come with me." He stopped after a few steps and said, "I hope you're smarter than you let on."

I think they call it the Rubicon.

CHAPTER 7

His name was Thomas Knoll, and he demanded to be called General Knoll. There were two others in the room, the two men who failed my ID of the man named Beryl. I learned Knoll's name when he shouted into a phone, "This is General Thomas Knoll! Who allowed that woman into this place! You better have an answer for me or I'll have you picking up cows chips from here to the Arctic Circle! Do I make myself clear!" He must have gotten an answer that pleased him because he grunted, "Knoll out," and killed the connection. Then he looked at me and said, "You better have a better answer than he did."

I still remember my grandfather. A gruff old man named Jack Collins, he taught me never to back down from anyone – and that included my mother. God bless him. Most of the arguments my mother and I had were because of him. We'd sit on the deck outside his second-floor bedroom and stare at the ocean. I didn't have to be impatient because I'd learned that he wanted to impart to me all the things he ever learned. Well, to be fair, he imparted them to my mother long before the doctor slapped my ass in the delivery room. He wanted both of us to be strong and independent. Well, he got his wish. It wasn't until a few years ago that my mother and me could discuss anything without smoke curling from our ears. What's all this mean in this context? You got it. Knoll had no way of intimidating me.

"How about this one," I said stepping up to him. "I was punched, tied, gagged and then bound to a pillar. I didn't have a whole lot of choice. If you're the head of this organization, then do yourself a favor now and quit because you're doing a piss-poor job of it."

Freeman remained stoic. Not that I noticed mind you. Knoll had my concentration. Well, the stinky cigar he held in his left hand did. When he held it to his mouth, I knocked it out of his hand and spat, "Don't you dare smoke in front of me!"

"Colonel Freeman!" he yelled. "Get this civilian out of my presence!"

Grandpa's basic approach to me was, "Baby? Don't be anyone's wallflower." Well, damn. No phony-assed general was going dismiss me. I stepped on his cigar, popped another button because I was so angry and screamed, "Look, your tin-plated, son of a heartless mother, you aren't going to get rid of me that easily!"

Well, he tried. He stood and said, "Madam…"

Yep. Roman candle. "Madam's sell their sex professionally! I get it medicinally!"

I again missed Freeman's small smile. Knoll didn't. "And that's funny, Freeman! I didn't see anything funny about it!"

I stepped between them and said, "Talk to me, asshole! Don't treat me like I'm the helpless one here because you're the guy that's at least fifty pounds overweight!" Yeah, and me thinking my butt was bigger than Devils Tower was giving *him* a lecture. Don't get me wrong. I don't know penicillin from the Piltdown man about fighting. Mario does. I think it's something about his man-genes. If he raised his swagger stick at me, then I'd look for a hole to run down. But know this: Freeman was sick and I was his doctor. Period. He came to me – specifically to me – and I was going to treat him until he was healthy enough for Mario to kill him. If you read that as confused, then congratulations. You win the prize.

He looked right down my split top and said, "Freeman? Am I to understand that she does not wish to be sent back to her home?"

"Yes, sir. You understand correctly."

Knoll looked at me and said, "Lady? Are you crazy?"

I thumped his lumpy chest with my index finger and said with as much frustration as I was ever able to assemble at one time, "Yes. I am crazy because men like you make me that way."

"Men like me keep daisies like you safe."

Well, damn. I slapped him. As my only weapon, it fell flat.

Before I could do it again, he grabbed my wrist and said with an undertone of threat in his voice, "Why don't you just tell me why you don't want to go home and let me make an intelligent decisions." Then he put his face in mine and said, "And don't bother to be cute. Just tell me."

Other than I wanted Freeman to put his arms around me and start the messiest divorce in Collins family history? Other than that? Well, throw in the fact that I still loved Mario and you had the makings of a seriously confused woman. But tell him? Well, not *that*. He'd tie me back to the pillar, call Mario and leave me for him. No, I couldn't tell him that Freeman had me seriously juiced up, or that he was suffering from a disease of some sort. I had to be quicker on my feet than I'd been. Hence, Freeman's line, "I hope you're smarter than you let on."

Well, show time. "Do you know how many tick-borne illnesses I've seen in the last two years? And did you know that one of them is entirely unknown and if not treated promptly can be fatal?" Well, okay. It's not fatal, or at least no deaths have been reported due to it. It's real, though. According to the studies I've read, the disease – as yet unnamed – is carried by a tick that does not carry Lyme Disease. Also, unless they were going to the Yellowstone River valley, then their exposure to the tick that causes the disease was almost nonexistent – and I didn't think they were going there because the river is more than a hundred miles from here.

He winced at me and said, "You want to be our medic?"

I poked his stomach. "Someone has to do it."

His eyebrows came together and he said, "No." Then he looked at Freeman and said, "And that's an order."

"No?" I said smiling. "Rash, fever, body aches, and lingering exhaustion," I said. "Are *you* going to carry one of your boys when he gets bitten?"

Knoll looked at Freeman and said, "Is she serious?"

He shrugged. "Got me."

That little aside between them should have been the clue – *the* clue – that started me to see what they were doing, what they were really doing. But, nope. Good old Doc Collins was always focused on medicine. Well, and Danny Freeman's eyes. And *every* time I saw them, I saw my future drying up and blowing away. I mean, how much crap can I dump on Mario before he gets tired of me and just leaves? Anyway, I missed it and never knew they had tossed me a plum.

Knoll, that fat bastard, looked at the two goons and said, "Remove the doctor from the room. Under no circumstances allow her back in here. Colonel Freeman will make a final disposition of her. Understood?"

"Yes, sir," one of the goons answered.

They approached me and both of them stared at my bosom. I gritted my teeth and resisted the urge to unbutton the rest of the tunic and said, "Here! Take a good look!" Hooray for modesty, I guess. Anyway, they herded me out of the room and I resisted another temptation to go scream, "Moo!"

One of them opened the door and put me in the hallway that exactly bisected the house on the second floor. One of them stood at one end of the hallway and the other at the other end. I wondered at the entrance requirements for their stupid militia because the stairway to the downstairs was to my immediate left. I could see the front door from my position at the top of the stairs. Well, I turned and looked at the man at one end of the hall and then turned and looked at the man at the other end. Then I turned back toward the door, grabbed the doorknob and before I could think, "Penicillin has saved millions of lives worldwide," a gun barrel was pressed to the soft tissue under my chin. "Go ahead," the older man said.

I turned the knob knowing he could shoot me. He didn't. The second man grabbed a handful of my hair, pulled it straight until I began to be forced to the floor. Then, my hair still in his grasp, he swung my head until it bounced off the wall. They say you hear bells. I didn't. I felt pain and nothing else.

"You going to behave?" a voice asked.

"Yes," I said surrendering.

"Good," the voice said. Then I heard footsteps that returned him to the end of the hall.

I sat against the wall, my head in my hands. My train of thought reduced itself to one thing: *You're a stubborn bitch.* I can't say that it gets me what I want because Mario makes sure that happens anyway. I asked him once if he thought I was spoiled and I thought he was going to start laughing. Instead, he looked thoughtful and said, "No, Evie, I don't. I think you are a rare person that is focused on what you want to do. If that makes you spoiled, then so what?" I argued, "But I treat you like dirt." He answered in a way that I will always remember, "We honeymooned in Paris. I walked down the Champs D'Élysées with you on my arm. I rode down the Seine past Notre Dame cathedral with you next to me. I had my picture taken under the Eiffel Tower with you under my arm. Evangeline Monica? We have a perfect life, you and I. It doesn't matter what you do because I always see your heart and remember all the things you said to me. Nothing that has happened has caused me to be anything but deeply in love with you."

And then Danny Freeman.

And then the damned disease he came to me to cure.

And then everything I said Mario became a lie.

And then I stood and considered letting that man shoot me.

Then my head cleared and I had a better idea. It might not even alienate Mario. When my heart felt better at that thought, I smiled. *Sorry, Danny. There's still some loyalty left in me.* I remained seated until the door opened. Knoll thought he was going to have his way, but I stood and said,

"Give me a phone and I'll call my husband. You can drop me anywhere and he'll find me."

"Blindfold her, drop her in the boonies and get rid of her," Knoll said to Freeman. Then he turned, went back into the room and slammed the door.

Freeman looked at the two men and said, "Blindfold, that's all. Put her in the Hummer. Five minutes. I'm going to talk to the general."

"Yes, sir," they said in unison.

He followed Knoll into the room and left me with Pete and Repeat. The older one pushed me toward the stairs but didn't say anything. The younger one followed us down them. I noted that the house was basically empty. No furniture, no appliances in the kitchen, but mostly no decorations on the walls, not even pictures. I tried to imagine what a headquarters would feel like, but had no idea. Shouldn't there have been maps on the walls, filing cabinets for old plans – or even new ones? The place seemed like an afterthought, like the sort of place they would know about, but not visit. Again. The clue they'd left me practically screamed in my face, but it had nothing to do with medicine, so I didn't see it.

The two goons took me downstairs and the older guy pulled a bandana from his tunic. Without a word, he wrapped it around my head and then made certain I couldn't see by pulling it down to my nose and up to my eyebrows. Then they took me out the front door, down the steps – down which I stumbled because neither of them cared to make sure I didn't – and then they put me in a vehicle, the Hummer, I assumed. Since the door didn't slam, I assumed they were standing there watching me. If so, it didn't last long because the driver's door opened and Freeman said, "Half hour and I'll be back."

One of them, the older one I guessed, laughed and said, "Yes, sir." Then the door closed, the engine started and we left. I had my hands folded in my lap.

We drove for no more than five minutes when he stopped and said, "Give me the phone number of someone that will pick you up."

I gave him Mario's cell phone number, told him the number and he dialed it. As it rang, he said, "Tell him you'll be at the store in the RV park in fifteen minutes and then hang up."

Mario answered on the first ring. "Hello?"

Damn. My hands shook. Was this a betrayal? "I'll be home in fifteen minutes," I said.

Then Freeman took the phone from me, snapped it shut and Mario was gone. I had no more than a few minutes to fix my life or Mario would know.

We rode in silence for a few nerve-wracking seconds before I said, "And now?"

"Forget about me." Then the Hummer stopped and his door opened. A few moments later and mine did, too. When he put his hand on my arm to help me out of the Hummer, my heart raced like it did *on my honeymoon.* "Please wait for five minutes and then walk in that direction," he said, turning me as he wanted. Then he added, "Don't worry about me. I'll be fine."

He tried to leave. I assume he turned toward his Hummer. But, no. I pushed it to the next level. I turned and wrapped my arms around a huge hunk of air. I stumbled and took off the blindfold. "You can't leave me here like this," I said helplessly.

He left me in the worst possible condition. He was a patient but I was putting my heart ahead of his condition. Knowing that wasn't bad enough. His reply made it worse.

"Try me," he said. Then he got into the Hummer and left nothing but a cloud of dust in the air.

Where was I? Kevin Road. From the looks of the situation, I'd say about two miles north of the RV park. I wanted to run away because this felt like a basic betrayal of Mario and my family. Worse? I still felt where he'd touched me. My arm tingled like a banjo.

But an odd thing began to happen as he drove away. I began to think like a doctor and his condition began to impress itself on me. He looked tired and that was one of the symptoms he came to me with. I needed to talk to Liz. I wanted to get the results of that blood test. But I knew Mario was going to happen first.

He did.

CHAPTER 8

It didn't take fifteen minutes to walk back to the RV park. It took most of an hour because I felt like a refugee. All that was missing was a cart full of the oddments of my life. I can't count the number of times I took a few steps, stopped, put my face in my hands and cried. Mario would know. He'd see it. He knows me that well. And I don't mean tears. He'd take one look at my eyes and know what I'd done to us.

Finally, I saw the store inside the entrance to the park. I expected to see police cars and their swirling lights, but saw nothing except the setting sun. I stood and stared at the scene for a few minutes. Nothing happened. The air remained thick and hot, the sky the color of the ocean and the air as clear as...*Mario's eyes.* Damn, it hurt. My heart, I mean. *He's going to know. He'll take one look at me and know.*

I'm not a very good wife. At least, I don't think so. Mario should take a look at Wanda and pair up with her. Becky's is cute and Maddy likes her. They'd make a good family. I stopped, looked at the distant motor home, turned around and started walking away. My intention was to leave and never go back. I felt that ashamed. *You damned fool. You're wearing a breakaway tunic, pants that will split the first time you sit down and besides...where are you going?* Right. The dusty road led straight to nowhere. I clapped my hands to my sides and cried – again. Tears rolled down my face and I made no effort either to stop them or wipe them away. Misery? Thy name is Evangeline Monica...whatever. Still, I couldn't face him. So, naturally, he came to me.

"Evie!" he cried in the distance.

I turned around and saw him sprinting up the road toward me. All too soon, he had me in his arms.

"What happened?" he asked. Then he asked a dozen more questions, but all I could do was cry as he held me. All of that nonsense stopped when he lifted my chin and said, "Someone hit you. You've got a bruise on the left side of your chin."

It is at this point that Americans usually say, "I'm calling a cop." Not Mario, not my man. *Are you, Mario? Will you still feel that way about me when you find out?* With his arm around my shoulder in a protective embrace, he guided me back toward oblivion. He stayed silent as we walked, his arm around my shoulder. I'll admit, it felt nice. Oh, hell. It felt wonderful, but I remained convinced he wasn't going to like what I'd done to us.

There is a bench outside the front door to the office complex. Nothing more than a weathered wooden bench of the type made in China, he sat me on it and knelt in front of me. When his arm slid from my shoulder, I felt as though I was falling through space. Yeah, splat. That's where this was going.

"Describe your condition to me," he said.

The damn man. He knows me well enough to ask about what happened in terms of an office visit. I'd asked that question to thousands of patients in the last two years.

I practically screamed, "No! I wasn't raped!"

His smile always works on me. Always. He smiled and said, "Well, let's thank our ancestors for that."

I did it. I threw myself at him, tumbled with him to the sidewalk in front of the store and cried, "I cheated on you! Now you hate me!"

Oh, lord but he has a beautiful face. It creased into a smile, his hands went to my butt and I was his – again. "You did, huh? Do I know him?"

"Freeman," I cried, my tears falling onto his cheek.

"Ah, the pretty boy." His voice got playful. "Is that his uniform?"

I screamed at his beautiful face, "It doesn't fit me! Why would you…" and he started rubbing my butt again and I lost track of where I was, who I was, what time it was and why we weren't in a bed somewhere. Then I started whining. "Mario…"

"So, it isn't sexual," he said in my ear.

"He has pretty eyes."

"What's wrong with them?" he whispered to me like a lover might.

"They…" and it hit me. "They're slightly yellow. He has jaundice." Well, damn. It had nothing to do with Freeman as a person. I saw his eyes and was attracted to them *medically*. I smacked his shoulder and wiggled off of him before he could rub my butt again.

He smiled up at me from the sidewalk, put his hands behind his head and said, "Love. Ain't it grand."

I put my foot on his chest and growled, "Don't laugh at me."

Travis and Woody picked that moment to come out of the store. Travis nudged Woody and said, "I think this means she can cut off his head and mount it over the fire place as a trophy." Then he said, "Hi, Mom. Cool outfit," and they left, headed toward the hills up Kevin Road. The last thing I heard from them was Woody. He said to his best friend, "I didn't know your mom was in the cavalry."

Mario pulled me down on top of him and started on my butt again. I began whining once more. "Mario…"

"So, what happened?"

"You didn't even call a cop," I whined.

"Why? All they'll do is a find a body. I kinda wanted you back alive. But I like your outfit, too. Did Freeman give it to you?"

"No," I said stupidly. "General Knoll did."

"He ranks Freeman."

But my mind was on Freeman's jaundiced eyes. "Yeah. He asked me if Knoll's bodyguards were the ones that kidnapped me."

Mario rubbed my butt. I laid my head on his shoulder. I rather liked his interrogation technique. "Kidnapped?" he asked rubbing gentle circles on it.

"Yeah," I sighed. "Some guy named Beryl punched me when I went to the store to buy batteries. That accounts for the bruise."

"Beryl punched you."

"Yeah."

He ran his fingers up and down my spine and I turned to mush. "Then what happened."

"I was taken to a house a couple of miles from here and tied to a post in the basement. One of the guys fondled me but that was it." I moaned.

"How long were you there?"

"Five or six hours, I think," I said deliriously.

"You were tied to the post for five or six hours?"

"Yeah. Don't stop. Please," I said. It felt so good that I had no idea what I'd been saying.

"Who untied you?"

"Freeman, I think."

"Why were you kidnapped and why were you released?" Then he kissed me and I lost track of everything. I think his hands were on my face, either side of my cheeks. I couldn't swear, couldn't have. He asked around a kiss, "Why?"

I gulped down that kiss, took another and said, "I think they're having a war of some type."

"And they took you why?" he said, then kissed me again. This time, I got his sweet tongue.

Breathless, I said, "They said I was proof that they had been infiltrated."

"So, you're safe?" he said looking at me from maybe three inches.

"No idea," I said and then stopped. *That's what he said. The same thing. "No idea". He said it the same way I just did, in an offhand way to a direct question.* It struck me in that moment: *they're equals, not general and colonel.* Why did I come to that particular decision? Because I consider Mario and I to be equals. Given that, the exchange I made with him was one equals would make. If that was so, then…

"Evie," Mario said kissing me softly on the lips. "Where were you?"

"Tell me about the army," I said.

His face went all grim and hard. "Soldier? Get off your stupid, civilian ass and give me a full and complete report about that action!"

I tried to hold it back, but I started giggling. Then I wrapped my arms around his neck and did in full public view what a lot of folks only do in their bedrooms. Kiss.

I might have married my uncle, but I'm not a perv.

CHAPTER 9

Damn. I did it. I said I married my uncle and now I have to explain it. My grandparents – Jack and Nikki – had seven kids, all adopted except for Uncle Albert. He was theirs genetically. All the others, Melodie – my mother, Dora, Tiffany, Stacy, Elaine and Mario were adopted by Jack and Nikki. If you ask Mario, he'll tell you that he wasn't adopted. He'll puff up his chest and say with great pride, "I was bought for three-hundred-sixty-dollars and a Happy Meal from McDonalds." So, the "uncle" I married was an adopted uncle. You want worse? Grandmother Nikki had a son when she met Grandfather Jack. That would be my father, Brian Sixkiller. If you've been following this, then you know that my mother *married her stepbrother*. I guess the apple didn't fall far from the tree, huh? All that means is that you don't have to worry about my genetics, or those of my kids either. Whew. I'm glad I don't have to go through *that* again. Still, it comes up maybe once a year. The best part? My uncle was only one year older than me when he got adopted into the family.

When the kiss ended? I smiled at him and said, "I can't believe I thought Danny Freeman's eyes were sexier than yours."

He kissed me back and I drifted away again. Then he said, "I need to get you back."

I put my forehead against his and spat, "If you *ever* expect to get into my pants again, you'll help me find that man because he's sick!"

Well, I have always been putty to him, so he started doing whatever he wanted. He started by caressing my cheek. I closed my eyes and acted like a three-year-old. "Mario…" Then he kissed me lightly on the lips and I was gone, just gone. Well, except for the sensory inputs, I mean. For example, when he runs his fingers up my arm? Well, I've experienced orgasm in more crude ways, but that one is pretty cool. Not that time, though. He needed me *here* and not *there,* so he pulled his caresses if you will. Then he said, "Debrief first? Then we find him?"

I was climbing a long ladder and enjoying every moment of it. The porno film in my head might have included food, I'm not certain. Hey, it's *my* porno film, okay? "M-kay," I moaned. I wasn't capable of anything else. He pulled me with him through the store. I don't think my feet touched the ground. Maybe. That's all I could admit. Maybe they had. Maybe they hadn't. He held my arm under his as we walked back toward the motor home.

Wanda saw me through the window and came rushing out the door, her red hair flying behind her. "Are you okay?" she asked, her eyes showing concern. Then she looked at Mario and asked the same thing. "Is she okay?"

"No," he answered. "She isn't."

"Am, too," I pouted.

"She was kidnapped and tied to a post for up to six hours."

"Oymygod," she said, stringing the words together.

Mario smiled. "She thinks Freeman is cute."

She shrugged, and with concern still on her face, said, "Well, sure, but that's beside the point. What happened?"

"You think he's cute?" I rallied with, "His eyes are yellow!"

She shrugged again. "Well, of course, but you're the wizard. I'm just the highly qualified assistant." Then her eyes narrowed and she asked, "Now, what happened?"

Mario put his arm around me, smiled and said, "Coffee?" I would have yes to arsenic at that point.

We went inside. Maddy and Becky were sitting in front of the TV. There was a camera setup on top of it and they were making faces at it. It was a tribute to Mario that the kids were as unaffected by my disappearance as they were. In fact, Maddy said, "Hi, Mom," and then Becky broke into giggles. Since neither of them remarked on my clothes, I assume that nineteenth century cavalry outfits have no great impact on seven-year-olds. She did notice the missing buttons on the tunic, though. "Button it up, Mom. That gross."

Mario and Wanda smiled. I just sat and expected Mario to slide on my side into the booth that was the kitchen table. He didn't. He pushed Wanda in next to me and said, "I distract her."

"Understood," Wanda said smiling.

"Don't either," I whined.

"See?" he said.

She nudged me. "So?"

"Tell me," Mario agreed.

"Us," Wanda corrected him.

Liz Dempsey crossed my mind. "Has either of you heard from Liz?" Freeman's blood test was still outstanding.

"Nope," Mario said.

"No," Wanda added.

"I need to call her," I said. Then I added, "And I need to cancel my phone."

Mario got out of the booth, walked to the rear where our bedroom was located and brought back my purse. He reached in it and handed my phone to me. "You might want to use this."

"You found it without me and didn't call the cops?"

He shrugged but made it look serious. "And that would have helped how?"

I know I've said it before, but this bears repeating. He is the most competent man I've ever met and I know doctors that can take your heart out, repair it and put it back. I don't know what I'd walked into, but Mario was involved now. Period. Maybe it was foolishness of the first order, but I felt better, safer. I'm not important to the police. I am to Mario. Whatever he does will be done with my best interests at the heart of it. The police? Maybe I'll be safe and maybe I won't. They won't lose any sleep over me no matter what happens. Trust Wanda to throw cold water on an orgy.

"You realize that whatever you're planning is illegal?" she said to him.

He shrugged yet again and said, "So?"

"If they catch you…"

"They won't."

"And you know that how?"

"So, you're saying that you're not involved?" he asked, his hands folded on the Formica.

Wanda waggled her finger back and forth between us. "How did me and Pocahontas meet?"

"Pocahontas?" I asked.

She looked at me and said bluntly, "You've been telling me that your father was half-Sioux. If that's true, then you're one-eighth Sioux. Right?"

"Right," I replied meekly. "I guess that accounts for my black hair."

"Hence Pocahontas," she replied. "Now. Answer the damned question. How did me and your dim-witted wife meet?"

He smiled. "You were on the Flathead County Search and Rescue Team when Cayn Wyatt asked Evie to help them."

"Right," she spat back. "Don't you assume even for a moment that I don't know how to take care of myself outside of a kitchen!"

"Sorry," he said smiling. "Won't happen again. So?"

"I'm in and that's that."

"What if you're caught?" he asked, his smile intact.

She answered with a growl that she aimed at both of us. Then she said, "I'm in or do I need to send smoke signals?"

Okay. I bit. "In what?" I asked Mario.

"In finding Freeman," he said with a smile I'd never seen before.

"Why are we finding him?" I asked stupidly.

"Because you asked."

"He didn't hit me. Beryl did."

"And that's a story you haven't told me yet," he said with the same smile.

"Us," Wanda said.

"Sure," Mario said to her.

"What about my kids?" I said a bit too loudly.

Maddy's head popped up, swiveled and she called out, "What, Mom?" Travis's head came in through the door and he said, "Did you call me?"

I smiled at them and said as happily as I could, "Nothing. You guys go on and play."

"Okay," they sang in unison.

I stared at Maddy and she became a symptom of what was wrong with me. This vacation – all two weeks of it – was supposed to be spent with them, not chasing some ersatz soldier all over northern Montana. I watched Maddy as she laughed at Becky's picture on the TV. Then Becky put her sticky finger – yes, I grimaced – on the screen and laughed at Maddy. They were having fun. Travis and Woody were having fun, too. God, my heart ached. I was ruining their childhood willfully. Why? Because I knew even before Freeman's blood test came back that I was going to run off looking for him. What did that mean for my children? Were they doomed to be doctor's kids? Were they doomed to a lifetime of anger because I treated their childhood so cavalierly?

Mario reached across the table and took my hands in his. "Evie? The kids are fine. The time you have with them is always enough. Don't worry about our life because there is nothing to worry about."

Wanda gave a light laugh and said, "Yeah. Becky wants to move in with you guys."

"Just tell me what happened," he said. "Okay?"

"Not unless you promise me than I'm involved, that I'm going with you."

"It's going to be rough country,"

I stared at him as though to say, "I know!"

"Okay, I promise," he said. "Just tell me the story and don't leave out anything."

I did. I started with my leisurely walk to the store and added the detail that the people working there disappeared when I entered. It seemed minor at the time, but as I retold the story, it gained in significance. Also, I knew better than to watch Mario as I spoke. His eyes would melt me to the seat and we wouldn't get anything done, so I spoke to the tabletop and held his hands. I gave him every detail I could remember including the one that painted me as unafraid, just annoyed that they groped me. When I finished, he surprised me by saying, "Okay, Again. From the top."

I took a deep breath – a thing that Wanda punctuated by saying, "Jesus, would you stop doing that" – and started again, this time after I gave her my best withering look. I went slower than the first time and even added details of Beryl that I hadn't remember before. He had red hair that was nicely cut. He wasn't a slob. I even recounted the lonely hours I'd been tied to the pillar and how I tried to occupy my mind during them. I added the other forgotten item, the one when Freeman told me all the episode meant was that they'd been infiltrated. Mario's eyes got harder them and I believe he saw something neither Wanda nor I did.

I asked, "What is it?"

He answered, "I'll tell you when I have it figured out."

So, I finished the story for the second time.

Then Mario said, "Let's get the kids to Cayn's."

I smiled, squeezed his hand, smiled and said, "Drop me at my office first. I want to see Liz."

He smiled back and said, "I'll pick you up at the hospital." He knew that's where the sample went. He knew I'd be there trying to track it down.

"You damn better or you'll have a wife tramping around Montana by herself."

"Noted," he said with a smile I recognized.

Wanda frowned, "Oh, get a room."

And that's where we started to get involved in a thing where we weren't going to be welcomed. While that might be true, I came to believe that our involvement was necessary to someone I'd never met. Personally, I thought things were going to get trivial, but wars have been started over worse things. On second thought, some people thought that what happened was war and nothing less.

    Me included, I guess.

CHAPTER 10

The first thing I did was change clothes. Mario kept dropping not-too-subtle hints that he rather liked the pants. Since the kids were strapped into seats that were right behind ours, he couldn't get as crude as he wanted. Still, I started giggling and had to look out my window just to avoid his face. I managed to get in, "At least they didn't split." He grinned and I kept laughing.

We got the kids – including Becky – settled with Cayn. He got curious, but Mario just said, "Hey, dude. Two weeks with hot broads. Ya know?" Well, Cayn's gay, so he had no idea. He was suspicious, though, and said something to Mario behind a hand cupped over his mouth. Mario thought for a moment and answered. They were discussing the school and who would run it if Cayn came with us. The only thing I could assume was that Mario downplayed where we were going and why because Cayn smiled and clapped him on the back. Given that Cayn is a big guy, Mario had to brace himself.

Then we went home and got our Hummer. We wound up pulling enough stuff from the RV to last a week and tossing it in the back of the Hummer. Wanda drove. I'd like to buy her one because she loves ours. She won't let me and gets adamant about it. So does the language she uses. Adamant, I mean.

Then we went to my office. All I wanted to know was whether Liz forwarded the sample to the hospital across the street or to a lab over in Billings. Well, she hit the fan. I mean, full force. She came out of the office and said in front of three patients, "Fourteen months without a single day off! And then what? Two lousy days! Sixkiller! Get your butt out of here!"

"Liz," I asked as my face turned red. "Where did the sample go?"

"Across the street, you buffoon" she bellowed.

I hugged her and said, "I promise I'll stop. Okay?"

"Really?" she said. She sounded worried.

"Really," I said. "We're going to work on another baby."

Her eyes bulged and she said, "Really? Another half-breed?" She had her hands clasped over her heart.

Even the patients laughed.

"Yes, and that won't happen unless Mario gets me alone somewhere."

"Well, okay," she said, stars in her eyes. "In that case, yes, the sample went across the street."

I hugged her. "Thanks, Liz."

I said goodbye to everyone and then followed the blood sample across the street to the hospital, Kalispell Regional. Just because I'm a doctor doesn't mean I know where the labs are. Yes, I had to ask for directions. Also, I didn't know who the lab manager in the facility was. Again, I had to ask. A lab tech flipped his thumb at an office and said, "Sandra. Sandy Peterson. I'll get her for you."

Sandy was an energetic faux blond that seemed to be everywhere at once. Also, she had me at a disadvantage; she knew me even though I had to be introduced to her. Her smile lit up her face and highlighted her few freckles. "Doctor..." and her energy had nowhere to go. It happens to me so much, the brain freeze people get when they are met with my impossible name, that I merely took her hand and said, "Six. Doctor Six."

That's when she betrayed her prior knowledge of me. "I've been wanting to meet you for so long, Doctor Six. You would think, 'just cross the street and introduce yourself', but I never have." She was one of those people who bent at the waist as they talked to you, her smile seemingly infectious. "Well, how can I help you?"

"I had a blood sample sent here. I'm trying to get its results." I know better than to send a blood sample anonymously. The identifications all belonged to Mario. That kept Freeman's name out of it. "It was a sample for my husband, Mario Collins." The only unknown was Private Donor. He could have done anything with or to the sample. Sandy's response indicated it had been delivered cleanly.

"Oh, yes," she said happily. "Let me get the results and I'll discuss it with you in my office."

Oka-a-a-y. I'm qualified to read the results of a blood test. I watched as she went to the lab tech that pointed me to Sandy. They spoke and his head went up. Looking at me, he nodded and came back to the office with her. His sandy blond hair was cut short, not buzzed. That was a plus for him. As an aside, I hate the stormtrooper look. Anyway. Sandy came into her office and sat behind her desk, her incessant smile accompanying her. She said, "This is Bobby Garrison. He ran the test."

Garrison was maybe thirty, roughly my age. Okay, okay. I'm thirty-*four*. Thank you for reminding me. Still, he looked younger than me. Damn him to hell. Okay. *Focus.* What I thought was a hit on me turned different as soon as he took a seat closer to Sandy than to me.

"Doctor Six. Right?" he asked.

"Yes," I said.

He sighed and said. "I apologize for not recognizing you." He paused and gathered his wits. That should have been a sign. "My son, Jeremy, goes to Mario and Cayn's school. I love what they do and Jeremy loves going there. They should consider extending the grade level to cover public school grades because he's going to hate leaving there next fall when he starts kindergarten." Then he looked bashful and said, "I'm sorry about not recognizing you. I've met Mario and Cayn many times and just didn't know you. So, I apologize again."

"It's okay," I said. "Perhaps you can tell me what you found?"

He bit his lip and that separated him from me because it seemed obvious that he had no practice at giving bad news to people. "Well," he said. "The first time I ran the test, it showed anemia. That's not uncommon. It happens a lot. But what drives the anemia? It's like a cowboy herding cattle. The cattle isn't uncommon. But what is causing them to all go in the same direction? The cowboy drives the herd. What drove the anemia?"

"What did?"

It was as though saying the words caused the disease to splash back on himself. "He has Gaucher's Disease. I did an enzyme assay on the sample and it came back positive. The only good news is that it's type 1."

Gaucher's Disease is marked by a buildup of fatty substances in several organs of your body. The liver, spleen, lungs, bone marrow and sometimes the brain lead to the inevitable problems with those organs. Type 2, which is found in children, is usually fatal by age two. Type 3 is the one that involves the brain and can be termed as the difference between types 1 and 3. While there is no cure for the disease, there are therapies that can be beneficial, enzyme therapy.

"But it could be type 3," I said. "That determination is made upon examining the patient. You should know that."

He looked sufficiently chastised, his head down, his angst pointed toward Mario and a disease he did not have. Daniel Freeman did. Logically, I was the only person to know that. Otherwise, only Sandy and Bobby knew that *anyone* had the disease. The issue became simple: should I tell them? I decided against it and couldn't say exactly why.

Sandy handed the paperwork to me and I looked at it idly. My mind was elsewhere, was trying to find – or to find a way – to locate Freeman in order to tell him.

"I'm sorry," Bobby said, his emotions running toward grief. Maybe there was a meeting in our future about who really had the disease, but it wasn't going to happen until I found Freeman and told him what I knew.

It isn't hard to commiserate with people when they're given this type of news. It's the most awful thing you can tell a person. It confirms your basic humanity, confirms what you knew when you first became self-aware. You're going to die someday. Now, Freeman had a good idea of when that was going to happen. Well, he was going to have a good idea when I found and told him. First, I had to look grieved. I pictured life without Mario and that did it. I couldn't. If something like this happened to him, I'd cry, scream and curse God. Then I'd find the best medical answer I could because God isn't much help in those cases. God tends to bury his creations.

I swallowed hard and said, "Thank you, but he isn't dead yet. With luck and treatment, he should be with us for years to come."

"That would be great," Bobby said and looked like he meant it.

"Maybe you should give some thought to having him treated by someone else," Sandy said with her ever-present smile.

My first inclination was to snap at her. I didn't. I held my ground, though. "That's a good idea," I said, "but I believe I can manage it."

Truthfully? I've already said I couldn't. I can't. Luckily, Mario is healthier than anyone I've ever known. Why? I've got some vague ideas, but nothing concrete. It is has to do with his immune system. Maybe one day I'll be able to find out, but Freeman comes first. "Is there anything else?" I asked, knowing there wasn't. The blood test would be all they had and they'd given it to me.

"No," Sandy replied. "That's it."

"Is this why Mario hasn't been at the school?" Bobby asked.

"No," I smiled. "We've been on vacation." Then I said, "It wasn't until I had the time off that I saw his condition."

Bobby nodded and Sandy said, "I see. Well, you know the results."

I shook Sandy's hand and hugged Bobby outside her office. He looked at me closely and said, "I can't imagine Mario without Cayn. You'll start treatment soon?"

"As soon as possible," I replied. "And thank you for your kind words."

I left the hospital with a secret that was going to cause immense troubles for me. Had I known, I would have done it anyway. Why? Because I'm a doctor.

It's a curse sometimes.

CHAPTER 11

Wanda was waiting in the parking lot with Mario. She waited patiently, her hands on the steering wheel. Mario sat beside her in the passenger seat. He looked patient, too. Me? Well, exhaustion was starting to settle over me like a plague. I felt it in my bones and behind my eyes. The only thing keeping me going was Gaucher's Disease as it pertained to Daniel Freeman. I knew he had it, but he didn't know, so it came down to this: I didn't care what they were doing out there. I had to find him and tell him what my diagnosis was. Only then could I go home and rest.

Mario asked as soon as I settled into the back seat, "What did they find?"

"Gaucher's Disease."

"What's that?" Mario asked.

Bless him. He's has always been supportive of me and my monomania. Even when I implored my mother to stop using aspirin, he backed me up by saying, "Come on, Mel. She knows this stuff."

Wanda's reaction was blunter. "You need a genetic test to confirm that."

"I know," I said wearily. "It will do nothing more than confirm it, though. I'm more worried about neutropenia."

"Okay," Mario said. "I'll bite. What's that?"

"A condition that destroys white blood cells. Given that, he'll more susceptible to infectious diseases and he's running around in the wilderness just waiting to be bitten by a tick. That man is in trouble."

Again, Wanda put her argument bluntly. "Cayn can call out the search and rescue team and make the whole issue moot. It's one of their functions, Evie. If he's sick, they can find him and get treatment."

The issue became me and my damned attitude. He came to *me*. Not to the search and rescue team. It was *me* that was tied to a pillar for six hours and left alone. It was *me* who was fondled and treated as an afterthought. Okay, that doesn't excuse what I wanted to do, but I'm a rich bitch who gets what she wants. No, I am. My family has lots of money and they've sprinkled it liberally on me. It pushed me through three different medical schools and allowed me to pursue my monomania with an intenseness reserved for most professional athletes. So, again. Yes, a call to the search and rescue team was in order. But. I had a good idea of where they were and we were about to get started anyway, so my reaction became typical of me. "No, let's just do it. He came to me, not to the damned search and rescue team."

"You sure, Evie?" Mario asked. "You need rest and not this."

Well, damn. I turned my exhaustion on him. I stabbed my index finger at him and said angrily, "No! I do not need rest! I need to find that man and tell him what's wrong with him!"

"Is it fatal in the near term?" he asked without reacting to my outburst.

"No," I said. "It eats you slowly."

"Then we have time?"

"Yeah," I said. Then, "Look, I'm…"

He leaned over the seat toward me and said, "Yeah, yeah. Just kiss me."

I did. It never gets old.

It's possible – no, likely – that had I been married to anyone else, that none of this would have happened. Someone more attuned to our society's yawning need for policemen would have just turned away and given the search to the authorities. However, he grew up in Clan Collins just like I did. He grew up with a family attitude that swam against that current. Grandfather Jack originated it, but my mother perfected it. She became a household name in the homes of three Portland police chiefs. And me? Well, as an example, take my constant yipping to get my mother to stop using aspirins. It worked. I kept one-upping her and them with endless reasons for her to stop. I threw in stomach pain, heartburn, nausea and vomiting as reasons for her to stop. It was like a disease that had me by the throat and would not let go. When none of those worked, I trumped her with *hemorrhagic stroke*. Then I gave her my best evil eye and said, "Do you want me to tell you what *that* is?" She stopped using aspirins and asked for a recommendation. My answer? "Grit your teeth."

So, the three of us were going to go looking for a man that any good search and rescue team could have found a lot easier than we were going to. One of the issues that separated those teams from me was my respect for human life. Oh, yes, yes. The search and rescue teams save lives, don't take them. In that respect, they would have done the same thing we were going to do – namely find them. Well, him. Daniel Freeman. It was the issue that put Freeman and his stupid militia in the field that was going to separate us from anyone else. Well, me from anyone else. My attitude – and can be a bitch – was going to sway everyone around me – even Mario. Well, especially Mario.

"So, where are we going?" Wanda asked. "Just point me in the right direction and me and this beast will get you there."

"Back to the RV park," I said.

Mario nodded. He wanted to go back there, but for entirely different reasons than I did. Look, I'm not that *that* stupid. He wanted a piece of the guy that got his hands on me and put them in places reserved for him. I've never said that he was nonviolent.

Wanda started up the Hummer and got us back on the road to Kevin, Montana.

We had at least four hours ahead of us, so I began by answering Mario's question. "Tell me about the guy you saw in the store." Yeah, him. Beryl. He knows that I can get extremely precise, so when I began to get that way, he remained silent.

Wanda didn't.

"Did you get horny?" she asked.

"Look, I'm trying..."

"And I'm trying to make this speech interesting. So, did you?"

"No," I said. My evil eye didn't work on her at all. But, then, she's a mother. It wouldn't. "Do you mind if I continue?"

She smiled. "That means yes."

"That means no," I countered.

"Damn, you're a stubborn bitch."

"So, you're going to drive or do I have to do that, too?"

She re-gripped the steering and mumbled, "Bitch."

"Bitchier," I answered.

Then we both laughed and that made the effort worth it.

"So?" Mario said, prompting me back to the story.

I learned as a kid that I loved traveling because it gave me time to read about doctors and how they practiced. Both Mom and Dad showed patience with me, too. If I curled up with a book, they held the interruptions to a minimum. If I engaged them in conversation, Mom took it as manna from heaven and talked with me until the next medical book grabbed my attention. Another thing I learned about my mother was that all she wanted was for me to talk to her. Instinctively, I knew that I could get anything I wanted from her as long as I did, but I held those extortions to a minimum. At least I think I did.

This? After all those years, the urge is still there. Human health still preoccupies my mind. Specifically, how to encourage and maintain it. Disease practices guerilla warfare against its human hosts. My job, as I see anyway, is counterterrorism. I watched the landscape – the human body – carefully in order to detect any moves by the enemy to disturb its delicate balance. That means, as I see it anyway, that I don't see my patients as often as I would like. It also means that I employ a clerk whose *only* job is to call patients I have seen recently in order to gauge how their visit went, if they have any lingering questions and then to return their questions with answers. Hence, fourteen months without a vacation.

If you read that as though I don't place my own health ahead of that of my patients, then you win. I started jogging only because my mother – who is fifty-seven – is in better shape than I am. Whenever she visits? I take her blood pressure and monitor her heart rate. Hers is always better than mine. But I started jogging when I lived in LA a few years ago. When I moved to Kalispell, I knew instinctively that I had to jog north along Highway 93 rather than south toward the medical center. Had I jogged south, the temptation would have been too great not to go across the street to my office and start work in my jogging shorts. So, I jog north toward the stock car track and not south toward my office. Yes, and I fight the urge to run all the way to my office every time I leave the house.

All these things led to my aborted vacation. Mario saw all the signs and started making plans long before it became real. I can't say because I didn't ask, but part of the trip to Kevin passed through the Blackfeet Indian Reservation in northwestern Montana. Since I'm one-eighth Sioux through my real father, Brian Sixkiller, I can't assume the trip through the rez was an accident. Still, I didn't even blink as we drove through it to the RV park just north of that town. Now? On the way back? I wondered.

"Why Kevin, Montana?" I asked him, forgetting about the precision I began to apply to Beryl. I put my face between the seats and followed that question with another one. "Of all the places we could have gone, why there?"

The look on his face was precious. Part smile, part deeply satisfied husband, he said, "Damn, you aren't stupid."

"So?"

"Evie, babe?" he said looking at me happily. "You're part Indian and those people need someone like you. Unemployment runs nearly seventy percent even though there are deep oil reserves there."

"You want me to move there?" I said not believing it.

"No," he replied. "But why not enquire to see if they need someone like you a few days a month? We don't need the money and the work would be as satisfying as any you have ever done."

I nodded and said, "Okay. I'll think on it."

"Now can you tell me everything you remember about the guy named Beryl?" he asked.

I sat back in the seat, crossed my arms and watched the rumpled countryside roll past. I started to think back to our meeting in the store. I recounted everything sequentially as it occurred to me, that he was fit, roughly my age and that by everything he'd done, he was deeply self-assured about whatever he was doing. I recounted waking up already tied and lying in the bed of a pickup. I even described how they tied me and controlled me. He interrupted.

"Did they threaten you?"

I wanted to be precise, so I paused. Then I said, "No. Just manhandled me."

"By fondling you?"

"Yes," I said with some worry in my voice. No one – *no one* – has ever done that to me except Mario. Well, and the human puke that raped me when I was sixteen. That doesn't count, however. It's also not germane to my store, the one I tried to tell Mario.

"Was it calculated?"

Good question. I gave it several long seconds of thought. Then I said, "No. I think he liked what he saw, grabbed the opportunity and took it."

Wanda sputtered into life. "Grabbed the opportunity and took it. Oh, good one, Evie."

I looked at her in the rearview mirror and burst into laughter. "Just drive, Wanda," I said. Yeah, she's my best friend and this is why. She makes me feel better.

The next part of the story needed careful consideration before I told it. Freeman said they had been infiltrated. What did he mean in that context? So I said to Mario, "Freeman said they'd been infiltrated. He referred to my kidnapping and the fact that I'd been left otherwise unharmed in that house." Then I looked at Mario and asked, "Does that mean there are two groups?"

"It could," he said thinking. "It could also mean there are individuals that don't like them."

I nodded and said, "You want me to finish?"

"Yes."

I did. I spoke slowly, deliberately and related everything I could remember. Then at the end, another salient fact dawned me. "He didn't try to hide where we'd been very hard. It was almost as though he wanted me to follow him."

"Or expected it," Wanda said eyeing me briefly in the rearview mirror.

The only thing I did wrong in my summary of what happened to me was taking the wrong intent on Wanda's remark. I took it to mean that Freeman's reason for wanting me to follow him were of the romantic sort. Wanda's intent was wholly otherwise. While she saw sinister reasons, I saw softer ones. While I was entirely wrong, she wasn't entirely right either. But she was closer to the truth than I was.

Lordy.

CHAPTER 12

Kevin has one motel. We checked in, Wanda in an adjacent room and called it a night. She looked tired and hugged me before locking the door and crawling into bed. Me? Oh, no. I might crawl into bed, but after the stupid stuff I imagined with Freeman, I clung to Mario like wet toilet paper and didn't let go until *he* was deliriously happy. And, yes, you may read sex into that as in we did *it*. I held out until I saw the happiness in his eyes and then allowed it to overwhelm me. Then I hung onto him until the alarm went off at six the next morning. Had I not been married to a man that didn't like clingy broads, I don't know what I would do.

Breakfast was palatable. The eggs may even have come from chickens. I resisted thinking about whether the sausage links really were. When Mario got up to go to the bathroom, I jumped up, held him in a ferocious hug and said, "I'll be waiting for you."

He smiled, kissed me and left it for Wanda to say, "Would you try toning it down? I went to sleep alone, thank you very much."

"That obvious?" I said with what I hoped was a small smile and not one of delirium.

"Is water wet?" she said.

"Okay, I'll try to control myself."

Mario returned, paid for breakfast and took us into the parking lot. "Okay," he said. "Where is this house?"

I pointed north along Kevin Road and said, "Freeman dropped me maybe two miles north of the RV park on Kevin Road. We hadn't driven very long before he stopped and left me on the road." Then I stopped and said, "It dawns on me that he dropped me not far from where Wanda and I first saw their group. If the house is part of their operation, then it isn't far."

"Well, let's get on the road," he said.

We did. Wanda got behind the wheel and drove slowly toward the RV park that sat north of town. All of us noted the few new RVs in the park. We'd been gone a single day and the park had begun to revert to normal.

"Hold it," I said. Wanda stopped along the side of the dusty road. "Someone in that office knows something." It was a part of the story I'd omitted. I recalled vague images of people leaving their desks when I walked into the store. "There were cars starting in the parking lot," I said. "The offices are to the left of the front door. I don't remember how many there were, but I remember the back door closing and people leaving. It didn't take long before the only people there were Beryl and me."

"Should we go back?" Wanda asked, her voice untypically serious.

"Yes," Mario said, his voice icier than I remembered it being. He looked at me and said, "Do you mind if I do the talking?"

"No," I said. I can honestly say that was the moment that I felt fear. No, not a lot, but some. It trickled down my spine and I began to recall all the physical reasons that stress and fear happen – and, no, stress and fear aren't synonymous.

Wanda turned around on the road and drove into the park. She settled into a space from where no one inside the store would see us until we entered. Mario went in first. My mind raced ahead of me and I let it. *You arranged all this with the people who run the park. You'd have names and know who had the authority to do this.* He made a left turn and bypassed a receptionist at a desk and entered an office. Wanda backed a skinny girl back into her chair without saying a word. Me? I became a bystander, part of the crowd, albeit one that was far more attached to the participants than usual. That means I followed Mario into the office, but kept an eye on Wanda behind me outside the door. I also noticed that the person behind the register in the store was a girl, a teenager probably.

Mario didn't mince words or waste time. He sat down in front of a woman who was probably responsible for the famine in Ethiopia. Even her fingers were fat. As much as I wanted to start lecturing her about heart disease, Mario got right to it. "My wife was kidnapped from this building yesterday morning. You know who did it and I want that name,."

The nameplate on her desk explained her to be Marianne Dawkins. She started to get indignant. Mario leaned across the desk and said, "Or would you rather talk to the police? You told me once that the only reason you took my deal was because the park didn't do enough business. If we go the police and ask them to investigate a kidnapping from this office, what do you think will happen to your park?"

Her earlobes were fat, too. The flab under her chin didn't help her be any more photogenic either. She stared at Mario for a few seconds, turned her gaze to me and then said, "Would you understand if I said his name wasn't Beryl?"

"No."

She looked at me and said, "He told me he wouldn't hurt you. Did he?"

"He punched me, knocked me out and aside from the miscellaneous fondling, I spent six hours tied to a pillar," I said with my best icy voice, the one I used on patients who seemed to disregard my best medical advice. She looked pained and I decided to allow her to feel that way. So, I rubbed it in. "The clothes he gave me to wear were too small, caused the other men to stare and made me worry that fondling wasn't all that was going to happen." Okay, that much was a lie and I don't like lying, so I decided to say nothing more.

She closed her eyes and looked like a virgin who dearly wished she weren't. "If I tell you his name and he gets involved in anything legal, he can shut me down."

"Why and how?" Mario asked.

Wanda came in and whispered something to Mario. He nodded and she came to me. "The other people out here are getting nervous. The phone rang once and no one answered it. The girl at the register is watching us and not the customers."

They knew. Also, I was right. They knew something was going to happen to me and their instructions were to leave as soon as they saw me. the fact that I vaguely remembered people leaving when I walked in had been verified. 'Thanks," I said to her. I didn't use her name and didn't know why either. She went back to the door

Mario leaned back in his chair and said, "Lady? Do you know what leverage is?"

She winced and said, "That means you're going to talk to people. You're going to ruin me."

Mario turned and gave me a look that I've seen ever since I was four years old. It's a mixture of love, peace and everything that implies. He sighed, turned back to Marianne and the tone of his conversation changed completely. "My kids, the kids that came with us all talked about a water slide. The boys talked about a climbing wall," he said, his voice as gentle as I've ever heard it. Then he asked gently, "Would those things make your life easier here? Would they attract new business?"

Marianne stared at him speechlessly. "A spa?" she said. "I'd kill for a spa."

"All three?" he said.

"Why?" she asked suspiciously. I mean, I would have asked, too.

He smiled and said, "Look, Marianne. I'm not going to tattle to the cops because my wife got out okay. And you were willing to keep your park empty for us. I appreciate all that you did." Then he looked at me and said, "Evie? Tell her about Freeman."

I saw this conversation as unethical. I was going to tell her about Freeman's condition before I told him. And besides that, I had no business discussing a patient's condition with anyone but that person. Period. And he knew it. Damn it. He got up from his chair and pointedly did not touch me. Had he I would have said anything he wanted me to say. Instead, he turned to me and said, "Tell her how sick he is, how he has a disease that will kill him. Tell her how he bruises so easily and how his skin is turning yellow. Tell him so that she knows. Tell him that unless he gets further testing, that it might turn out to be a more virulent strain of the disease." Then he winced pretending that he didn't remember the name of the disease. "What's the name of it?" he said, the look on his face distinctly painful.

"Gaucher's Disease," I murmured. "He has Gaucher's Disease."

Bless the damn man. He told her everything she needed to know in order for Marianne to make a decision.

Two things happened then. One, she immediately melted. Her defensive attitude became one that told all of us that she was going to tell us what she knew. But also, she betrayed that she knew Freeman. If that was relevant somehow, I couldn't see it.

"Oh, that poor man," she said. "And they just had a baby."

No. *It's hereditary.* The odds that the baby had the disease were high. I murmured, "Then the chances of the baby..."

That was all it took.

"His name was Arthur Bridges. He's from Helena. That's about all I know about him.

There were so many questions Mario could have asked at that point. *Who was he that he could command your office to empty like that? What did he offer you? Or was it a threat? Or is he a relative of some type?* But he asked neither these nor any other question. Instead, he pulled out his cell phone and dialed a number I didn't see. It became quickly apparent who he'd called.

"Cayn, buddy," he said. "You remember the company we used to fix up the house before we opened the school?" He paused, then said, "Yeah, them. This is Marianne Dawkins at the Kevin RV and Motor Home Park in Kevin.

She has some work she wants done. Have them do it and bill me, not the school. The next voice you hear will be hers." He handed the phone to her and said, "This is Cayn Wyatt. We run a school in Kalispell. He's my partner. Tell him what you want done and he'll arrange it."

He picked up the phone and said to Cayn, "He'll call you back," and killed the connection. Then she slid it across the desk to Mario.

Before she could saying anything further, Mario smiled and said, "She doesn't believe me, babe."

"Obviously," I agreed.

He picked up the phone, made another call and said, "Cayn, buddy? Have Harry call me." Then he waited a few seconds and said with a wide smile, "Thanks, dude."

The next twenty minutes were spent waiting for something to happen. I wanted Marianne to be a bitch, but when the girl from the register came to her door, she took the time to sort out her minor clerical problem. Then we went back to waiting, none of us speaking. Marianne had her hands fold on her desk. Mario had his in his lap. He smiled at her, she just sat there looking confused. Me? I already knew what was going to happen. It did. His phone rang.

He answered it. "Harry! How's it going?" Harry Riggs is a gregarious man with a black beard that is slowly turning gray. Mario wants to invite him to our growing poker game, but we haven't had one in a while. My job is to make sure the refreshments are fresh. My added touch is to do it while wearing a Playboy bunny outfit. It probably doesn't fit anymore. It's also possible that all my jogging is in vain. But, Harry.

Mario talked with him for maybe ten minutes and left it that Harry was going to drive to Kevin to talk to Marianne personally. He told Harry to do whatever Marianne wanted – including nothing if that's what she decided. In that case, Mario told Harry that he would give him a thousand dollars just to drive to Kevin to talk to Marianne. That ended their conversation. Then Mario got up to leave. He slid his arm around my waist and I walked out of Marianne's office with him knowing that she was going to cave. She did.

"This is ridiculous," she exclaimed. "You can't just give me all this stuff! You don't even know me!"

"Then tell him you don't want it," Mario said and then turned away, his arm still around my waist.

"But…" and she had no more words.

Mario kissed me on the cheek and said nothing to her. He did, however, turn to face her. My part was loving that his arm was around my waist. Mmm, delicious. His part was to smile and wait for the inevitable.

She came around the desk and said, "You can't do this."

"You'd rather I came across as a cop? As someone who assumed you were guilty of something and worked from that point?"

"But…" and this time all of us knew something was lurking in the woodwork. Her hands fluttered like dying butterflies in front of her. Her eyes looked convinced that this was a cruel joke.

"Miss Dawkins," Mario said at last. "You don't owe me anything, but I owe you two nights of happiness with my wife that money will never be able to repay." Then he put his hands over his heart and said, "I cherished every minute I had here with Evie." Then he kissed me again, this time on the lips. My knees weakened for a moment.

But it was there, lurking in the shadows, a piece of information that all of us knew we were going to get. We did.

She looked at the floor and trumped all of our expectations. "Arthur Bridges is a businessman who deals in rare artifacts. He says that there is something coming across the border soon and he wants it. He said that if I said anything…"

All that meant was that Arthur Bridges was out chasing rainbows, his. It also meant that the other shoe had dropped. But our job – mine – was simple: find Daniel Freeman, get treatment started and go home.

Yeah, right.

CHAPTER 13

"Mario?" Wanda said as we drove slowly north along Kevin Road. "I need a spa, too."

"Move into a home that's anything but a rental and we can talk."

She hooked a lock of red hair behind her right ear, glanced at him as she drove and said, "Really?" She rented an apartment near our home.

"Really."

She wiggled her fingers back and forth between them. "Are you trying to get into my pants?"

"Hey," I said. "I'm right here."

"Ignore the babble from the back seat because it's not very helpful," she said.

"Wanda?" he said. "You're Evie's best friend, and as such there is little I won't do for you." Then he smiled and added, "Except that."

"So the spa is still in?"

"Sure. Buy a home first."

She looked into the rearview mirror and said, "Doc? You and me are going house hunting."

While they were jabbering, I was leaning forward between the seats and staring at the terrain up Kevin Road. Nothing but jumbled terrain was ahead of us. The road made a left turn a few miles from here in deference to it. A low plateau with farmland atop it was to our left. Also to our left was Montana's newest oil field. I had no idea how much oil was pumped out of there and didn't want to know.

A road branched off to the left. I said, "Stop there."

Wanda did.

I opened the door and walked out into pure Montana sunshine. Big sky country. I regarded none of it as worthy of note. If I haven't said it, let me address that issue. I tend to be monomaniacal and my current monomania was Daniel Freeman and not vacations and/or license plate slogans. I stood on the road looking south toward the RV park and Kevin. It looked familiar as it should have. Freeman dropped me here somewhere close by. I closed my eyes and tried to remember the drive from the house to this point. Did we make a right turn? *Yes. I was sitting there trying to be calm and the vehicle turned to the right.* I opened my eyes and pointed down the road that branched to the left and said, "That way."

We piled back into the Hummer and drove slowly down the dirt road toward the badlands that spread out before the plateau. Highly rumpled ground rose six to seven hundred feet before giving way to lush farmland. Somewhere between where we rode along another dirt road and the top of the plateau was a house I was going to recognize. I only hoped we'd find something that pointed at where Freeman had gone. "Slowly," I said. "I want to be able to turn back if I think we're going in the wrong direction."

Wanda inched the Hummer westward toward the plateau. It took maybe twenty minutes for us to reach a tangle of roads, one of which led off to the north, another that led west and another than circled back toward Kevin Road. I didn't have to say anything, Wanda stopped. And drummed her fingers on the steering wheel.

I got out and looked at the area. There are few trees here. Squinting, I looked in every direction, shielding my eyes from the sun as I did. What was I looking for? Trees. There had been one behind that house. Freeman took me out the back door *as though trying to make me see it.* Still, trees were sparse here. Worse, I saw no buildings at all, just a few pieces of construction equipment. However, the more I looked, the more I saw trees to the northwest. I pointed in that direction and said, "There. We're going there."

I stood looking at the area for several moments. Finally, Wanda said, "Are you coming with us or are you going to stay and appreciate the view?"

I smiled and said, "I think I'll join you." After I got in, I said, "Slowly."

Memory meant nothing now. The last time I'd been here, I'd been blindfolded. Even had I been trying to remember my surroundings, it would have been impossible *because Freeman had been talking to me.* Hmm. He hadn't made it easy for me because nothing was familiar. *Think, girl. If you believe he gave you clues, then why didn't he just tell you?* I looked out both windows and tried to force something to take a shape that I'd recognize. Nothing did. So, I did. "Stop. I need to think."

The Hummer came to a slow stop.

He took you outside. Why? Nothing came. *There were any number of empty rooms in that house he could have taken you into. Why take me outside?* Still nothing. *Ask him. He's involved just because you are.* "Babe?"

Wanda said, "How many times have I asked you not to call me that?"

I smiled and said, "I keep forgetting. Sorry."

She smiled back. It's okay." It was her way of staying involved.

"Why would Freeman take me outside to talk to me when the entire building was empty? All he had to do was walk across the hall and we'd be out of earshot. Instead, he took me through the back door. Why?"

Mario said, "Simple. The house was bugged. Outside was the only place he could take you without fear of being overheard."

"But the house was empty," I said confused.

"Maybe it's not going to stay that way," he countered.

"I have to walk," I said.

I opened the back door and got out of the Hummer.

To me, the problem was a medical one. It never dawned on me that something else might be going on until Mario got out from his side, walked to where I was pacing along the side of the narrow, dusty road and said, "There's oil from here to the Blackfeet reservation, Evie. Is finding this guy worth the trouble we might encounter?"

This is where I usually snap and remind him – again – how important medicine is to me. I don't mean to imply that Danny Freeman is more important than my husband; he's not. That said, I stopped myself before I started ranting because he asked a good question. Was it worth it? Wanda got out from the driver's side and added more medical fuel. "If Freeman has type 3, he could die within a few months without treatment." Then she waved her arm at the terrain and said, "And if he's out here? He isn't getting treatment and that compounds the problem."

I sighed and my irritation bled off. "Yeah. I know."

"We need to find him, Evie."

Mario stepped up and said, "Well, before we do? Consider this: by everything you've told us about the disease, his presence in that group could be a hindrance to them. They might exacerbate the problem by lashing out at him physically – which, if I understand everything you told us – could cause so much damage to his body that he wouldn't be able to continue. Am I right?"

"Yeah," I said thinking about the bruises he'd already shown me. If left untreated, he could start to show skeletal deformities that would probably remain irreversible. Worse, his kidney and spleen problems would get worse and so would the buildup of lipids in not only those organs but others. If his brain became involved, he could start convulsing or worse. He needed to be found and treatment started. "We could call the police and they could find him faster than we can, huh?" I said turning away from them.

Mario put his hand on my shoulder and turned me to face him. "Babe? Just say it."

"I can't keep screaming at you," I said tearfully.

"But?" he said smiling.

"What if they're up to something illegal and the manhunt kills him?" I said as calmly as I knew how. But the urge to scream and treat him as an outsider – and thus an idiot – was still there.

"Wow," Wanda said with a whistle. "You didn't scream at us. Does it hurt?"

"Funny, Lansing," I said. "But that's my fear. The police will compound a medical problem by making it a legal one – and our track record isn't too good in those cases."

"So, you think we should keep looking?" Mario asked.

"Yes," I said. My fear was that he didn't agree – or wouldn't.

He nodded up the dirt road and said, "Well, then. That way?"

Wanda threw her hands in the air and said, "Yes, yes. I know. Slowly."

"Wait a minute," I said. "You guys agree with me?"

"Always have." Mario said opening his door.

"And you?" I asked Wanda.

She stared at me deeply. "Sooner or later you're going to let me open up this Hummer and I'm going to have an orgasm doing it. That's my involvement. It's my weird sexual fetish for Hummers."

"Wanda," I said softly. "Seriously. Why are you here?"

She closed her eyes and wrapped her arms around herself. "I'm an ER nurse, Evie. It's what I do. You know that."

"Yes, I do," I said calmly.

"Do you know how many people wind up in my ER because the police got involved? Or don't you remember things like the Jennings Fiasco?"

Walter Jennings was a man going through a divorce. Separated from his wife and two small children, he'd gotten laid off after they separated. After three months, he was evicted from his small apartment and was living out of his car. Nothing in his background had prepared him for a life that included forays into dumpsters looking for food. Out of money and gas, he tried to go home to see the woman who was bent on becoming the ex-Mrs. Jennings. The one thing he brought with him that he shouldn't have was a cap gun in the shape of a Saturday Night Special. He didn't have enough money to buy caps either. He'd found the gun in a dumpster. A neighbor saw him approach the house with it and called 911. The response was almost instantaneous because, unfortunately for Walter, he lived near the police station. Or had.

Marcy, his soon to be ex-wife, was terrified of him as soon as she saw the gun. She called 911, too. With sirens closing in on him, he did to him the only logical thing left to him. He forced open the front door and tried to talk to Marcy. In the process, he was waving the toy gun around in frustration. The police came to skidding halt at just that moment. As Walter was asking Marcy, "Can I please sleep here? In the garage?" he swept the toy gun toward her because she was standing in the part of the living room that led ultimately to the garage. A cop saw this through the window and signaled a SWAT officer to take him out. The team took three shots and hit him twice.

No, he didn't die. He's spending twenty-five years to life in the maximum security facility in Deer Lodge, Montana. The fact that he's carrying a colostomy bag is irrelevant. The fact that his "weapon" could not have hurt anyone is also irrelevant. The most salient fact of his case – that he was looking for a place to sleep – is also irrelevant. Walter Jennings is there *only* because the police got involved. Had they not, he would have tossed the toy gun into his son's bedroom and left.

"Yeah," I said. "I remember."

"He wound up in my ER and I had to help treat him. He wasn't criminal. He was cold. Or don't you remember that it was February and there was a foot of new snow on the ground? I don't normally get involved in the lives of patients but I got curious because of you two," she said nodding at Mario and I. "You have some friends who are cops, but you make your attitude toward their professional lives very clear. Or again, don't you think I've heard all those internet rumors about the stuff your mother did when she was younger? I'm here because I agree with you. The world needs less violence and more understanding of one another. I'll be entirely satisfied if we find him and get him treatment before the police get involved."

I don't hate the police or even find them unnecessary. That's first and foremost. I support them and always will. However, as a culture, we have come to rely on them and the guns they carry than anything or anyone else. If I can find Freeman and get him treatment without the police getting involved, then I'll consider this vacation a roaring success.

As it turned out? One out of two ain't bad.

CHAPTER 14

The road curved to the left and there it was. The house. The rumpled land and the lone tree behind it were as I remembered it to be. Fortunately for us, no one was there. At least no cars were parked around it. Even so, Wanda stopped about one hundred yards from it and said, "What now?"

"Drive up to it," Mario said. "We lock the door, sit for a while and no one gets out."

Wanda gripped and re-gripped the steering wheel but only nodded. I said, "Okay."

We sat. Gray siding faced us. The window sills were painted white. None of the windows were broken. I tried to see the house as having been empty for a long time, but failed. Someone was taking care of it. There were no signs either; nothing that proclaimed it to be a business of any sort.

"Five minutes," Mario said from the passenger seat. "I'm going."

Well, naturally. Wanda got out of the driver's side and I opened the passenger door behind Mario. "Not alone, you're not," I said.

"What she said," Wanda agreed.

I would have walked up the steps and into the house. Mario started walking along the front looking at everything. Wanda started in the opposite direction doing the same thing he did. I stood at the foot of the steps and looked up at the front door. Mario disappeared around the corner of the house to my left and Wanda disappeared around the corner to my right. Me? Yep. I walked up the steps and looked at the porch. It was empty of anything, even something as decorative as a swing. That left the windows and the door. Soft white curtains covered the windows. Since I saw nothing moving behind them, I reached for and found the front door unlocked. I turned the knob and pushed it open. It swung smoothly and did not squeak. Still, it was the same as I remembered it being - at least from what I could see through the open door.

I stood on the porch looking into the living room. Nothing moved and no one came to see who had opened the door. After as much as a minute, I stepped into the room. It was as empty as the first time I saw it. The stairs hugged an inner wall to my left. The room where Knoll talked to me would be up them and to the right. The door to the basement where I spent a frustrating four hours of my life would be through the living room and in the kitchen. The voices I heard at the back of the house proved to be Mario and Wanda as they came in the back door.

"There's nothing outside and that includes any obvious transmitters or antennas," Mario said. Wanda just nodded. That meant Mario checked her side of the house as well. He looked toward the stairs and said, "You said that Knoll talked to you in one of the rooms upstairs. Which one?"

"Follow me," I said.

I went to the stairs and climbed them to the second floor. As I walked down the hallway, Mario signaled for Wanda to open the doors at the other end of the hallway while he opened the rest. Neither of them found anything or anyone.

"This is it," I said nodding at the last door on the right.

I stood aside as he opened the door by pushing it inward. It bounced off the wall behind it and stopped. He ducked his head inside the room but said nothing. I decided to stay that way myself. I looked at Wanda. She made a zipping motion across her mouth.

After Mario cleared it, I entered the room with Wanda. It was the same as I'd last seen it – empty, barren with not even curtains in the windows. There was a closet that took the entire space on the wall to our right. Mario slid the door open to view first one side and then the other. When he stopped, I knew he'd found something. He stuck his head out of the closet and motioned for us to come to him. Neither Wanda nor I spoke. He pointed to a black object stuck on the wall at the end of the closet that met the outside wall. He mouthed, "Microphone."

It struck me that they knew someone was here. I thought about it and then whispered in his ear, "Would there be a video camera somewhere?"

He shrugged. Then he paused and whispered in mine, "Probably. Good thinking."

I pulled him from the closet and led him down the stairs and through the backdoor. Wanda followed. I led him out to the tree and asked, "We're not here to debug that house. We're here to find something that Freeman might have left."

"Well, you need to know that they know someone is here and if they're any good, then they know who it is."

The rumpled landscape was behind him. I stood looking at it and tried to make a connection between it and whatever Freeman was doing and couldn't. "Any idea what this is?" I asked him.

"None," he said.

I looked at Wanda and she said, "A scavenger hunt?"

To me it remained simple: find Daniel Freeman. I looked back at the house and said, "I'm going back inside and start looking for whatever I think is there. Personally? I don't care if they know I'm here looking."

He shrugged and looked at Wanda. She laid her red hair behind both ears and said, "I didn't come this far to chicken out now."

"Let's go," he said.

The only place I thought about looking was in the basement around the pillar to which I'd been tied. If something wasn't there, I had no idea where to look. I said before we got to the back door, "I'm in the basement."

"First floor," Wanda said.

"Upstairs," Mario added.

I entered the back door and walked down to the basement. I stopped on the third step from the bottom and scanned the room. Logic seemed to escape me because I couldn't think of anything to apply to it. For example, if there was a camera down here, then Freeman would know it.

Would it affect where he put whatever it was? With no experience thinking that way, I decided to look. Naturally, I found nothing either on the pole or around it. *What now?*

Deciding that nothing ventured was nothing gained, I stood against the pillar the same way I'd been tied. I even put my hands behind it. Closing my eyes as though blindfolded seemed stupid, so I simply stood against the pole and saw nothing.

Until.

I can't say it was a glimmer of light because nothing in the room changed. But I saw it. Whatever it was An object was peeking from the top of a beam that crossed the stairs. I had no idea what it was. It would be easy to get to, easier to destroy. Taped to a two-by-four, it looked like nothing more than a cable of the type that makes our HD television work. Don't ask because I don't know. A small piece of glass was affixed to the end of the cable, the part that I saw. Walking up three steps so that I could see where the cable went, I saw it. I actually smiled and said softly, "You devil." A piece of paper was taped to the two-by-four in a place that even if the cable was attached to a camera, it wouldn't see the paper. I gingerly removed the tape and slid the paper from the wood.

I walked up to the top of the stairs, pulled the door closed and unfolded the paper. Written on an eight-and-a-half by eleven piece of printer paper, it was a note addressed to me. "Dr. Collins. I cannot stress this enough: do NOT approach me. Please check in at the Cut Bank Motel on Main Street in Cut Bank and leave instructions with the desk that will allow them to tell me which room you're in. I need to talk to you because my condition is deteriorating. I am exhausted almost all the time and I think I might have a broken bone in my wrist. If you don't get this? I assume I will die." It was signed, "Colonel Daniel Freeman, FCMM."

It was enough for me. I'd keep looking for him until I found him. Considering I had ten more days of vacation time left, I thought I had more than enough time. While I had no idea what the cable on the two-by-four represented, I smiled at it anyway and went back to the top of the stairs and went into the kitchen.

I caught Wanda pulling out drawers in the kitchen. Without saying a word, I stopped her and gave the note to her. She mouthed, "Cut Bank?"

I nodded.

She pumped her arm like a jock and did a dance on the kitchen floor. Well, I joined her. Sue me. I like to dance, too.

That left Mario. We found him upstairs lifting the lid off the toilet. I showed him the note and he smiled. "Where was it?"

"The basement."

"I mean where?"

I motioned with my head and said, "I'll show you. You can tell me what the cable it was taped next to is."

"Back cable?"

"Yeah, like the one that goes to our TV."

He smiled. "Fish-eye lens. It would be able to see the entire basement if placed correctly."

We went back down to the basement and I showed him the cable. He smiled and said, "Video only. No sound. But I was right. It can see the entire basement from here."

"Did it see me if I was standing here?" I asked.

"Nope. You were invisible for all intents and purposes."

"Then our next stop is Cut Bank," I said feeling as though our chase was at an end. Freeman would come to our room, I'd give him the diagnosis and stress that it needed to be confirmed with another test. All he had to do was accompany Wanda and I back to the hospital and he'd be as fine as someone with Gaucher's Disease was ever going to be again. His therapy would be ongoing but he'd be alive.

But there were two things wrong with my emotions. One, I'd forgotten he had a baby. Two, things never go as planned.

Unfortunately for me.

CHAPTER 15

Cut Bank isn't far from Kevin. But even though Cut Bank has barely thirty-one hundred people living in it, the contrast between it and Kevin was like the contrast between Los Angeles and Portland, Maine. Day and night.

We got there at dinnertime, checked in and gave the woman at the desk the instructions given to us by Freeman. All we had to do was wait for him to show up. I agreed to wait for him while Mario and Wanda went in search of dinner.

The room did not adjoin Wanda's. Another room was between us. That didn't matter. We were almost home. As motel rooms went, it was a nice one. A queen-sized bed, a small flat screen TV and a small couch that I would have called a love seat made up the basic room. I settled onto the love seat content in the knowledge that I could convince Freeman to come back to Kalispell with me.

Then someone knocked on the door.

This is it, I thought. *I'm home free.*

I got up to answer the door and found two men in it that I recognized. Private Donor and Sergeant Custer. Both were out of uniform; in civilian clothes, in other words. "Yes?" I asked.

"We're here about Freeman," Custer said. Donor nodded in agreement.

I smiled. *Freeman wants to know if I'm here.* "Well, come in."

They did.

Donor is slightly older than Custer. Not that it means anything. But since Custer ranked Donor in their petty army, he did the talking. "Colonel Freeman is waiting for you. He'd like you to accompany us to see him."

"Let me call my husband and tell him where I went," I said reaching for my phone.

"Could you do that in the car, ma'am? We don't have much time."

It seemed reasonable, so I said, "Sure. Lead the way."

Things seemed so easy and so straightforward that I had no problem going with them. Donor even opened the door and bowed slightly to me as we left the motel. The same Hummer he'd driven to Kalispell was parked next to ours in the lot. He opened the passenger door and said, "Please." I got in and he walked around to the driver's side and got in. Custer sat behind me.

The heavy vehicle rumbled to life as I gripped my phone. That's when geography took over. Cut Bank, Montana, runs basically northwest-to-southeast. The motel was on the southeastern-most part of town. All Donor had to do was pull out onto the road – which I did not know the name of – make a right and he'd be in thick farm country. A huge combine sat in a field alone but looking ominous in a green sort of way. Yes, I'd taken the time to play tourist. I can't say that it became the difference between what happened and what could have, but it didn't matter in the end. Had I promptly dialed Mario's number, the outcome would have been the same. But it started when I held the phone in my hand and tried to dial his number.

Custer reached between the seats with a club of some type and smacked my knuckles. Pain trumped everything and before I could react in any deliberate fashion, a hand came around the headrest, a knife was pressed to my throat and Custer said, "You need to remain silent, lady. Otherwise? Private Donor is going to have to hose out the Hummer." Donor reached into my lap, took the phone and slid it into his shirt pocket.

"Why?" I asked. "All you have to do is tell me what you want."

His voice sounded wet somehow. "I wanta fuck ya, lady. Still think we can talk?"

Donor pulled off road and snickered as he did. "I get sloppy seconds."

My head was back against the headrest as far as it would go. The knife was blade-first against my neck. I turned my head to lessen the pressure of the blade but Custer adjusted the knife to meet the new angle. I reached up with my hands to try to dislodge his hand and he pressed the knife so far into my neck that blood begin to roll into my blouse.

"Just keep your hands in your lap and you'll get to where we're going. Understand?" Custer said, his voice hot in my ear.

"Where are we going? You said to see Freeman. Is that it?"

Custer sneered, "Oh, yeah. Freeman. We're going to see Freeman. Right. That's what we're doing."

I could hear the voice of Uncle Alex in my ear. *Stay calm. No one ever did anything good while panicked.* That message was given to me eighteen years ago; I was sixteen. Alex played for the Patriots and was All-Pro at least twice, so his message to me was delivered as a middle linebacker would do it. "Destroy the enemy. Their job is to protect their fancy quarterback from people like me. My job is to send him back to his mommy in tears." Mario helped him teach me. But this? After medical school? After watching people like I'zzak Jenkins pour brutality on themselves? Could I be brutal to either Donor or Custer after all that training? Well, no. But I still took Uncle Alex's advice and stayed calm. It wasn't easy, though. For example, Custer seemed to have a sadists handle on the world. Or a bully. Either one, just choose. His voice dripped with what he wanted to do to me. Had I panicked, I might never have found out that his orders were to deliver me in one piece. To whom was still to be debated.

To stifle his bullish tendencies, I crossed my arms and smiled as I said, "So, either you're in to necrophilia or all you can do to me is what you've already done. How close am I?" I dabbed at the blood on my neck with my index finger and sucked it dry my sticking it in my mouth. "I imagine your blood is probably sweeter than mine. Am I right?"

That's when I discovered that the knife was a bayonet because he hit me on the side of my head with its butt. I can't say that bells rang, but it hurt. I winced, put my hand to my head despite his threats and said, "Damn, that's sweet. Have you been talking to my husband?" For the record. No, Mario has never hit me. And, no, I've never asked him to hit me. I was yanking Custer's chain; that's all.

Donor slowed; a house was in the near distance. I counted exactly two vehicles in front of it. The Hummer they'd driven was parked next to a rusted red pickup. Custer's bayonet dug into my neck again as Donor got out of the Hummer, walked around to my side of it and opened the door.

"Out," Custer said releasing the pressure from my neck. He scrambled out as Donor held a handgun leveled at my inherited bosom. *Thanks, Mom. I've got two horny wannabes in front of me because I inherited your rack.* Then I noticed that neither of them were staring at it. They were watching *me* and not *it*. *Well, thank you. Here I fret over my ladies and you two don't even notice them.* There was a trip to Victoria's Secret in my future and it was entirely ego based.

Custer motioned with his knife. "Walk."

"Should I wiggle my ass?"

"Don't matter. You ain't that great."

I knew it. I have a fat ass and floppy tits. Mario was right, that bastard. I would have wiggled as I walked but I realized I had no practice at it and didn't know how to do it without looking stupid. So, I walked to the house like a puritan might have.

This house was much less impressive than the one north of Kevin. One story, its walls were made of old logs, old weathered ones. A chimney on the roof was belching smoke. I noticed the windows were covered, sealed.

"Around back," Custer said pushing me.

Donor kept pace with his gun still leveled on my disinteresting rack. I felt like flashing them and screaming, "See! They're the best you'll ever see!" However, I don't think my ego could survived the laughter such a move would have caused. We went around back peacefully.

The first thing I noticed were the kitchen windows. They were not sealed. Frilly red and white curtains hung in them. Donor opened the door and Custer pushed me and spat, "Inside." I went and didn't argue with them.

I entered a room full of sweaty men. In another time and place, my hormones would have turned on full blast and I might have swooned. However, I have *never* been that girl and didn't swoon. Also, I didn't grow scared when a phalanx of four men sealed off the back door by closing it and then standing in front of it with their rifles at the ready. Donor and Custer faded into the crowd.

The only other person I knew stood from a small table spread with maps.

"General" Thomas Knoll. He was about to make my day real interesting. Had I known? I might have taken my chances with the four men with guns behind me. Why? Well, because I'm a doctor and fairly good at cause-and-effect.

And it was about to be aimed at me.

Like I said, had I known.

But I didn't.

CHAPTER 16

He started simply. "What's wrong with Colonel Freeman?"

I stated the obvious. "That's confidential between him and I."

Knoll had the usual Nazi haircut as practiced by the US military. Short, immaculate and liable to cut your finger if you touched it. The color was immaterial. At any rate, it was mostly gray. Also, the buttons on his tunic strained to remain attached to it. Especially over his stomach. Shorter than me – and I'm five-eleven – his weight easily approached three hundred pounds; a heart attack waiting to happen.

"I can make your life difficult," he said.

I restrained from laughing.

"Well?" he said. "What's wrong with him?"

"His condition is the same as yours. Paranoid fantasy."

That's when I noticed the winter weather gear piled on the table at which he stood. The only other thing upon it was a roll of duct tape. I felt uneasy and didn't know why.

"Please, doctor. I am a reasonable man and I have always believed that reasonable people can make reasonable decisions. I simply need to know if Freeman will be able to perform his mission. That's all."

"I can't talk about his condition with anyone but him. Is he here?" I said.

"You won't change your mind?" he said.

I struggled to stay calm and didn't know why. Still, I managed. Even in a den of wannabe soldiers and their guns, I managed to stay reasonably calm. "No," I said.

He looked at a man to his right and said, "Proceed, Lieutenant Green."

Without a word of warning, he punched me in the stomach. I folded up, dropped to my knees and men began putting a heavy coat on me. I was confused because I thought – at least in the beginning – that this was a gang rape. Heavy winter gloves slid over my hands. What was this? A pair of heavy winter thermals slid over my legs and up my body. As I began to get my breath back, Green said calmly, "Stand her up again." They did. And he punched me the same way as before. Then he slipped my shoes off and someone put heavy boots on the feet. Then they lifted me into a hard-backed chair. Green knelt and said, "Can you breathe?"

A man stood on either side of me holding me upright against the back of the chair. All I wanted to do was folded over and gasp for air. I shook my head instead.

"Let me know when you're okay," the man I knew as Green said.

Huffing and puffing, I finally said, "Yes. I'm okay."

He reached out, pinched my nose shut and I instinctively opened my mouth. A red ball was stuffed into and a piece of duct tape went over my mouth. A stocking cap slid over my head and face making me all but blind. Then another long strand of duct tape went across my forehead and wrapped around the chair. Tape went over the heavy gloves and obviously wrapped around the arms of the chair. The last piece went around my waist. I was stuck to chair more firmly than a bug on the end of a pin.

Knoll stepped out of the crowd and calmly asked, "Are you sure about this, doctor?"

It was difficult to answer his question, but I managed to say, "uh huh," behind the ball.

"Do it," he said, obviously to the men in the room.

They picked me up and carried me somewhere. It didn't take long to realize what their plans for me were because as soon as what I assumed was the kitchen opened, a wave of heavy heat enveloped me and I began to panic. They were going to induce hyperthermia – and if they were wrong on the timing, I could die.

Panic tried to swamp me. That's as easy as I can say it. I heard the snapping and roaring fire even though I couldn't see it. The heat hit me as though it were a hammer. *Don't panic, don't panic, don't panic,* I started telling myself as they sat the chair on the floor. From the immense heat and the popping sounds from the fire, I suspected I was as close to it as they could make me.

Knoll said, "I'll be back and we'll talk again."

And the door closed.

It didn't take long for sweat to begin popping out all over my body. Given the intense heat and its inability to bleed off – I assumed that's why they put a stocking cap on me – I tried to estimate how long I had before the first signs of hyperthermia began to appear. Of all the symptoms of hyperthermia, the one that I could not afford to happen to me was delirium or confusion. If that happened, I was dead because I'd never get out of the chair. On the other hand, if they wanted an answer to the question of what was wrong with Freeman, then they had to keep checking on me. A delirious doctor would be no good to them. So, my best bet was to let them keep track of how long I'd been in that room.

If a headache started, my task would become more difficult. Among the symptoms, that was one of the first. My blood vessels would start to dilate in an effort to dissipate heat. Given the heavy clothes I wore, that seemed unlikely to work. Nausea was another symptom, one that I could not afford to allow because given the fact of the ball in my mouth, I could choke to death on my own vomit. When my blood vessels began to dilate, my blood pressure would drop and I could easily faint as well. No, there were no good signs among the symptoms. That meant I had to do something. But what?

I wiggled my hands against the tape holding them to the chair and my right hand was looser than my left. That meant nothing because the tape wouldn't give. Unless my hand was smaller than the tape would allow, I was stuck to the chair. *Relax. Take the time to be thorough.* The tape held the glove firm. It didn't move much. My hand did. *Try.* I pulled my hand straight back and thanked their clumsiness that they hadn't taped my forearms to the arms of the chair. Otherwise, I wouldn't get even this slim chance.

The heat tried to grab my attention. It grabbed all the oxygen from the air and kept trying to distract me. I took a deep breath and knew that the first signs of hyperthermia were near. Given the level of heat, I had maybe a few minutes before *something* started to debilitate me. The first signs of irrationality began when I tried to spit out the ball. Failing, I groaned and pulled against the tape. I fought for control and wiggled my right hand inside the glove. My hand slipped through its confines just a bit. I wiggled and rolled it until it slipped further from the glove. The tape did its job and did not give. At all. *If you can roll your thumb into your palm, it might work.* With all my heart, I wanted to jerk my hand free but could not risk tangling the tape. If that happened, I might not be able free myself. So I rolled my thumb into my palm and moved my hand left and right, up and down until it magically slipped free from the glove. I wanted to cheer. I didn't.

I decided to remove the tape from my left hand. As much as I wanted that damned ball out of my mouth, I decided to free my other hand first. I noticed that my hand shook, the right one. From fear, exaltation or the effects of the heat I did not know. Inside the heavy mask, I closed my eyes and tried to calm myself. *Find the end of the tape. That's the easiest way.* Working blind isn't much fun, but I did. I ran my right over the unyielding tape and felt where they'd ripped it from the roll. My blunt fingernails weren't much use on the stubborn tape, but I finally got a grip on it and began unwinding it from my wrist.

My hands were free. The urge to shout in triumph was still there. The ability to restrain myself was fading, however. *Free your head.* I did the same thing to the tape around my forehead and found the place where they'd ripped it. This time it was easier than before. Someone had gotten careless and hadn't smoothed the edge of the tape down. It came off easily. I slipped the stocking cap from my head and spit the ball across the room. It rolled to the front door. I noted briefly that the door wasn't sealed, just closed. It was getting difficult to think, the heat was that bad. Sweat rolled from my forehead in streams. I used the heavy coat I wore to damp it away. Then I found the end of the tape around my waist and struggled to unwind it. I'm not sure who did it or when, but a single piece of tape went down between my legs. Had someone groped me? Realizing that it didn't matter, I finished my effort to remove the tape from my waist. The effort almost left me screaming. I didn't, but it was getting more and more difficult to keep my temper intact. *Just finish the job,* I chided myself.

The tape around my ankles hadn't been applied very well. Both strands came off easily. Once done, I stood, free. But free to do what?

The first thing I did was to strip off the winter clothes. It made conditions in the room more bearable. Still, it was hot, very, very hot.

My first mistake seemed to be a final one. I wanted to investigate the door a bit closer and took a few steps toward it. The sound of the boots clomping across the floor almost panicked me. How could they not hear it? My footsteps seemed as loud as gunshots. If I took off the boots and escaped, would my socks provide enough protection outside? *No. Leave them on. You can be more careful.*

I stood still and looked at the room. Nothing, not even a carpet. The windows, as I already indicated, were covered with black paper. I moved carefully to a window to the left of the door and inspected the paper. *Tar paper.* Its only purpose was to keep the heat inside. Back in Maine, people used plastic sheeting. Was this any better? Well, it was enough because the heat was intense. My clothes were sweat-stained and I kept dabbing the back of my hand across my forehead. *Take a look.*

I'd lost track of time and was a bit surprised at the darkness outside. I punched a hole in the bottom of the tarpaper and peeked through the window. Once done, I peeled the paper over the hole so anyone outside wouldn't see the bright light from the fire. Then I sat against the wall and another piece of irrationality crossed into my mind. *I'm not even attractive enough to rape.* I squeezed shut my eyes and a few tears escaped. *Don't you dare! You do this because you have no choice!* I decided that the thought of my rape being overlooked was a sign of mental confusion. So I let myself to think about what I'd seen through the window.

There were still only two vehicles in front of the house. It begged the question, how did all the people get here? It did not answer the question of how I was going to escape. Whatever I did, I had to move quickly because of Knoll's warning, "We'll talk again." They would be back to ask about Freeman again. Given that I thought I'd already experienced a few signs of hyperthermia, the chances were good that Knoll's people were going to come in here soon. So how was I going to get out there?

The idea came to me as I stared hypnotically at the fire. I smiled to myself and hoped I survived my answer.

Time, short time, would tell.

CHAPTER 17

I was going to burn down the house. Old logs were stacked next to the fireplace. They gave evidence that Knoll and his people were going to take their time with me. My plan was simple: start the fire at the front door, so that anyone outside it would at least pause before he came inside. Then throw the chair through a side window and hope no one was there. If I stopped and thought about it too much, I wouldn't do it. So I did.

I used the old coat to pick burning logs from the fire. The logs ignited the coat, but I persisted and laid it against the door. Then I repeated the process three more times. By the end, I was lucky I didn't have burns on my hands or arms.

The only part left was to wait for either door to open. Then I'd throw the chair through the window and hope for the best. Panic rose in my throat once again when I realized I hadn't checked the windows for obstructions. What if they were barred? What if there was a bush or a tree that would prevent me from slipping away? I had to check. I poked my finger through, and damning the consequences, peeled away enough of the paper to see that the outside was clear as far as far as I could see. At least the window would break and let me outside.

Smoke began to fill the room. As stupid as it sounds, it was a consequence I hadn't foreseen. If someone somewhere didn't notice the smoke soon, I might be in no condition to make a break. I pulled my blouse over my nose and stood by the window, the chair in my hands.

The flames licked the door and it started to burn. If anyone was out there, they'd see the smoke and then the flames. Since the door was unlocked, it was possible that someone out there would or could enter. That made me grip the chair in readiness. I also had to watch the door that led back to the kitchen. If I hadn't been sweating already, the situation would have made me do so.

While I thought it most likely that the door to the kitchen would open first only because there were so many more men back there than in the front, that didn't happen. I heard the doorknob turn and then immediately stop. It took a few moment for me to realize the doorknob was probably hot. I waited. Then a gun butt hit the door and I threw the chair through the window. Yep. Shards of glass. My perfect plan had a drawback. What to do? I looked back at the fireplace and decided that the logs were my only hope.

Not caring if they heard me, I ran to the fireplace, grabbed the longest and narrowest log and carried it to the window. The men outside the front door were hammering on it with gun butts because I could hear them each time they hit the door. It wouldn't be long before they were inside with me. I used the log to clear as much of the glass from the broken window pane as I could. When the door splintered, I went through the window shoulder first.

And stayed there. My off-the-cuff logic went this way: if he goes to the window, he'll look into the distance and not straight down. That would allow me time to disarm him. Naïve? Completely. There were any number of reasons, too. First among them was the second soldier. *He* could look down. Or any of the men in the kitchen. They might not even be back there, but might be outside the window waiting for me. Knoll was probably the key man here. If his organizations skills were better than his appetite, then he might have his men spread around the house. If so, I didn't stand a chance.

All I could do, though, was lay beneath the window and hope that I could grab his gun and yank it from his hands. It didn't take long for me to find out how well thought-out my plan was or wasn't because the gun barrel came through the broken window and it was show time.

They say that all high thoughts disappear when you are afraid. I can testify to that because I was terrified when I reached up grabbed the gun barrel with my right hand. All thoughts of being a doctor were gone. All pacifistic thoughts evaporated. All pretenses to being a better person than you just disappeared as I pulled that gun down toward me. In that moment, I was prepared to use it, too. That is, if I managed to get it away from him. It fell toward me.

You can't be the daughter of Melodie Chang and not know how to hold a gun. While I didn't like it, I knew how. I stood and pointed it at the man who stood in the broken window with his life in my hands. You can't know how it feels to *want* to kill someone unless you've been in that situation. Sure, it isn't uncommon to feel hatred toward a person that includes the obscene thought, "Why, I oughta…"

The commotion stirred the men in the back because the door opened and a head popped into the room. I was going to get killed. There were no other options for them. At least that's how I saw it. They couldn't afford to take the chance that I would finally go to the police. So, I did the only thing left to me. I ran. Well, I dropped that hideous gun first. Then I ran.

I heard shouting behind me. The only assumption I could make was that it was directed at me. Maybe it was. I don't know. But I ran blindly and fearfully. In truth, I expected to be shot in the back. It never dawned on me that I'd made a good decision about wearing the boots. The ground I ran across was broken and full of sharp rocks. But like I said, it never dawned on me.

The first stupid mistake I made was running parallel to the road. Any help I could get would on it and not next to it. Why? Because I was running toward pure farmland. Stacks of hay stuck up in the darkness. The second stupid mistake I made was diving into one of them. Why? Because I became a stationary target. If they found me, I was theirs to do with what they would. It totally trumped the reason I burned their house down. All I knew was fear. I hunkered face down in a huge pile hay and just shivered. *Go away,* I said to myself and then kept repeating it. *I'm a doctor, not a contestant on Survivor.*

Slowly, though, the noises and voices abated and I felt alone. I'd dived head-first into the hay and hadn't moved. All I'd accomplished was to tuck my long legs into the hay. If necessary, I would lay there all night.

I'll never know how long I lay there before a voice said, "Lady? You okay?"

I know this much. I screamed. Then I heard laughter and that settled my stomach. A lot.

I swam through the hay until the stars popped out in the heavens above me. Even though I was more settled than I'd been, I became wary when I saw a single man standing in the moonlight. It got even more weird when he put his hand out toward mine and said, "Hi. My name is William Moon Owl Moore."

My reply was full of dignity.

"Huh?"

His laugh was gentle "I'm Blackfoot."

"Oh, I'm Evie."

He asked again. "Are you okay?"

"I think I wet myself." I said *stupidly.*

"Maybe we should call a cop."

That did it. I was no longer addle-brained "No. I just need to go home." I grabbed his hand and he pulled me from the hay.

I couldn't know it, but he was the answer.

The Answer.

His being there was not a an accident, not even a fortuitous circumstance. He was there only because Knoll and his people were. Of course, all that lay in the future. I couldn't know this man with long black hair was going to weigh his future with me in the balance. As it turned out, his decision was to kill me until I told him my name.

"You got a last name?" he asked.

"Doctor Evie Sixkiller-Collins Collins. People tend to call me Doctor Six."

That did it. He spared my life based on my name. And no, he'd never heard of Doctor Six. He knew the name Sixkiller. I couldn't know it, but my life was saved by my ethnicity. And one more wild coincidence that I'd learn soon enough. And, no, I'd been taught not to believe in them. But here he was.

My own very coincidence.
Thank you, Great Spirit.
Or whatever you are.

CHAPTER 18

His first command sounded harsh. "Stay down."

I crouched behind him and looked in the direction he faced. The house had caught fire. The living room where I'd been placed looked to be totally involved. I expected to hear sirens, but didn't.

"You came from there," he said, his back to me as he watched what I did.

"Yes."

"What happened to you there?"

I stood and didn't care what his reaction was going to be. "They dressed me in winter clothes, tied me to a chair and then put me in the living room of that house. The fireplace was full of burning logs and they sat me next to them. That's what they did to me."

"Why?" he asked.

"Because one of them is sick and they wanted me to breech a confidence."

He looked back at me and said, "That's it?"

Savior or not, *that* was something I couldn't allow. "I'd protect you the same way. Daniel Freeman is my patient and I will not spread his condition over half of Montana!"

"Danny Freeman is sick?"

"That's none of your stinking business!"

"Then how did you get the name Sixkiller?"

"My father was a quarter Sioux. His father was full-blooded. My father was Brian Sixkiller and his father was a man named Danny Sixkiller. I've seen pictures of him, but he died long before I was born."

It became possible that I would never know what those names meant to him because he turned on me and put his huge right hand around my throat. Oddly, the pressure he exerted on my windpipe left me as clear-headed as I'd ever been. I stretched my neck out and held my arms wide. With the voice left to me, I said, "Here. Let me make it easier for you."

"I'll tell you why I'm going to kill you."

"Sure."

"If all that is true, then you'd be the daughter of Melodie Chang and that is impossible."

Despite his grip on me, that was enough. I knocked his hands away and spat, "That bitch! Everywhere I go, she's there! It doesn't matter how well I do, what pains I have or even how successful I am! I get Melodie Chang thrown in my face every stinking time! Just once I'd like to do something without her damned name come up!"

He put his hand on my shoulder and said, "Excuse me. I have to do something."

"Whatever!" I half screamed.

He one-punched me. Just curled up his fist and laid me out. I was ranting and pissed one moment and the next I was gone. Well, unconscious. I woke on the passenger side of an old pickup. I might have screamed, but I felt a hand on my shoulder. Then the Blackfoot I knew as Moore said in a flat voice, "I apologize. You were starting to get loud and I didn't want Knoll and his people to find you."

My jaw hurt. Again. Tied up and punched twice in as many days. It got old real fast. "Well, if you that again, I'm going to take out one of your eyes."

"I haven't decided. I might still kill you because I think you're lying to me."

"You got a phone?"

"Yes."

"Dial this number and put it on speaker."

"Why?"

I smiled. "Don't trust me. How white of you."

"What's the number?"

I gave it to him and he dialed it.

"What time is it?" I asked.

"Nearly nine o'clock."

"Damn. It nearly midnight where she is. She might not answer."

"If she doesn't, I'm going to kill you."

"Yada yada. Better people than you have tried."

Still, the phone rang once, then twice and I began to worry. Not about me, but about her. She has a thing for ringing telephones and the number I'd given her sat on their nightstand not three feet from her head. It was impossible she couldn't hear it. Unless of course they weren't home.

"Come on, Mom," I said to the ceiling of the cab as I leaned back in the seat. "How hard can it be? Just pick up the phone and say…"

"Hello?" she said at last. "Who is this?"

"Hey, Mom," I said to the top of the cab. "Planning any breast reduction surgery?"

"Evie?" she said.

"Who else besides anyone else in our family would wake you at midnight and not fear for their life?"

"What's wrong?"

Bless you, Mom. You always worried about me.

I elbowed Moore and said, "Say hello, asswipe."

"If you really are Melodie Chang, then you should know Daniel Sixkiller's middle name." Danny Sixkiller was my grandfather on my father's side.

"Horesemount," she said in a voice that made me worry for Moore.

"Really, Mom?" I said laughing. "That was his middle name?"

"Yes, and who is the imbecile with you. It isn't Mario."

"No, Mom. I'm not planning an affair. Just straightening out a few facts."

She'd be sitting on the edge of the bed running her left hand through her long hair. She'd be worried, too. So it fell to me to take things down a notch. "Hey, Mom? I'm really sorry to wake you like this, but we're planning on a last-minute visit to Portland and hope you'll still be there."

"Evangeline Monica," she said with gritted teeth. "You tell me what's wrong and what that man is doing to you or I'll call the FBI myself."

"Oh, relax, Mom. Me and Bill here…"

"William," he said.

"Whatever."

Mom stopped. I could see her. Whatever his name meant to her had caused her to sit straight up on the bedside. Her eyes were focused, clear and alive. "Young man? What is your name?"

"William Moon Owl Moore."

"Oh, lord," she said. She'd sighed, relaxed and probably laid down next to Brad, my stepfather. "Evie? Meet your cousin."

That sat me up straight Mom had been. "Mom? You'd better explain that."

"It's simple," William said. "My mother and your father were brother and sister."

"Mom? Dad didn't have any sisters. Grandma knew better. What the hell is this?"

William put his head on the seatback and said, "Half brother and sister."

"In order for that to be true, then grandfather Danny had to…"

"Dabble. Yes. William's mother was the result of a one-night stand Danny had in Bozeman while he was in a training class. William's mother is older than your father. In fact, he hadn't met Nikki, your grandmother, yet."

"And grandmother didn't know?"

I could see the smile. "How do you think I know? She told me."

"And you couldn't find it in yourself to tell me! You do know that I live in Montana!"

"William?"

"Yes, ma'am?"

"First? Knock that shit off. I'm Melodie. Second? Your cousin tends to get hysterical."

"Yeah," he said calmly. "I got that."

"Hysterical!" I screamed. "Mom! I'll show you hysterical."

"William?" Mom said. "She's harmless."

"I got that, too. You have a good night, Mrs. Chang."

"Thank you. We need to meet some time."

"My guess is that your daughter will arrange it."

"Evie?"

"Yeah, mom?" I said angrily.

"When that meeting happens? Make sure it isn't midnight."

And she hung up.

William extended his hand to me. "Welcome back to the world."

It was so stupid that I started giggling and couldn't stop. "Where the hell are we anyway?" I asked.

"I was going to dump your body in the creek down here," he said. "But a higher power advised me to not to kill you."

"The Great Spirit?"

He shrugged. "Well, unless his name is Melodie Chang, then sure."

"I can't call you Bill?"

He shrugged again and said, "Sure. Just once and then I'll risk any great spirits named Melodie Chang, kill you and throw your ass in the creek down there."

"Which means we are where?" I said looking over the end of the hood.

"Let me show you," he said and got out of his side.

The Moon was nearly new, a sliver hanging in the sky. I got that much about astronomy from Mario and our visits to the roof of the RV. I knew gibbous Moon, waning crescent Moon, first quarter, third quarter and several other phases. How Mario knows all that stuff is beyond me.

We went to the edge of a cliff. He looked down and said, "It's not quite one hundred feet from here to the bottom." Then he turned on me, grabbed me by the neck and held me out over nothingness. If he released me, I was dead.

"You're going to arrange that meeting," he said.

"Okay," I said holding onto his arm.

"Sooner rather than later," he said.

"Not until my business with Daniel Freeman is over."

"You realize what will happen to you if I let you go?"

"You realize you'll never meet my mother if you do?" I responded.

"Are you too stupid to be scared?" he said, his face twisting.

"How about this? I'm not afraid of you, but the fall is something else because I can't swim." Well, I could, but I was being a wiseass.

He pulled me from the brink, but held me three inches from his face. "Why is Daniel Freeman so important to you?" he growled, his long hair waving around his face. Then he held me nose-to-nose and said, "And note that I did not ask what is wrong with him. I only want to know why he is important to you."

"Have you been eating garlic?" I asked irreverently.

He growled and threw me so that I rolled a good twenty feet. At least it wasn't over the cliff. Then he stood over me and held down his hand again. "I could do worse than have a crazy cousin," he said stoically.

I stood without taking his hand and brushed myself off. "I need your phone," I said.

"Answer my question and I'll let you have it."

I sighed. He was asking me why I cared about my patients. I went to the edge of the cliff and looked upon the dark land. The city lights from Cut Bank were off to the left. It was darkness that pulled at me, however. Every disease ever identified by man rested in the city lights. It was the darkness where all the unknown things that can harm us lurked. Freeman was out there in the darkness. Yes, I knew he had Gaucher's Disease, but that was nothing more than a preliminary diagnosis. Anything that lurked in the night could be afflicting him. I owed it to him to find out, treat it and make him better. He was merely the latest incarnation of my mother.

"William? I'd feel this way about you if you were sick. It started with my mother and continues through Freeman. Yes, I have a preliminary diagnosis but I need to make certain that there is nothing else wrong with him. Nothing else matters but Daniel Freeman."

"You're a healer."

Other people have called me that. The name never seemed to describe how I felt, however. I've tried to put a name to it, but nothing comes as close as "obsessive". Obsessive doctor? Obsessive healer? I push myself ragged and then keep pushing. Once I saw Mario staring at me. I'd gotten out of the shower and my mind was on my latest obsession. But it was the look on his face that I'll remember until I die. Adoration. Complete devotion and a mesmerizing love that I cannot comprehend. Naked, I feel bloated, fat and ugly. Clothes just cover my imperfections. But that look? He saw Aphrodite while I thought I reflected Medusa. When I take the time? Oh, god, I love him. But do I do it often enough? No. Categorically no. My obsession runs to people that are ill or who are about to become that way, not to my family. I asked Mario once, "Why do you stay with me?" His look betrayed a man who knew the answer, who knew exactly why he stayed with me. "There are many reasons. Do you want the complete list?" I said, "Yes. Please. I need to know because I'm horrible to you."

And he told me. He unwrapped his heart, peeled away the layers and said, "You're in here. You have always been in here. Since I first saw you when I was five, you have been in my heart holding my life together." And I cried. I felt unworthy of his commitment. Then he took my chin, forced me to look at him and then he said, "You cannot fail me or us. No matter what you do, you will pursue it with a vengeance that makes me feel sorry for others. Please, Evie. You are a great success here in our home. And in my heart? There is no one else."

I said these things to William Moon Owl Moore, a man who was my titular cousin. I felt no attachments to him, felt no tugs of strings, felt no obligations toward him. Yes, I have a large family and I feel many of those things to them, especially Aunt Tiffany back in California because she taught me what being a Collins meant when I was a kid. But I felt nothing toward this man who came out of nowhere and swept me to…safety? I mean, was I safe? I don't know.

But as I finished, he nodded in the dark, his question answered. He gave me his phone and I held it for a moment. Then I asked the big question, the one that was going to propel me across the next few days. "Are we okay?" That one. So simple it was, so direct, so straightforward, so easy. It held all the emotional attachments that a man like him would covet.

His answer? One word.

"Sixkiller."

And he walked back to his truck. And I missed a connection that might have made things easier. But then, I've got a lot of practice figuring out stuff that tries to hide from me. I also have a lot of recent practice at being tied to immovable objects. My point? I was going to be tied to him – metaphorically speaking – for the next few days and he was going to prove to be every bit as immovable as that pillar had been.

Fortunately or unfortunately for me.

Depending.

CHAPTER 19

I followed Moore back to his pickup. As soon as I settled into it, he handed his phone to me without saying a word.

I called Mario.

"Evie!" he said with clear surprise in his voice. "Where are you!"

I smiled. "You are not going to believe who I ran into."

"Who?"

"A cousin on my Dad's side. A guy named William Moon Owl Moore."

"Yeah," he said calmly. "Yeah, his mother's name is Trudy and she lives on the Blackfoot reservation in Browning."

He knew? And I didn't? "Mario!" I said hotly. "How did you know about him and I didn't?"

"Can I have the phone?" he asked.

I gave it to him without saying anything to Mario.

"Is this Mario Collins?" he asked, still stoic. He must have said yes. "Been wanting to meet you, too. Talked with your sister a bit ago. Interesting ladies in your family." Whatever Mario said, Moore grunted. Then he said, "Yeah. Does your wife look like her mother?" Moore looked at my chest and said, "Yeah. That would be too cool." Then he looked out the windshield and said, "We're outside of town a bit. Tell me where you are and I'll take her there." He nodded, nodded again and then said, "Yeah. I know where it is. We'll be there in five minutes."

He started the truck and it rumbled to life. He found a road in the darkness and drove until things got familiar again. We were back on the main street in Cut Bank. I wanted to learn its name, but felt a need to keep my eyes on Moore and not the street. He turned into the Cut Bank Motel parking lot and I saw the Hummer in front of our door. I breathed easier when he parked next to it.

Mario threw his arms around me and kissed me, or tried to. I put my elbows between us and pushed him away. "Explain how you know him!"

He looked at Moore and said, "Are you him? William Moon Owl Moore?"

"Yeah."

"Mario!" I insisted. "How do you know him?"

He shrugged and stared at him. "I don't. I know his name. Nikki told me once when I was maybe nine or so."

"Grandma?" I said quizzically. "Why did she tell you and not me?"

He smiled, but was looking at Moore. "You were reading the labels on aspirin jars in the bathroom and she told me that Moore's name would mean nothing to you."

Moore nodded at Wanda. "You related?"

She crossed her arms and said, "Best friend."

He grunted. "Practically sisters."

"Amen," she said. "Good thing you didn't hurt her."

He shrugged." I was going to kill her, but then she said her name and I figured she was the best way to meet her mother."

"The senator?" Wanda and Mario said simultaneously.

"My mother says that Melodie Chang has powerful magic."

"And the boobs to go with it," I said. Then I grumped, "I lost my purse again."

Mario smiled, but kept his focus on Moore. "It's on the bed."

"But I took it with me!" I stammered.

"Found it outside the door here." Then he said, "You got a place for the night?"

Wanda hooked his arm and said, "Yes, he does."

They left.

"This family gets weirder by the day," I grumped again. Then I went to the bed and pulled my purse into my arms as I slumped to the bed.

Mario sat next to me and slid his arm around my waist. "Wanna make another one?"

"Why?" I sniffled. "You'd wind up raising him."

"Her. It's going to be a girl and her name is going to be Anne."

"Naturally," I grumped again. "That's Mom's middle name."

"Oh, yeah," he said distractedly. "But I was thinking of Anne Hathaway." He whistled. "That girl is hot."

I hit him in the ribs with my elbow. He says I have sharp ones. "Pig."

"You mean she isn't?" he said pulling me down to the bed next to him.

"Mario," I whined. "We can't have another baby. When would I stop to nurse, have her and do all the other things?"

"We hire someone."

"A surrogate?" I said clearly not believing him.

He snapped his finger and then pointed it at me. "Yeah! We take an egg and a few little wiggly men and mix them in a surrogate and Anne is born!"

"Wiggly men?"

He kissed me on the cheek. "You know what I mean."

"I don't know," I said. "I mean, what with my schedule and…"

"Well, think about it," he said kissing my cheek again.

"Anne Hathaway or the baby?" I said smiling.

"Both," he said. "But she'll never be as hot as you."

He stared at me and I began to fall away again. It was always that way. He could have me whenever he wanted me and always could. Maybe the magic between us was that he never took me until he knew I wanted him. Well, I did just then, but the damned room phone rang.

"That would be Anne," he joked.

I stretched to reach it, then pulled to my ear and said, "Hello?"

Wanda said, "Breakfast is on you. Bill said we go together."

"He doesn't like to be called Bill," I said fearfully.

"Here, Bill. Tell the bitch," Wanda said to him.

"Except when she does it," he said. "And she's right. We go together."

"If you..."

"Don't bother to threaten me, lady. Just be ready at six."

He hung up.

I scrambled to dial her room number and Mario took the phone from me and put back in the cradle. "She's okay."

"But..."

"Trust me, girlfriend. She's as safe with him as you are with me."

I stood angrily, put my fists on my fat hips and spat, "And you want in my pants! Is that what you're telling me he wants?"

He lay back on the pillow, put his hands behind his head and smiled. "Yes to both."

Speechless. Trust me. That doesn't happen to me very often. But my mind went blank. I stood and stared at him, then turned my focus to the wall where Wanda lay with a crazy Indian just two doors down and then returned my focus to Mario. I might have stammered. It's possible. I'm fairly vocal – even when I'm speechless. His smile remained wide, hopeful and happy.

"But..."

"She is. Safe, I mean."

"But, he's... she's..."

"That's right. They are."

Dumbstruck. That follows speechless. Well, at least in my dictionary it does. When that happens? Not even squeaks. I'm completely mute. And it doesn't end until I get an outside stimulus. It didn't count when Mario gently reached for my hand and pulled me onto the bed either. It very definitely counted when ran his finger up my crotch. Then he said, "I've been meaning to ask you about this duct tape you have on your pants."

I rolled on top of him and said, "Who cares about duct tape." I kissed him, felt him caress my fat butt and moaned. He was right about another thing. Like they were, I was. In love, I mean. Willingly. Who knows, maybe Anne won't need a surrogate.

The alarm rang at five the next morning.

I can say one thing about our night. Mario straightened out all my kinks.

Lord, did he ever.

CHAPTER 20

I think I was purring when we sat down to breakfast at a restaurant near the motel. Unless I missed my guess, Wanda was, too. God, it was worse than prom night. We stared at each other across the table and started giggling like teenagers.

Moore looked at her and said, "Are you going to do this every time?"

"Oh, god, I hope so," she said hugging his shoulder.

He slid his massive around her, pulled her into him and that caused me to turn to Mario and say, "Ahem. Dude?"

"What?" he said feigning stupidity. Trust me. He's not stupid.

I put my nose to his and said, "Hug me, jerk."

Well, he did and it didn't seem forced either.

"We need to talk about why I didn't kill Mrs. Collins last night," Moore said as bluntly as he'd done everything else.

Mario sipped his coffee, then said, "That would be a good thing to know."

Wanda looked up at him and asked, "Are you ever going to kill me, Bill?"

He hugged her and said, still stoic, "Wanda? There is a very good chance that I'm going to fuck you to death."

She looked like she ready to go, too. She patted her chest and said, "Oh, good lord, yes. Bill? Can we…"

"Later, Wanda. We got the rest of our life. First, I have to tell this story."

She murmured, "Fucked to death. Oh, lord. Oh, my god."

I took her hands and said, "Should I worry about you?"

She squeezed them and said, "Only if he does it wrong."

"Ladies?" Moore said. "Can we return to the subject?"

I didn't think it was possible, but both Wanda and I blushed. "Sure," I said feeling hot.

Moore looked across the table and asked Mario, "I know your wife is looking for Freeman, but my agreement was with Knoll. I was supposed to meet him last night and ran into her. My business with Knoll was supposed to be simple: take him to the transfer point, collect the money and leave. Nothing in our agreement mentioned a nutty doctor running around looking for yet one more patient." Then he looked at me and said, "Or do you not know how close to death you came?"

Mario was about to answer him when I just waved my hands at him and said, "I can handle the stupid Indian."

Mario sipped his coffee. Wanda tried to sip hers, but fell into a spate of giggles. It got so bad that she put her forehead on the point of his left shoulder and giggled until her entire body shook from them. Moore kissed the top of her head and said, "Is she always this dismissive?"

"No, sometimes she's asleep," she said between giggles that wouldn't stop.

I waggled my index finger at Moore and said, "Dismissive? Don't you assume for one rotten second that I can't defend myself. Or did you not get it that I escaped from a burning house?"

"You did?" Mario said.

I stared him into silence without saying a word. Then I turned back to Moore and continued with, "I don't give a good you-know-what about why you and them were out there. Or haven't you been listening? Freeman needs medical attention and I'm going to give it to him. You got that?"

"If that's true," he said, "then why would they try to kill you in a burning building? Nothing we arranged said anyone was going to be killed."

"Unless you did it," I snapped.

"That's correct," he said stoically.

"Um, Evie?" Wanda stammered. "I'm going to need another hour or so."

"Oh, put a cork in it, Wanda!" I snapped. "We're here to find Freeman. Remember? And his diagnosis is a condition that worsens over time. Remember?"

"Damn," she muttered. Then she said, "Sorry. Never felt this way before."

Mario folded his hands and asked, "And what were you exact arrangements? And you mentioned a transfer point. What was being transferred?"

For the record: I didn't care. Whatever illegal plot they had arranged was moot as far as I was concerned. Pot, cocaine, it didn't matter. And, yes., I aware of all the hallucinogens that get smuggled into this country every day. I see the people who buy, who sell, who find them and try them, who purchase bad lots and die, who overdose and the ones who do it as a last resort. I see all of them and know the score.

He looked at me, but answered Mario. "I was to receive a package about five feet long and one wide. It was to be left at a specific coordinate easily identifiable by my GPS unit. Once in possession of the package, I was to take it to another point on the reservation and hand it over to whoever showed up and gave me the corresponding password. That person gives me an envelope with money in it." Then he added with fierce intentness, "The contents of the package were not revealed to me. In fact, I don't care what I'm transporting as long as I get paid."

Mario turned to me and said, "And she's the only reason you didn't?"

Moore turned on me and said, "Correct."

"And her mother is the overriding reason?"

"Correct."

I had just one word for the situation but I try to be a good example for my children. Hell, I said it anyway.

"Fuck."

Moore looked at me long, steady and hard. Then he said, "It would be better if you came to terms with her."

"I've always wanted her to come to terms with me," I replied icily.

"She deserves your respect. Unless, of course, you can show why she does not."

"And what does she have to do with smuggling?" I asked.

I'd like to say that his answer fulfilled everything I could have asked, but it didn't. Well, maybe it did because he kept talking after he gave the first part of his answer.

It started when he said, "I never thought I would ever hear that name, Sixkiller. Then you said it as part of your name. Lady? I know every adopted son, daughter, brother and relation you have." That part. The part where he mentioned my father's name. Sixkiller. That name. No, it wasn't anything bad; it just started a cascade of recent memories in my brain. What memories? These: When Freeman first saw me on Kevin Road, he held up a picture of me and called me, "Sixkiller."

How did he come to know that name? And from where did he get my picture? It was at that point, when those questions and a few others ran through my mind, that I stopped Moore. "Hold it." He stopped. Maybe it's not merely Mario who sees the look on my face that screams, "I'm thinking here! Shut up!" Maybe others see it, too. Maybe those others include distant cousins who want to meet my mother, the freaking magic goddess of the Blackfeet Reservation.

"How would Freeman know my name?" I said to no one in particular. "Moreover. Why would he know that name?" When he identified me with a photograph and said that name, I didn't ask him why or how he came by it. I got angry and made a rudely dismissive remark. Maybe I have to stop doing that and listen to people who aren't sick. Had I known Freeman was sick, I might have been nicer to him. I turned to Mario *again* and sniffled. "I'm sorry, Mario. I promise…" He kissed my nose and, for once, it wasn't enough. I needed to be a doctor as well as a human being. I needed…

"Evie," he said as calmly as ever. "You think better than anyone I know. Who would tell Freeman that your name was Sixkiller?"

An answer didn't come until…

I looked at Moore and said, "You told him."

Finally, a smile.

"Correct."

Wanda put her hand on his shoulder and said, "You aren't going to kill us, are you?"

"No."

She sighed, put her forehead on his shoulder again and said, "Oh, thank god. I have this pretty little outfit that I can't wait for you to see."

"That and Melodie Chang are why I won't."

I smiled and said, "Well, thank you for that, but do you mind getting your face out of my girlfriend's crotch and tell me what you and Freeman are up to?"

The story, as it was told, implicated so many people that I finally told Wanda to take Moore back to her room because I needed time to think.

I didn't have to ask her twice.

CHAPTER 21

"Do you believe him?" I asked Mario over coffee.

"And what does the answer to that question have to do with Daniel Freeman?" he replied.

Indeed, what did it? My tongue itched with unspoken sarcasm. It was difficult to hold back, but I managed. Mario knew, but didn't say anything. Bless him. Still, the question was a valid one and I needed to provide an answer that would satisfy him or we were going back to Kalispell.

"Because if Moore is telling the truth, then we might become involved in a police case."

He smiled. "Dear? We already are, or what do you call being tied up two days in a row and threatened with death?" Before I could wax sarcastic, he added, "Your answer merely confirms what I already knew. We're going to find him regardless of his legal circumstances."

"Are you okay with that?"

He batted his eyes at me and said, "Your beauty blinds me to anything but your desires."

"My beauty," I muttered dismissively.

"Evie? How much do you weigh?"

"What's that…"

"How much?"

"One thirty-five."

"How tall?"

"Five-eleven."

"And your butt?"

"Isn't fit to barbecue."

"Look. Can we put this to bed? You are the most delicious-looking woman I have ever seen. Period. There isn't an ounce of fat on your body, you work-out regularly, watch your diet and yet you see a person that I don't. Can we agree to disagree?"

"Well, I'm glad you think I'm pretty, but this isn't making any decisions about what we're going to do next."

He smiled again. "I thought we'd already decided."

"And if we get involved in a firefight with the cops?"

"We set up a triage area and start tending the wounded."

I still didn't like it. "Mario? If Moore is right, then he admitted to us that he's at least a smuggler. Can we afford to trust him?"

His answer put the question to rest. "Evie? You admitted that you trust him as soon as you let Wanda go back to her room with him."

True. As much as he thinks that my logic is firm, his is firmer. If my butt was as firm as his logic, I'd be drinking lattes on the French Rivera that were served by ignorant French waiters. Well, no I wouldn't. I'd still be a doctor, but maybe to ignorant French waiters and pool boys. "Do we wait until they're done, or interrupt them now?"

"We wait," he said.

"Damn," I said. "I'm getting impatient."

"Still."

I looked out the window and let my mind slide away to…Anne. I had to admit that I thought my childbearing days were over, but the thought of having another daughter – and one with my mother's middle name – was almost intoxicating. "What's her middle name?" I asked with a small smile on my face.

"Whose?"

"Anne's."

"Tiffany," he answered.

"Anne Tiffany?"

"Anne Tiffany Sixkiller-Collins Collins," he said adamantly.

"No. Anne Paula-Tiffany Sixkiller-Collins Collins," I countered.

"Anne Tiffany-Paula Sixkiller-Collins Collins," he said with a smile that made it final.

"I like it. When do we start?"

"As soon as you stop taking the pill."

"Are you serious about Anne?"

"Well, can I return her if she turns out to be a him?"

"No. That means we need a boy's name," I said.

"Let me think on it," he replied.

That took us to Wanda's room whether or not they were done. I knocked on her door and a *completely* satisfied voice said, "You may enter."

She was *smoking*. A sheet pulled up to her chin, her smile of the Cheshire variety and a smoke ring hanging over her head. "Dear, dear Evangeline," she said with a voice that pictured her purring somewhere. "Please come in." Moore had her under his massive arm. She took another puff and exhaled another smoke ring.

"Since when do you smoke?" I asked.

"That was so wonderful that I don't care if I die right now. Nothing can top that."

Moore looked at her and said, "I need to try harder?"

She kissed *him* on the cheek and said, "Oh, lord, no. Any better than that and I wouldn't survive it."

"Then please care about your own survival, Wanda," he said, entirely nonplussed.

"Look," I said. "Can you two get dressed because we've decided that we're going to ask Moore to take us to Freeman." Then I looked at him and said, "And don't turn yourself into a liar by saying you don't know how to find him."

"I do," he said. "But she stays out of it."

Naturally. Wanda shrieked, "What!" Then she climbed onto his lap face-first and started snapping orders in his face. Well, this looked like fun. I crossed my arms and Mario slid his arm around my fat waist. That left us to watch Wanda start jerking her head as she spat, "I am *not* staying behind! You will *not* treat me like I'm a weakling! You will *not* leave me here! You will most certainly take me with you and bring me back horizontally!"

Stoic to the end, he looked at her and said, "Horizontally?"

"You need a frigging picture! Horizontally, the same way I get laid!"

"Mario?" I said turning my head toward his but keeping my eyes on Wanda. "Is it a coincidence that the words 'whore' and 'horizontal' sound similar?"

"It's not a coincidence. It's a certainty."

Moore looked at her, then us. "I would feel better if she were not involved."

I bumped Mario and said, "He probably feels the same way. Get over yourself, Moore."

"And you, Mario?" Moore said.

Mario looked at me and said, "Get Wanda ready. I'll talk to Moore."

"Better you than me," I responded.

And, yes. She was naked. And, no. It didn't bother me. I did, however, have to pull her out of the bed because she wrapped her arms around Moore and wouldn't let go until he kissed her lightly. Then she unwrapped herself and allowed me to lead her into the bathroom. I turned on the shower – cold – and pushed her into it. Naturally, she started screaming at me and making up words as she went along. Resigning myself to a change of clothes, I got in and wrapped my arms around her. It was as cold as I intended it to be. Still, I was wearing clothes while she was naked. All that means is that it was worse on her than on me. "You need to be clearheaded here, Wanda," I said. "He could be wanted. We don't know. And I'm not saying that you should stay here, I saying that you need to be less star struck than you are."

"Star struck!" she screamed as cold water pummeled both of us. "All Mario has to do is look at you and you're sloshing around in wet pants!"

"And he knows it," I said. "He doesn't do it when we're working. Moore? All he needs to do is say your name and you swoon like a teenager on her first date. So, Please? Be as level-headed as you always are and then jump his bones in private?"

"Two conditions," she said.

"And they are?"

"One? Warm water. Right now."

I leaned over, turned on the hot water until the spray was warm and then said, "And two?"

She reached down, picked up the bar of soap and said, "My pubic hair needs to be washed. If you start now, you can finish in time to do my hair."

We both started laughing at the same time. "This is why I don't shower with you," I said. "It always leads to sex."

It was fun.

The last we were going to have for a while.

CHAPTER 22

We approached Browning, Montana, from the east. It isn't thirty-five miles from Cut Bank to Browning, so it wasn't much of a trip. While I didn't like it, Moore insisted on taking his own truck and Wanda insisted on going with him. Mario drove the Hummer because I was too worried about Wanda to concentrate on something as mundane as driving. Worse? She sat right next to him on the seat. Moore had his right arm draped over her shoulder. I resisted the temptation to stick my head out the window and scream, "Take your filthy hand off my friend and drive, asshole!"

Mario studiously avoided giggling.

Our first stop was at a sign just inside the reservation. It's nothing more than one of those big ones that proclaim "The Blackfoot Reservation". He told us he was going to stop and we did. He even told us why. There was going to be a sticker pasted on the back of the sign in its bottom left corner. It would have numbers written on it in ink that wouldn't run when it got wet. It would be the geographical coordinates of where Moore would meet Freeman. He would know where the coordinates were by the GPS unit mounted on his dashboard. I suppose all good smugglers have them.

His brake lights came on and he made a left turn onto a single-lane dirt road. Farmland rolled past us on either side of it. I had no idea what they were growing and didn't care to learn. It might have been corn. It might have been lettuce. Hell, it might have been marijuana for all I cared.

He drove slowly through it and we came to a dirt parking lot that serviced a lake. "Mission Lake," Mario murmured.

"How do you know?" I grumped.

He smiled. "The internet will never tell."

Yes, there was a car parked at the end of the lot. The last time I saw Freeman, he drove a Hummer, a different model than ours, but a Hummer nonetheless. Now he was parked in a dark blue four-wheel-drive pickup that had one of those compartments in the bed just behind the cab. I wondered if whatever Moore was smuggling was in it. If so, did that make Freeman a smuggler, too?

Moore parked to the left of Freeman's truck and we parked to his right. There were two boats in the lake, both of them showed people fishing. A man cast a line toward the deep water in the center of the lake. I'd never been fishing.

Freeman was alone. On that score, I had no expectations. I'd heard that he'd had a baby and I knew the disease to be hereditary, so that chances of that child having Gaucher's was at least fifty-fifty. It depended on a genetic evaluation I was not prepared to do just then. Later, yes. Not now.

The first thing that painted Moore and Freeman's meeting as different was when Moore wanted to clasp him in a bear hug. Freeman simply put his hand in the middle of Moore's chest and said, "Can't. I got something wrong with me and you might break a bone." That left me. He turned to me and said, "So? Do you have any idea what's wrong with me?"

Again, it seemed over. After I gave him the diagnosis, he'd come with me and we'd finish it. He'd get treatment, the baby would be tested and each of them would get a test to see who passed the gene to their baby – if the baby had the disease.

"I have a preliminary diagnosis," I said. "Gaucher's Disease. It's a genetic disease in which fat accumulates in parts of your body. It affects organs such as your spleen, liver and kidneys and even possibly your brain. We need to get you back to Kalispell, or barring that, to see your own doctor. The disease can be serious and can also affect your children. I was told that you have a baby. If so, that child needs to be tested."

"What did you call it?" he asked distractedly.

"Gaucher's Disease, named after a French doctor who first described the disease in the 1880s."

He sneered. "He was probably Jewish."

I shook my head and said, "What's that got to do with anything?"

He looked away and mumbled, "Nothing."

But the seeds for what was going to happen had been planted. Possibly, quite possibly, the few days since I'd last him had been just troubling enough that his off-the-cuff remark about Jews popped out unwanted likes pimples on your first date. And, yes, they did the first time Mario and I went out on a serious date. Damn the luck. Anyway, while he might not have wanted to drop that remark like he did, he had dropped it and it stood like a pregnant girlfriend in front of your parents.

"We need to see your wife and baby, get DNA samples from them and then retest you. Are you and they available right now?"

His jaw moved uneasily. I saw bruises on his forearms and his back was starting to bend under the insistent pressure of his enlarging spleen. In fact, it dawned on me that his remark about Gaucher being a Jew could be a symptom of brain involvement. I seriously hoped not, but only testing would confirm it.

"Um, no," he said. "I was hoping for a pill or something." He nodded toward Moore and said, "We have business."

Moore said, "Not any more. The redhead has my loyalty."

"That would be me," Wanda said like a girl who'd just won the Miss America pageant.

Freeman became animated for the first time. "Look, Moore. I can't do this alone, especially not in my condition. We had an agreement. Your freedom for your help!"

While the remark meant nothing to me, Mario stepped up and asked, "Does this have anything to do with what we talked about, Moore?"

"Yeah," he said and nothing else.

While even Mario's aside meant nothing to me, Freeman trumped all of their conversation when he said, "You can't change our agreement or I'll escort you back to Helena in handcuffs!"

Okay, I tend to be a bit dense. But that remark made me think aloud. "You're a cop," I said.

"Fuck," he said as he turned toward the lake.

So many questions popped up in my mind that they seemed endless. Among them was the one I stepped next to him to ask. "If that's true, then why did you seek out me?"

"Never mind," he said and walked to the lake's edge.

Well, I followed him and asked, "My guess is that you already have a doctor and that Moore, for some reason, sent you to me with my maiden name. Why? And why shouldn't I just go home right now? You don't need me."

He sighed, but it looked like one of weariness. "Do you remember Debbie Hollis?" he asked as he watched the man in the nearest boat cast a line into deep water.

"She ran my mother's election campaign for senator," I said, starting to feel a bit uneasy.

His smile looked weary, too. "Yes, she did. Right after she tried to kill your mother."

I smiled and said, "Well, that's…"

Freeman smiled back. "Debbie told me the story just before I went undercover. All for a man. She expected to spend the rest of her life in jail and your mother hired her to run her campaign." His smiled got wider. "There's a rumor that a lady named Paula Watkins got pissed and wouldn't take an apology without lunch."

Okay, dammit. Yes, that's true. Deborah Hollis tried to kill my mother about eighteen months ago. Mom's answer was to hire her and turn her into a friend. By everything that I have heard, Debbie counts herself as Mom's left-hand man. Paula has her right. "How did you hear that?"

He kicked at the dirt along the narrow beach. "I work for Governor Layne," he said referring to Governor Donald Layne. "Debbie came here as part of a delegation after your mother got elected to help set up negotiations with the

Blackfeet for rights to oil on their land. The tribe wanted to set up casinos, but your mother thought that the oil would bring quicker economic relief. Debbie with a few representatives from Alaska who gave their recommendation that the money the leases gained should be spread among the tribe. They need it and Debbie fought for it. The Governor made an appearance at the negotiations and I met Debbie. While I was staring at your mother and not doing my job, she was waxing eloquent about what a terrific person she was. I asked why and she told me."

"What's that got to do with Moore and him being a smuggler and me and why you're telling me this story rather than telling me to go home?"

Moore moved next to him on the other side and said, "Mario told me to tell you everything. I will even if you don't." He looked like a mountain and spoke as deliberately as one might. His long black hair lay thick on his massive shoulders. But above everything, he looked calm.

Freeman looked anything but. Weariness hung on him like a curse, but he came alive enough to say, "I'm not sure I believe everything you said, Moore. Everyone that works for Layne is a Jew. They're deep into his administration and they're looting everything that isn't nailed down." Layne was a narrowly-elected Democrat.

"Really?" Moore said. "Ramos is a Jew? And that lesbian he has working for him? What's her name? O'Toole? She's a Jew, too?"

Moore referred to Arthur Ramos, a Blackfoot who advised Layne about Indian affairs, and Hayley O'Toole, who advised him on social issues. I smiled, but Freeman got upset. My smile was of the secret variety because I knew something about Freeman that he obviously did not. When I looked at Mario, I could see that he didn't know either. I smiled and winked at him. He shrugged and I mouthed, "Love you, dude."

Freeman continued to murmur and mumble about how Jews and socialists had penetrated not only federal government but state as well. Considering he used my mother as a means to seek out my services as a doctor, and my mother has been accused of being everything from a Nazi to a Communist, I thought I might have been looking at a type 3 Gaucher's patient. If that turned out to be true, then a test would be moot.

"Can we go sit in your Hummer?" I asked him.

"Yeah," he replied. "I need to sit down."

What I had up my sleeve was going to tell me if a further test was necessary at all. He turned and headed toward the Hummer. I kissed Mario and said, "Just us. Okay?"

"I'll be here with Moore."

I smiled and said, "And who's going to keep Wanda down?"

"Oh, ha ha," she grumped.

"Me," Moore said. "This has all the trappings of a sadistic movie. I'll protect her while you defuse Freeman."

"And me?" Mario joked.

"Don't worry," Moore said. "I'll take care of you, too."

That left Freeman and I. I was going to give him the best medical advice I had and frame it in a way that might tell me if his condition warranted immediate help. Meanwhile, he was going to counter with something that I hadn't even considered – and counter with something that made me revise what I thought about his condition.

Yeah, you may read that I thought I was holding all the cards.

Well, no.

CHAPTER 23

I started bluntly. There was no reason to beat around the bush. "Mr. Freeman? You have Gaucher's Disease. It's a hereditary disease that is characterized by the deficiency of an enzyme – one named glucocerebrosidase. This deficiency causes a fatty substance known as glucocerebroside to build up in your body, specifically your kidneys, liver, spleen, bone marrow and in the worst cases, your brain. It also affects the blood cells, hence the pigmentation issues. It is not curable, but is treatable. I recommend immediate treatment. You and I should return to Kalispell and the do an enzyme test to get a confirmation of the diagnosis." I paused and then added, "I have heard that you had a baby recently. Is that true?"

He held out his bruised arms and said, "Will he look like this?"

"How old is he?"

"Barely three months. Mary worries about his development. She says he seems slow."

"Three months is fairly young to notice things like that."

"You're telling me that Marcus has this thing, aren't you?"

"Are there any other symptoms?"

He shrugged and said, "Well, I'd call it sway back. His spine seems really deformed."

"That's his spleen pushing against the spine."

He looked out his window. He gripped the steering wheel so tightly that I had no doubt it would come away bruised.

"Mr. Freeman?" I asked, getting down to it. "How long has your family been in the United States."

Without looking at me, he said to me, "Since the range wars end at the turn of the twentieth century. My great-grandparents settled in Wyoming. They homesteaded land in southeastern Wyoming but were driven off by cattlemen. Why?"

"Because there needs to be a determination made over how you got the disease and from who. It would help if your parents were alive. If not, the doctors will ask you about them. Start by telling me." The last part was to see if I was right. I had a fairly good idea of where this was going and needed him to cooperate.

His face got hard and I thought he was going to argue with me. Instead, he said, "I don't want Marcus to have this."

"He'll need to be tested. Your wife, too. What's her name?"

"Mary," he said sadly. Then, "What do you need to know?"

"Are your parents still alive?"

"My mother is." He frowned as though something had upset him suddenly. "My father died when I was young."

"Where does she live?"

"Bozeman," he replied. "I grew up there."

"Would she consent to a DNA analysis in order to see if she carries the gene?"

He shrugged. "You'd have to ask her." Then he frowned at me and said, "You aren't talking about Marcus. Tell me he'll be okay, that he won't have this thing."

"You want an honest reply? I can't tell you that until I both see him and have him tested. It's a painless procedure that will tell me everything I need to know about him. But please remember; it's an hereditary disease. You got it from either your mother or your father. That's certain."

"I live in Helena. Mary and Marcus are there."

"Then we need to got here and see them."

"No," he said with what sounded like an adamant voice. "We need to finish this." He curled his right hand into a fist and almost pounded the steering wheel with it. Then he looked even angrier. "I have a chance to bag a few Jews in this and I'm going to. Layne and his ilk can go fuck themselves as far as I'm concerned."

Well, there's no time like the present to tell him. I laid my hands in my lap, looked out at the blue waters of the lake and said, "Gaucher's Disease shows up primarily among people of European descent, central European to be exact, Ashkenazi Jewish Europeans to be even more precise." Then I looked at him and said, "In all likelihood, you're Jewish, Mr. Freeman." Then I added, "Your name was once probably spelled with an 'ei' rather than a double 'e'. It would make your name German in descent. Either way, you have a disease that is common to people of Jewish heritage."

However, I'd made a crucial mistake here and wouldn't even become aware of it until much, much later. My only defense is that I'm a doctor and not a religious scholar. The mistake? Well, it passed among us without any of us catching it.

His reaction was immediate and emphatic. "Get out," he said with a spurt of anger that didn't surprise me.

"Why?" I said as calmly as the situation warranted.

He leaned to my side and spat, "Get out; because if you don't…"

And I interrupted him by leaning toward him. We were nose-to-nose over the center console. "You're planning on doing something spontaneous and stupid. Given your condition, you're going to need a doctor with you. So just do it and let me tag along."

"I DON'T…" he screamed.

Yep. I interrupted him again. "Yes, you do," I said, my voice still calm. I'd admit to some nervousness at this point, though.

Mario came to my window and said, "Are you okay?"

The door locks all popped into the lock position. I rolled my eyes and said to him, "Yeah. Just be ready follow us."

That did it. He put the Hummer into reverse and shot out into the dirt parking lot, a clouds of dusk masking us. Then he put it into gear and shot out of the lot northward toward the exit and Highway 2.

I knew two things about where we were. One, that if he made a left turn, that he could go either north or north once he got to Browning. Given that he said he lived in Helena, my bet was south. But, two was that the Great Plains basically start here. The high country and the trees that go with it were basically to our north. That meant Freeman had nowhere to hide because the terrain was mostly open. Yes, there were rolling hills that he could have used, but it didn't look as though he had any intention of doing it. He turned hard left on Highway 2, not stopping for the sign and roared toward Browning.

Have a cool head, girl, or you could get killed. "You know," I said. "If you tell me where you're going, I could drive."

He turned his face toward me and lost full sight of the road. "This is your fault, Jew lover!"

I smiled because Mario says I have a nice one. I hope he's right. "I was kind of hoping that you wouldn't kill the messenger."

Browning was approaching rapidly. I couldn't see the speedometer but I wouldn't have been surprised had been doing a hundred. He slowed when he saw the sign for 89 south. Well, that's relative. His speed dropped to maybe seventy-five. Huge plumes of dust rose into the sky when his front tires went off the road. And, yes, it was tourist season in Montana, so the roads weren't empty. If he kept this up, someone would call a cop and we'd be both be thrown in jail. My best bet was to smile again, hope that Mario wasn't merely horny when he said it and said, "Oh, come on. You can rant at me while I drive."

It never dawned on me – because I had the stress of being killed in a rollover accident – that Wanda was following us in our Hummer and that one of Freeman's issues was losing her. Of course, it likely never dawned on Freeman that he was getting irrational and sounding that way, too. He ranted and raved about Jews and Communists in government, basically sounding like he was a teabagger looking for a camera. That said, imagine my surprise when he slowed to maybe fifty, maybe even less, looked normal for a moment and then went off-road between two folds in the terrain to the right.

I didn't see how Wanda could miss us because Freeman threw up another plume of dust as the Hummer slid to a stop in the thick grass. Actually, I wouldn't have minded seeing Wanda right about then because I had to admit to fear. Yes, I was scared. I'd invalidated everything that Freeman felt about the world and then expected him to take that news rationally and calmly. I turned my head toward the rear and tried to see if Wanda either drove past us or stopped and went off-road where we did. I neither saw the Hummer nor anything that looked faintly like it. I was alone to defuse a man who could easily be in the grip of a debilitating illness that could easily rob him of any grip on reality.

He put his head on the steering wheel and moaned.

"Um, Daniel?" I said trying to sound familiar. "Is this your way of letting me drive?"

That started a long string of profanity that made it obvious he was used to working around men. Most of the language was sexually appropriate. It took maybe five minutes for him to run down – and I mean that literally. Exhaustion popped out on his face like police lights in your rearview mirror. "Yeah," he said sounding on edge. "Maybe you should."

"Give me the car keys," I said with a very forced smile.

"Shit," he said smacking the steering wheel. Then he grimaced and used a few female specific curse words.

"Let me see your arm," I said. I hadn't forgotten that he'd already gone on record as thinking he had a broken bone in his hand.

He extended his right arm to me. His face was toward the window on his side. "My wrist," he said. "Hurts like a fuckin' bitch."

I ran my fingers along his wrist, both dorsal and ventral, top and bottom. The scaphoid bones below his thumb did not seem normal. There are many bones in that area of the wrist and most common way to break one was to catch yourself when you fall. "Did you fall recently?"

"I didn't fall, but I caught myself from falling. I put my hand to the wall and felt something odd in my wrist. Is it broken?"

"My opinion? Yes. One of the bones below your thumb." Then I smiled and hoped it didn't look phony. "That's another reason I should drive. Please? The keys?"

It appeared that he was holding his temper only under a lot of pressure. He bit his bottom lip and then pulled the keys from the ignition and threw them at me. Then he opened the door with a hard push and exited into a tall stand of Montana grass. I compared his actions with those he'd shown me back at the RV park. He'd shown patience there that he wasn't showing now. Could I ascribe pressures to him now that he didn't have then? Or was this an example of behavior as dictated by his physical condition? My best answer? A little of both. All of which meant that something had changed for him, changed personally. Maybe I should try to find out before we got to his home, or to his mother's home.

He was waiting for me at the front of the Hummer. I got out on my side, keys in hand and stood at the right front fender. "I could disable you and leave you here," he said.

"You could try. I doubt you'd succeed."

He wasn't convinced. Maybe he needed a lesson. I stepped up to him and said, "What would be your first move?" I stood ready before him, stood on the balls of my feet ready to move in any direction. His move was a jab at my chin. I deflected it with my forearm and stopped my counterpunch at his chin. "I can do this all day, Danny."

"How did they catch you then?" he asked.

"The punch in the store? Easy. I walked into it. That was the last thing I expected. And the house over in Cut Bank? There were at least a dozen men in that room. Despite how things go in the movies, I literally had no chance but to submit." I stood easily in front of him and asked, "So, what now? Do we go see your mother or your wife?"

"My mother," he said. "It will take all day to get there." Bozeman was easily a four or five-hour drive.

"You ready?" I asked.

There was nothing he could say that would convince me that he was ready to face his past, especially in front of his mother. And what happened at her home beat all of my expectations – and they weren't real high to begin with.

But the stakes were getting higher. It would have helped had I known that.

Pity that.

CHAPTER 24

Freeman's mother lived on Alderson Street, just north of the Montana State University campus. The house was pale blue. There were towering oaks on either side of the property as well. He'd told me her name was Petra Freeman and that she worked in the admissions office at MSU. He told me a lot of other things about her because we had those four hours to fill. Well, five because we stopped for dinner in Helena. I asked about Mary, his wife, and he grew nervous and emotional. He even changed the subject to his condition and finally asked what it would do to him if left untreated.

"Death," I said. "Your organs will fill with fats that it can't clear and you will die. You need a definitive test and then treatment." Then I looked at the house and said, "You want some advice?"

"No," he said and got out of the Hummer.

I got out and followed him to the front door. Under a sloping porch roof, the door was pale white with an old-fashioned knocker in its middle. Without using it, he opened the door and called out, "Hey, Mom! Where are you?"

There was a big red Ford SUV in the driveway, an Explorer. If it was hers, she was here. Since there was a Dodge RAM pickup next to it in the double-car driveway, she might have company.

The house looked like Mario had been there. He decorates our home. I just live there. This looked like one of his better efforts. The room looked comfortable and an easy place to rest, relax and recuperate. The couch looked plush and inviting, the layout of the room invited you to sit and talk. Given what Freeman told me about his mother, she entertained a lot, so the room probably had lots of practice being used. As an aside, since he told me she hadn't remarried, I didn't want to know why she was living in a three bedroom home when Danny was an only child – and he lived in Helena.

I thought I'd gotten an answer to that question when a fairly attractive woman came out of the hallway to our right, a man following her. It wasn't until I recognize the man – it was Knoll – and the fact that he had a gun pressed to Petra's head just behind her right ear that I saw our situation as being a bit more precarious than I thought it might be.

"Well, mother," Freeman said spitefully. "I see you run in the best circles."

Knoll said with a hateful smile, "Freeman? You're coming with me and your mother is coming with us."

Well, no. I stepped into the middle of the crowd and said to Knoll, "Not until I get an answer to a few questions." Petra, for one, looked absolutely terrified. She wanted to scream but was afraid of what Knoll might do to her if she did. I smiled at her and said, "Knoll? Could you exchange me for Petra? She's pretty scared and I'd like to alleviate her tension. Okay? That way I can still ask my questions and Danny can take care of his mother." I even held my arms out as an invitation. I wiggled my fingers hopefully. I smiled, too. "Come on. Let her go. I'm willing."

Knoll wasn't exactly willing to oblige Petra. Instead, he tightened his left arm around her neck, pressed the gun further into the soft spot just behind her right ear and snarled, "I should have killed you when I had the chance."

I smiled, wiggled my fingers on my outstretched hands and said, "Well, you still can. Come on. Let her go."

Freeman growled, snatched his mother away from Knoll and pushed me into the General's arms. Then he snapped at Knoll, "When was the last fucking time that gun was loaded? Or let me ask it another way. Do you even have ammunition for it?"

Knoll started waving the gun around, so I turned my back into him, slid his left arm around my neck and slapped his hand when it fell onto my boob. "I've had enough of that crap," I said adamantly. Then I gently guided his gun hand behind my head and said. "There. Feel better?"

"Are you crazy!" Knoll shouted.

Meanwhile, Freeman slapped his mother and said, "Bitch!"

That made me mad, so I lifted Knoll's gun hand, stood nose-to-nose with Freeman and said, "Do NOT do that again. Do you understand?" Then I went back to Knoll, wrapped his left arm around my neck and then lowered it onto my boob. "Just this once as a manner of apology." Damn the luck. He didn't squeeze. I put it back around my neck and said, "I can take a hint."

The scene would have devolved into bedlam had not Petra gathered her wits, stuck her fingers in her mouth and pushed a shrill whistle into the room. "Quiet!" she shouted above Freeman and Knoll as they screamed at each other.

It happened. Silence.

"You first," Petra said looking at me. "Who are you?"

"Doctor Sixkiller-Collins Collins at your service," I said with a smile.

"And you're Thomas Knoll," she said looking at him. "I thought you had better manners than this." Then she turned to Danny and slapped him so hard that I was afraid he was going to walk around for the rest of the day with a bruise on his cheek in the form of a handprint. "If you ever do that again, Daniel, I will personally emasculate you with the rustiest pair of scissors I can find!" Then she stamped her foot and said, "Into the living room where we can talk like civilized people instead of Bedouins around a campfire."

Knoll looked pissed at Danny, so I stepped between him and Freeman, my arms extended into each of their chests. "Petra is right. Let's go talk," I said to them.

Freeman knocked my hand away, but walked toward the couch behind him. He sat hard on it and looked like he wanted to eat a Democrat. Knoll settled into a chair near the door. I noticed that Danny was holding his hand. He'd hit me with his right hand, the broken one. As clear as that was, it also seemed clear that nothing was going to happen here

Whalebone

until I found out what was separating Knoll and Freeman. They were friends a few days ago. What happened? But, Petra first.

She stepped into the middle of the room directly between Knoll and Freeman. She eyed them equally evilly and then looked at me. "You *let* him fondle you? You should have…" and she turned toward Knoll and said, "Up. On your feet." He stood. She put her knee halfway to the moon and he folded up worse than a three-legged card table. Then she looked back at me and said, "That."

I looked at him and said, "He might need medical attention."

Petra looked annoyed and turned her attention to her son. "And what brings you here besides a crazy friend?"

Freeman went right at it. "Am I Jewish, mother?"

She deflated. That's the only word that came to mind because the air seemed to be let out of her. She floated to the couch where her son sat and fell onto it as though dropped from a great height. I sat in a chair opposite Knoll.

For his part, Knoll sat up from the floor and said, "What? You're Jewish?" Then he looked at Petra and said, "Is that possible?"

Petra looked at her son and said, "You know that I am not."

"Was my father Jewish?" he asked again, getting persistent.

I suppose none of us, including Freeman himself, was quite ready for what was going to happen. Oh, sure, Petra said the proper and completely true thing when she replied, "Yes. He was Jewish." She even looked awful when she said it. She looked like she knew she had thrown a lie over his life and might even have been sorry for it. The fight that was brewing between mother and son might even have been a classic one, but neither of them would ever know. Why? Because Knoll said calmly, "Really, Petra? You know, you know could have mentioned this a lot earlier than now."

All three of us stopped and stared at him. Me? Well, to that point, I was a serious bystander. My *only* reason for me being there was Freeman and his condition. If I could get him to return to Kalispell – or barring that, to see his own doctor – then I'd be happy and ready to resume being fat and lazy on my vacation.

Freeman's reaction settled for me once and for all the issue of whether he'd become mentally impaired by Gaucher's. He looked at his mother and then at Knoll and looked disgusted. "Oh, please, mother. Don't tell me you've been doing *him.*" It was delivered on time, on cue and told the rest of us that he was appalled by what Knoll had implied. Freeman stood – a bit shakily, I thought – and said, "If you've been doing *him*, then you're on Layne's side and that's even more disgusting than anything you could do with him."

Well, men will be boys, I suppose. Why? Because Knoll stood to face Freeman and Petra got between them. Knoll looked ready to defend himself – and I didn't think it was because he'd been doing Freeman's mother. No, he looked ready to defend himself from whatever Freeman had implied. Whatever that was. For the record, I didn't care what that implied. At least right then I didn't. It was when Freeman's face turned into a scowl and looked like he wanted to destroy Knoll's whole family that I began to care. Being the daughter of Melodie Chang, I've seen my share of senseless violence and this seemed to be leading to it.

I stood, went to Knoll and said, "You know that story about injecting a bubble into your blood stream?"

"Yeah," he said *nervously.*

"Well, it's bullshit, so don't make me do something that isn't. Sit down." Then I looked at Freeman and said, "In your condition? You've got to be kidding. Sit down and verbalize this conflict so that even dunces like me can understand. Otherwise, Freeman? You're probably going to die and not because you can't fight old, fat white men either."

Petra turned to me and said, "He isn't fat."

"Really?" I said. "His BMI reading is higher than the national debt."

Okay. All that meant was that Petra came down on Knoll's side. Maybe she had conflicts over it, but as they say in Rome "A fat chance he has in a Speedo". Or something to that effect. Anyway, it seemed that I was the cool head in the room – and Knoll had tried to induce hyperventilation, Freeman needed a doctor before parts started falling off him and Petra was sparring with the guy who'd just held a gun to her head. That left me.

With my first consideration still Freeman, I asked, "Look, can we all sit down?" Okay, I was standing when I said it, but I sat in the chair opposite Knoll when I did. Then I added, "Please?"

The players started to sort themselves out when Petra pulled a chair from the dining room and sat next to Knoll who was sitting in the same chair near the door. Freeman sat on the couch again and that left me – and I was sitting so far outside the circle that I sat cross-legged on the floor. "Can we start at the beginning so that those of us who don't have any idea what you're talking about can get up to speed?" I looked at Freeman and said, "That would be your cue."

"And you worked for Layne," Knoll said, clearing indicating that he considered Freeman to be a traitor.

"This is about Katy Layne," Freeman said holding his hand gently against his stomach.

"The First Lady?" I said skeptically.

"Yes," he said.

Well, I was going to be right about one thing. I wasn't going to care at all about why this was about Katy Layne. I cared about my patient – Danny Freeman – and he was going to be so stubborn about what he saw as his mission that I was going to have no choice but to be the third wheel. And it all depended on what he was going to say about the Governor's wife.

I suppose empires have fallen on worse grounds.

CHAPTER 25

Freeman nodded at Knoll and said, "He was assigned the task of doing it."

Knoll jumped straight up and almost put Petra on the floor. She stood, put her knee into his Cadillac position and he sank back to the couch, his face turning a lovely shade of purple in the process. Freeman obviously didn't care if Knoll was involved in the conversation because he kept talking.

"The governor, that fat bastard, did this for her."

"Did what?" I asked feeling a disconnect that was going to stay with me all the way to the end.

"Got that idiot Moore involved in this. He's been smuggling everything from drugs to Inuit's out of Canada for most of his adult life. He waved a pardon under Moore's nose if he got Katy a shipment of ivory. That's what we're going to get when we meet him. He knows where the rendezvous place is and that's where I was going to bust him, pardon or not."

Smuggling with the approval of the Governor. That was his story. I had no doubt he was going to stick to it, too. But was it legit? What better way to guarantee that the governor wouldn't get a second term than by allowing the smuggling of *anything?* It sounded specious. I put voice to it.

"And your point by being involved with Knoll is what?"

Freeman paused as though considering whether or not to say more. He blinked and everyone knew he was going to babble like a baby with a noisy toy. "I was brought into the operation by Layne's Chief of Staff, Ted Hentley. Hentley has been with Layne like that broad Watkins has been with your mother," he said looking directly at me. That he referred to Paula as "that broad" I would steadfastly keep to myself. She's the second-most deadly person I know. My mother is the first – and not just because I tested the bounds of teenage dating when I was that age.

Mom threatened me with reckless behavior unless I started coming home on time. The one thing that scared me the most was when she said she'd start taking double the prescribed dose of acetaminophen unless I came home at midnight the next time I dated Mario. It made my stomach rumble and I got home half an hour early and actually woke her up to find out if she'd made good on her threat. I was in tears. She wearily looked at the clock on the nightstand, smiled and said, "I feel so wonderful that I won't even take the prescribed dose." I cried like a baby because it was the best news I could have heard.

Freeman looked out the window and said, "It was all cloak-and-dagger stuff. We met on a dark road outside the capital. Layne told me to go with this guy he was with and do whatever I was told. My job was to protect him and I thought that's what I was doing. I mean, I was part of his bodyguard detail." His eyes grew clouded and he continued. "Hentley was there in a big car. There was a partition between the driver's part of it and where we sat. It seemed appropriate. He told me that the operation he wanted me to perform would not have any written orders associated with it. It was just what him and he talked about."

"How long ago was this?" Petra asked.

"About eighteen months ago."

She nodded.

Freeman nodded at Knoll and said, "They were after you. Why? Well, they saw your piddling militia movement as a threat to their rule. My orders were to infiltrate the movement, ingratiate myself with you and then turn my evidence over to the attorney general's office."

I leaned back in the chair, smiled and said, "What happened? I mean, you have no love lost for either of them." For what it's worth? I didn't care. I figured that if I helped him through this, then I might get a chance to treat him – and that's all I wanted out of this.

He stared at Knoll and said, "The things I had to do to ingratiate myself with you. You fucking pig, you damned Jew-lover. You were taking orders from Layne himself. In time, I figured that my part of the operation was to find evidence against you that would put you away forever and break whatever hold you had on him."

"And?" I said edging him closer to whatever this was.

Freeman stood, but Knoll remained seated. "You and Moore are in this together with Layne. Any pardon Moore gets will be to keep the operation going."

I wiggled my fingers at him. "Um, yoohoo?"

"What!" he snapped at me.

"What role does my mother play in all this? Ever since Moore found out that Melodie Chang is my mother, he's been willing to dump everything he's been doing in order to get a meeting with her. What's all that about and should I be worried about her?"

Petra said, "Your mother is Melodie Chang?"

I rolled my eyes and said, "Yes. She's my mother. My father has been dead since I was a young girl."

"He's not Brad Chang?"

"Stepfather," I said. "And, yes, I can get you an autograph."

Petra's eyes glazed. Then she said, "Oh, I'd love to meet her. If you could. . ."

I smiled and said, "Sure. The next time she's here." Then I looked at Freeman and said, "You started with Katy Layne, the First Lady. Why not stick to that subject? It will give me a chance to relax and maybe even time to figure out who's going to tie me up again and maybe even plan a getaway."

"Funny," he said.

"And every time it happens, you two are around."

"You want me to stick to Katy Layne or help you plan your getaway?" he said sarcastically.

I smiled. "I'd like to hear how Katy Layne prompted all this."

"That's easy," he said. "The bastard married a bitch. And their kids inherited double doses from both of them."

"Katy?" I asked, trying to keep him to the story.

Freeman stared down at Knoll and said, "It's got something to do with what Moore smuggled into the country. That's all I was able to find out from his people. Knoll was going to rendezvous with Moore, exchange the cache of whatever he'd smuggled into the country for a wad of cash; non-traceable stuff, too. Personally? I wouldn't trust any of them. My opinion? As soon as Moore gets the money, the alert goes out and he winds up in federal prison."

Hmm. While it explained a lot, there was one item that it did not. "And what's all that got to do with me?"

"Him," Freeman said nodding at Knoll. "He had to know that you were related to a US senator. When I went to you asking if you could help me with my condition? He already knew you were there and that I'd gone to you. He planned your kidnapping and probably knows who Beryl is. It probably isn't even his name. And then the scene you described in Cut Bank? The fat bastard has his own doctors. I wouldn't be surprised if one of them told him how to induce hyperthermia. It's something a Jew-lover would do."

Well, okay. That explained both Knoll and Moore. They fit the rolls that Freeman assigned to them - paranoid as all hell and willing to do anything to get their way. It even explained Moore's role in this until he met Wanda. Of course, if anything happened to her, I was going to have a meltdown of such proportions that not even Mario would be able to pull me back from the edge. The issue became Freeman's mother, Petra. So I asked her, "You have a part in this or Knoll wouldn't be here as comfortably as he was. I figure you come down on Knoll's side only because of how things were when Danny and I got here. How close am I?"

Freeman echoed my question, only his tone made it something much more sinister. "Yes, mother. How do you figure in this?"

She fidgeted and everyone in the room knew she was going to lie. "Um, I'm not involved in whatever you're talking about." Then she looked fiercely at Knoll but didn't say anything. She didn't have to. That was the look of blackmail, maybe sexual. Mario makes *certain* that I never have to resort to that sort of thing, so I was getting out of my depth. I am beginning to think that everything outside of medicine is out of my depth.

Freeman stepped up to where she sat and said down to her, "If Knoll is in this with Layne, then so are you. Given what I've learned about my own background – namely that I am Jewish, that you knew and yet never found it appropriate to tell me – I have to assume that you have a roll in this with both the Governor and Knoll." He leaned down until his face was mere inches from his mother's and said, "And I want to know what that roll is, *mother*."

God, flashbacks. I hate them. I can't remember the countless times I did to my mother what Freeman was doing to his – namely, putting my face hers and demanding that she do *exactly* what I said. Of course, most of my issues were distinctly minor ones, like the effects of aspirin and such. Thankfully, my mother was always up to keeping both of us in the game. The one time I can remember it being otherwise was when I was sodomized when I was sixteen. She knew I'd been kidnapped and knew I'd suffered horribly at the hands of my kidnapper. Had I not *insisted* to the responding medical attendants that I had *not* been raped, Mom would have gone ballistic and gotten herself killed. Had not Uncle Alex been there to help me swim past the shoals that appeared with maddening regularity, neither one of us would have survived that awful time.

My point here is that it seemed likely that Petra and Daniel Freeman had not been on the same wavelength at any time in their lives.She may as well have been speaking German as he spoke Yiddish. Or vice versa. Unless someone intervened, I could see the need for a trauma team in about five minutes.

Well, I've never been shy, so I stepped up. Or in. Never figured out which way I went. But I went. Into the fray. Mixed it up with them. Wasn't afraid to get dirty. Or any those things. All I know is that I *still* didn't care what they were up to – either of them - when I stepped between them. My concern was still for Daniel Freeman, his son, Marcus, and his wife, Mary. Everyone else was a peripheral player.

Lord, how that was destined to change.

CHAPTER 26

Group dynamics are very interesting – especially if you have time to observe them. To that, I once asked my PA – my Physicians Assistant, my almost-doctor, Norma Young – to watch patient reactions on a webcam that we set up. As a rule, the younger the patient, the more people are involved in treatment. My part was to forget there was a camera recording everything I said and that I'd asked Norma to judge my words and actions. I did my part by forgetting she was there and she did her part by laughing her ass off when she came to me with her reactions. "Evie?" she said. "You define the word 'concentration' better and more aptly than anyone I ever saw."

Okay, I bit. "Why?" I asked.

A digression: the appointment I had was with Gayle and George Kendricks. Their three-year-old daughter, a livewire named Stephanie, had been running a slight fever and they wanted to be certain she wasn't in any danger. She wasn't. In fact, by the time of the appointment, Stephanie's mild temperature had faded away entirely and she was healthy. When pressed by Gayle, I told her that asthma sometimes manifested itself in that way. I prescribed an inhaler for little Steph, but warned her mother not to use it unless the fever returned. It didn't. Again, when pressed later, I told Gayle that Stephanie could have had a minor sinus infection. I even told Stephanie that I wanted her to blow her nose – and I showed her how to do it – every time she first saw her mother. It would tend to keep her sinuses clear and would be an activity that would draw mother and daughter together.

If you've noticed that George had no part in any of this, you win a prize. When Norma played back the video, she was laughing so hard that she had to stop and pee. "Watch George," she said giggling.

Again, a digression: I knelt in front of Stephanie, hands on my knees, Gayle right next to me kneeling the same way. Stephanie had our attention, our completer attention. My ass had George's attention. No, don't. George Kendricks is a good man, one that I called into the office a few days later. I told him to come alone, that I wanted to see him about a matter that concerned him and no one else. But what did the video betray? Well, the worst thing he did was stand behind me and make an hourglass motion with his hands and then reach out with his right index finger and pretend to touch my butt. Retracting his finger as though it had been burned, he retreated to a chair in the corner and slapped himself. He even stuck his hands in his armpits and tried to look away. But his eyes kept coming back to my butt as I talked to his daughter.

Three days later he showed up in my office. I applied a new layer of lipstick, walked into the patient room and placed a sloppy red kiss on his left cheek. He reached to touch it and I slapped his hand away. "You tell Gayle that you had a physical today in my office and that was my reward for being as healthy as you are." Then I stopped and stared at him. Yep. Guilty. He blushed brighter than a Christmas ornament and tried to back away from me. I smiled, caught his arm and sat with him on the table. It was my turn to blush. "George? I owe you both an apology and a thank you. First? No more video cameras in the patient rooms. I should have known better. Second?" I placed my hands over my heart and said, "I never think of myself as being that pretty, as being capable of attracting that sort attention. Having two children just makes me believe the worst for myself. You rewarded me in a way that I cannot thank you and cannot tell anyone." I smiled again and said, "Thank you and this will stay between us."

"I was a pig," he said. "Gayle would call me worse."

"It was normal and I will not allow you to castigate yourself over it." Then I smiled and said, "But maybe I should learn not to turn my back on male patients."

"Do I get a physical now?" he said, still embarrassed.

"Yes," I said patting his hand. "Norma will do it. She's my PA and she's even prettier than I am."

He got the last word. "Um, Doctor Six? No, she isn't and that has nothing to do with your behind and my juvenile reaction to it."

What's this got to do with Petra Freeman? Well, nothing. Except what men and women find to start a relationship. Daniel Freeman had been a straightforward asshole ever since I first understood that I was drawn to him because *he had a physical condition that should have been apparent to me.* That's important. His eyes weren't as yellow as a crayon box, but were yellow enough that any doctor not out of her exhausted mind should have seen it. He was chasing Governor Layne in a straight line that led from Kevin, Montana to Petra Freeman's living room. Meanwhile, Petra was following another line of logic that twisted among several of the players, but didn't become obvious to any of them until she tried to downplay her involvement in whatever Moore smuggled into the country.

It was, however, Petra's reaction to her son's observation that put the entire episode into the back stretch, if not the home stretch. Why? Because she dropped a name. Oh, sure. It was absolutely inadvertent but she dropped it anyway. Her reactions started meekly, if not slowly. She backed away from Daniel and ,looked at me and said, "I have no interest in this." It was what followed that throwaway line that drew all of us into the story. "Ted told me…" and then she stopped dead and stared directly at me, the knowledge that she'd given away a key player in the drama. Ted Hentley may as well have been running around naked in the room for all the good her denial made. "I don't mean Ted Hentley. He didn't tell me anything. I mean, well, I mean that no one told me anything."

Daniel wanted to strangle her. Me? Well, I just put my hand in the middle of his chest and said, "Please?" Then I added that part that got to him. "Daniel? You've been like a dog with a bone over this stuff. Take a gigantic step back and see that your son and you both need medical attention. Take a break from this and let me handle your mother?" I don't think I was being disingenuous when I added, "I have a lot more experience with mothers than you do."

In truth, I was doing nothing more than protecting him from any further physical damage than he already had. I couldn't know it, but it became possible that I saved all of our lives by mentioning his son. Daniel Freeman was a mess and that had everything to do with the sudden knowledge that he was Jewish. The specter of my crucial mistake still hung over us like a sword, but none of us were actively Jewish – and that told the tale as it unwound from a tangled ball of old wives tales. So, Freeman withdrew, mentally at least. I pushed into the gap only because I tried to protect Freeman from himself. If only someone had tried to protect me from myself, maybe things would have been easier. But, no.

I turned to Petra and said, "Let me guess. You met with Ted Hentley before your son did. Maybe even on the same dark road where he met Daniel. But, you know? I really don't care what you talked about. I only care about getting Daniel the medical attention he desperately needs. You could make his life easier and healthier if you just told him the story, let him process it and then let me take him to a testing facility."

I can't say that maternal instincts run deep in every mother. They don't. I've seen the medical results of parental neglect, so I can testify with firsthand knowledge that Petra Freeman's reaction to my little speech ran true to course in several respects.

First, she continued to lie by saying, "I've never even met Ted Hentley."

Second, she threw in another detail, one that only Moore, Mario and Wanda knew about. It stopped me completely when she said, "And William Moore is smuggling ivory out of Canada in violation of federal law. He should be arrested!"

Freeman looked at me and maybe saw that a detached viewpoint might go farther because he said a lot more calmly than he'd been saying anything, "Ivory? And you know that how?"

If the last tumbler hadn't fallen until that point, it did then. Freeman became a cop and not one dying from an obscure disease named after a Frenchman who wasn't a Jew. Well, okay. Gaucher *might* have been a Jew; I have no idea. I just thought it was unlikely.

She'd just drawn a straight line that connected Governor Layne, Ted Hentley, William Moore, Daniel Freeman and herself. It seemed likely to include Knoll as well. If I understood it, Layne asked Hentley to get involved with a smuggling outfit headed by Moore and smuggle ivory into the United States. Why? No idea. None. Not a clue. Did I care? Resoundingly no. I did not. That news did not impact me at all – and it wouldn't until something threatened Freeman's health. Oddly, nothing did until Freeman went home to see his son, Marcus. That, however, was still in the future.

But now? I took a giant step backward and did something that Norma asked me to do. Take the long view. I turned away from them and walked into the kitchen. She had a nice view through a window over the sink. It could have been the Statue of Liberty for all I saw because I was concentrating on them as a group. I traced a line from Governor Layne straight through to William Moore and saw criminal activity all along the path. Worse, I was involved in whatever they were doing. It brought to mind a woman named Mary Surratt.

I'm no historian, but I know her story through my grandfather, Jack Collins. She was hanged by the government on July 11, 1865 for her part in the assassination of Abraham Lincoln. There was evidence either way that she was guilty or not. One of the other condemned, Lewis Paine, said she had no part in the plot to kill Lincoln. They hanged her anyway, guilty or not.

And that was my problem. If Layne was guilty of smuggling ivory into this country, then was I guilty as well simply because I was always practicing medicine and one of the perpetrators was sick? My coherent mind was telling me to go home, to leave these imbeciles to whatever fate awaited them. I almost never listened to it. Had I, I would not have married Mario. Why? Well, jeez. He's my *uncle*. Okay, okay, there's no blood between us, but I grew up with him and always knew the score. No, my logical and quite coherent mind told me that Mario Collins was going to be more trouble than he was worth.

But. Yep, but. The mind I use to practice medicine, the one that is monomaniacal in its pursuit, the one that sees the road and not the gullies that line either side of it, saw Mario Collins as the most romantic person I'd ever met. Period. There was no question I was going to marry him and give him a family. So, which mind was I going to use? Actually, it wasn't much of a fight. Freeman was in medical danger and that meant I had to use every possible treatment that his condition would require.

And, Lord, sometimes the medicine tasted awful.

CHAPTER 27

When I turned around, all of them were watching me from the doorway. Of their number, Freeman logically was the person to whom I should direct everything. Why? Well, as my number one patient, I was going to guard his well-being like a mother hen protects her chicks. I mean, period. That was always my driving reason. He's my patient. Period. But beyond that, there was the nagging feeling that William Moore was going to play a part in this beyond what he'd already revealed. What role he had to play in this vis-à-vis Freeman was anyone's guess. Maybe I should just talk to Moore and get a story without all the angles, twists and turns. He seemed straightforward enough to tell me from the hip what was happening here.

But. My patient's best interest won the day.

I looked at Freeman and said, "You and me are going to Helena and we're going to take you, your wife and son to a doctor. We're going to get both you and your son tested for Gaucher's and once treatment starts, we're done. Got it? Because I'm tired of running around Montana chasing you. We're going to get you tested. Period. End of story."

That put Knoll in front of the small crowd. "You really think I'm going to let you just leave?"

"Yeah, fat general. I do. You are going to let me take Freeman to get tested for a disease that might ultimately kill him unless you do." Then I added, almost as an afterthought, "And don't threaten me with you damned gun because I already know it doesn't have an ammunition."

"Layne is committing a crime against the state! He's smuggling ivory into this country from Canada!"

I rolled my eyes and said, "Well, as crimes go, that's not very high on my list." Then I asked Freeman, "You ready?"

He murmured, "I should stay here and make sure Layne, Knoll and my mother get justice."

"But you aren't," I said. "You're coming with me and we're going to get you and your family tested for Gaucher's. Got it?"

I figured Knoll was due to start acting like a pompous jackass. Well, I've made better guesses, but he did. He stepped in front of the group and approached me. "I rather disagree," he said. "I think we're going to Browning, to the rendezvous point on the reservation. Moore will show up sooner or later and I can finish my part in this."

I crossed my arms and said, "Really? You're going to stop me?" I motioned toward Freeman and said, "If he does anything? All I have to do is tap his wrist and he starts crying like a baby. And Petra? You have got to be kidding. As a modern day Annie Oakley, she has all the ability of a carnival barker."

Well, maybe so. But she picked that moment to trump my best speech. She opened her purse and pulled out a gun. I thought, *Naturally*. I assumed this one had bullets in it. Still and all, I wasn't going to get pushed around by a broad who was trying to grow a dick. That's how I saw Petra. She was compensating for the fact that she wasn't born male by resorting to the one thing that almost all men will resort to if given a chance: a gun. The ultimate phallic symbol, I know. Point-and-shoot. Pull the trigger. High caliber weapon. Hair trigger. High velocity ammo. I've heard them, being related to my mother and so many more that I forget. She stopped using those expressions when I started asking for the references they referred to. I might have been nine. It didn't matter that she stopped, though. Mario filled me in. He'd give the expression, tell me what it referred to and I'd say, "Got it." If I didn't get it, I'd look up the reference in Gray's Anatomy – and I don't mean that stupid TV show.

She walked up to me, stuck the gun in the soft tissue under my chin and said, "You and me are going with Knoll. Freeman will come only because he's after us, Knoll and me.

It doesn't matter that we're on opposite sides of the same coin. He'll follow."

Oh, bro-ther. As near as I could tell, this particular coin had at least four or five sides to it. In other words, everyone was out for themselves. Knoll wanted to continue smuggling whatever it was he was smuggling. Moore, my suspicion told me, was in this to tweak the nose of Whitey, the white man. Petra? God knows. Layne had all of them chasing and threatening each other to a point that they began to look like the Keystone Cops. All that was missing was the Bennie Hill music.

But threaten me? Maybe she hadn't been paying attention. Why? Well, I hate this shit. Guns and such. Ooh. Icky. I raised my hands in mock surrender, let her see my bottom lip tremble and then swiped the gun from her hand in one easy motion. Then I head-butted her. Damn, that hurts. Never did it before and only did because Mario taught me how to do it and bought a soccer ball for me to practice on. Still, Petra folded over and I offered my arm to Freeman. "Shall we go?"

"Then gun?" he asked pulling my arm to him.

I gave it to him.

He dropped the magazine, emptied the bullets from it, cleared the chamber and then tossed the gun to where Petra was still hands-on-knees in the kitchen. While that sounds as cool as hell, I described all that to Mario much later and gave him the details. I said after he described what Freeman had done, "Gosh. I didn't even know guns could read. Who knew they had magazines." Then I grinned.

But Freeman. He looked at Knoll and said, "You?"

"We're not done."

Knoll was destined to have a role in this much different than the one being played out by Petra. Oddly, had they only talked to one another while they were bumping ugly, it's possible that their plans would have been far more advance than they were. Of course, that's giving an awful lot of credit to a group I have already described as the Keystone Cops.

Since I still had the Hummer keys, I drove.

It was dark as a welder's heart, nearly nine o'clock, when we got back on the road headed toward Helena. Since it was nearly one hundred miles between Bozeman and Helena, we were looking at almost eleven o'clock before we got to his home. I'd admit to being tired, but not as tired as Freeman had been. He fell asleep almost as soon as we got on the road. Had I not foreseen that and gotten an address, I would have felt bad waking him up once we got to town.

The traffic isn't as I remember it being in LA. It's like I remember it being back in Maine. There were long stretches of empty road. The weariness began to wash over me, so I stopped at a convenience store I saw and got a cup of coffee. Freeman woke groggily and I put him back to sleep by beginning to cite from the Pharmacist's Manual verbatim. He tried; I'll give him that, but he fell asleep faster than Mario did when I pulled the same stunt on him when I thirteen. Of course, then I had to read from it. Now? In my sleep.

The best surprise I got was Mario, Wanda and William Moore were following me and had been ever since Mission Lake. I began to tell him what had happened and he put his index finger over my lips and took my purse from me. He reached into it, rummaged a bit and then pulled out a black box from it and said, "I've been listening."

He's often accused me of having a one-track mind and I'll admit to being guilty to it. I suppose, had I known that I was carrying it, that I might have acted different, might have deferred to him in some odd way. I'm glad I didn't know. Still I hugged him and felt an immense sense of gratitude, love and romance when he grabbed my butt. "Damn, girl," he said. "It's as fine as ever. Don't you forget to bring it home." Then he caressed my cheek and said, "And don't forget the best part. Your heart. I've been in love with it since I was five."

I hugged him and said, "Oh, damn. I was so hoping it was my butt."

"It's part of the deal," he said holding me, his arms wrapping me tightly into him.

"Are you okay?"

"Yeah."

"Girl? We need to talk to Moore. You got time?"

"I'll make time."

We went to our Hummer. Wanda was face-first in Moore. I'd call it a kiss but that would be like calling the Sistine Chapel just another building. They were in the back seat and that meant they had the entire expanse of it to unfurl their devotion to each other. Wanda seemed willing, but Moore sat like a stone on his side of the seat.

I leaned in and tapped Wanda on the shoulder. "Um, girlfriend? I need him for a few minutes."

She turned on me like a mother lion. "Go away! I need him! I do!"

Well, it would have gone like that had not Moore touched her cheek and said with a deep voice, "It is okay, my Fire Dawn. It is also necessary. I need to talk to your friend."

All her fierceness turned to whining. "Bi-ll," she whined sounding worse than a child.

His hand on her cheek stopped her. His gentle kiss caused her to scramble off of him and out the door. She stood next to me and was smiling contently. I would have sworn that she...well...*completed* the act because she looked so serene. I stared at her and she just wiggled her fingers at Moore. "Go on. You can have him." Then she added, "For now."

Well, ok-kay. I'll say this – Moore never changed. His taciturn face, his stoicism and his basic static demeanor was as I remembered him. "Mr. Moore?" I said. "If you were listening to what was said in that house, then you heard Moore claim that the package contained ivory. I need to be clear, Mr. Moore. Did you know you were smuggling contraband into this country?"

His smile was disarming. I mean, it snuck up on you. Around it, he said, "Pot, coke, so many other things. Ivory? It may well have been the contents of King Tut's tomb for all I cared."

"What was your payment?" I asked.

"Fifty grand."

"Payable when?"

"When I reached the exchange point."

"Which is where?"

That smile again. "Violet's living room."

Wanda's voice warbled. "Who?"

"Violet. I owe my life to her. I swore I would take care of her son and I will."

"Oh," she said, her voice sliding over every octave ever recorded.

He touched her cheek and said, "I hope you understand that I made Violet a promise. To break it is wrong."

She nodded only because she was unable to speak. Her mouth formed the words, "I see."

He pulled her to him and said, "She is my sister. David is my nephew."

Well, damn. Red hair exploded all around him. "That was mean!" she said smacking his massive chest.

He touched her cheek again and all was quiet. "I make the same pledge to you. No one will ever hurt you. I swear."

She looked back at me and said, "Um, I fight with her all the time, but she's my best friend. Can you exclude her?"

"And her family," he said.

I walked up to him, looked directly into his eyes and said, "It will never work. Everyone knows there is no such thing as red-haired Indians."

Her laughed and pulled Wanda to him. I'd say it was the perfect ending to a shitty day, but we hadn't gotten to Mary Freeman's home yet. *That* was going to be interesting.

It was a good thing I'd had that coffee.

I was going to need it.

I noted that Freeman was awake as we came out of the store.

Oh, goody.

CHAPTER 28

Before we left, Mario got with an awake Freeman and said, "You got a minute?"

"Yeah," he said, his voice distant and slightly on edge.

"You know that all of us heard what happened in that house. Right?"

"Yeah," he answered the same way.

"Well, can you explain to me how it felt when you discovered that you're Jewish?"

"Why?" he barked. "Why would you care?"

Mario shrugged and said, "I was curious. You've been pretty nasty toward them and now you find out that you're one of them. How do you feel about that?"

Well, physically he was a mess. Since I had no way of knowing if the disease had affected his mind, it was possible that anything he said would be specious. His eyes were yellow, his spine was starting to deform a bit and he looked exhausted. Also, I had to admit to the possibility that the broken bones in his hand might be forming an infection. If that was true, then we needed to get our business with Mary Freeman concluded as quickly as possible.

Freeman turned his back on us and walked to the back of the Hummer. Mario didn't follow him, but stood next to me and even took my hand in his. I love his touch, love it no matter where it lands. But Freeman...

He held out his arms and said to the sky, "Why? Why was I cursed like this? To hate them and then be shown to be one of them! How can that be?"

Mario held his voice. "Why do you hate them?"

Freeman turned and said with an intensity that I always associated with mental instability, "They're behind everything that happens. They're the cabal behind every social ill in this country!"

"Really?" Mario said. "Name a few." When Freeman started to get angry, Mario smiled and said, "Humor me. I'm not up on some of this stuff and I just wanted to know."

Well, *that* was the purest bullshit I've heard in an awfully long time. As near as I can tell, Mario is up on *everything*. If he wasn't baiting Freeman, then my name isn't multisyllabic and doesn't confuse most people who don't know me.

"Money!" Freeman said like that explained everything. "They control who has it, who uses it and how. Layne is a perfect example. He's giving that Indian fifty thousand dollars to smuggle ivory into this country!"

Mario held up a finger. "As a point of contention? Moore contends that he has no idea what he's smuggling."

Freeman took a step toward Mario and said, spat, "It doesn't matter! It's illegal! He should be in jail and not fucking in the back seat of your car!"

"Hey!" Wanda shouted. "We never got that far!"

"Whatever," he said beginning to sound irrational.

Was I seeing a symptom or a belief? Mario smiled and said, "Suppose Layne wasn't guilty of anything. Assume he's just a governor doing the best job he can. What then? Is he still guilty of something only because he's a Jew?" Then he added, "And are you?" Freeman looked ready to growl, but turned away instead. Mario slipped from my hand and followed him. "Freeman?" he asked. "Are you guilty of anything only because you're Jewish?"

"I don't know," he answered emotionally.

"Why" Mario continued. "It seems to follow logically. If Layne is guilty because he's a Jew and it is shown that you're a Jew, then you should be guilty of the same things he is. Or is my logic failing somewhere?"

Prejudice is hard to shed. Extreme prejudice is extremely hard to shed. I'd say I was sorry for Freeman, but I wasn't. My guess? This had nothing to do with his condition and everything to do with his beliefs. Otherwise, I think I would be seeing erratic behavior and I wasn't. I was seeing a steadfast belief being questioned and saw the answer as confusion because Freeman seemed to be confused.

He turned away again and walked into the parking lot. Mario followed him and I followed Mario. I'd like to lie and say that the condition of my underwear vis-à-vis Mario was why I followed him, but that would only be half true. The other half was Freeman himself and what he was driving himself toward. Okay, an answer. He was driving himself toward an answer, one that neither of us could see.

"Why?" he screamed at the empty sky. "Haven't I suffered enough?"

Mario said, "My mother and father were murdered. I could ask the same question, but I'd rather lead the life they taught me. My question becomes the obvious one. What have the Jews done to you that you resent being one of them?"

He turned on Mario quickly. I'll give my husband this: he didn't flinch. Still, Freeman was in attack mode and did. "Are you kidding? Think of the kids in this state that need food! Think of the adults who don't have a job! Jews are behind all that!"

Mario remained calm. "I meant personally. What Jew ever came up to you and started berating you for being a gentile? What Jew ever accused you of the holocaust? What Jew ever accused you of half of the things you have attributed to them?" Then he thumped Freeman's chest with his index finger and said, "And don't forget that you're one of them."

Freeman could only look at Mario and steam. He clapped his arms to his side, rumbled something incoherent, turned and walked away. I almost stopped Mario when he pursued Freeman. The only reason I didn't was because he knows me that well. He turned and said lowly, "Don't worry. We'll be okay."

"Are you sure?"

Whalebone

He smiled, turned his head and said, "You don't know, do you?"

"Um…"

He kissed my forehead and said, "Bless you for being so single-minded."

Mario went to where Freeman was simply looking at the dark sky. I stood next to Mario and took his hand. He slipped his fingers inside and around mine. It was better than sex. Still, his concentration was on Freeman and maybe helping him. How? I had no idea. All I could do was watch him as he started to speak again.

"Mr. Freeman?" he asked. "Do you know what is to be Jewish? Do you know how it is passed from one generation to the next?"

"What's that got to do with this?" he asked. "I'm as guilty as they are."

"Why? Because your father was Jewish?"

"Why else? That makes me as guilty as he is. Was."

"You know what you inherited from him?" Mario asked.

"Yeah, the fact that I'm a filthy Jew just like he was."

Mario smiled. "Actually, no. You inherited Gaucher's Disease. That's all. The Jewish heritage is passed from generation-to-generation through the mother, not the father. Mr. Freeman? You're merely an asshole, not Jewish. You inherited one thing from your mother and the other thing from your father. Not many people are given a glimpse at their soul as clear as the one you are getting. You want some advice? Listen to that voice you're hearing. It's your conscience telling you to get your act together. If everything I've heard about you is true, then you're a cop and you were siding with everyone except the one guy you were hired to defend. Governor Layne deserves more from you than he's getting."

With that, Mario walked away. He had to pull me gently along with him because I was as stunned as Freeman appeared to be. I wanted to ask Daniel if he was okay, but instead I followed Mario because he was shaking his head and saying, "No. Don't."

That left Freeman alone to consider what Mario had done to him. And exactly what was that? Well, Freeman's face went blank as he stared at a retreating Mario. He started to say something, but caught himself before he did. Mario stepped beside the rear door and just watched.

"You're saying I'm as guilty as Knoll," Freeman said.

"I'm saying you need evidence before you can convict anyone and you have squat. You want more advice? Start acting like the ccp you're supposed to be and put all that prejudice away because it doesn't serve you very well."

You know that famous last tumbler? Oh, you know, it's the one that falls into place and opens everything to plain view? Yeah, that one. Well, that didn't happen. Things were destined to stay murky as Freeman tried to figure out his life. He had maybe forty-five minutes to do it, too.

Unfortunately, for him.

CHAPTER 29

Freeman's home on Fifth Avenue in Helena wasn't as pretentious as it sounded. A tree-lined street, it was an eclectic mix of one and two-story homes. There were some lights on in the neighborhood despite the hour – it was midnight – but Freeman's home was dark. That figured, he told us he didn't want to wake Mary or his son, Marcus.

His was a one-story home. The porch was of the wrap-around variety and came complete with a swing, three chairs and what looked like a chessboard. It might have been checkers. It was too dark to see and there was no porch light. He unlocked the front door and entered, shushing us as we entered his home. "I don't want to frighten Mary. Please, quiet."

That wasn't hard to do. Even Wanda belayed her latest moan. We all waited as Freeman went to the back of the house and their bedroom. There were still no lights on anywhere. It was only then that we saw a light go on in the back of the house. That meant he was in their bedroom waking up Mary. Then another light came on and we heard him cry out, "Mary! Where are you?"

Okay, I think all of us heard the panic in his voice. I can't say that it fell to me to find out what caused it, but I almost immediately started down the hall toward where his anguished voice continued to cry out.

Lights went on; Mario had found a switch and flipped it. Freeman came hurrying down the hall shouting, "Mary! Where are you?"

Okay. Mary wasn't home and it was midnight. While that might not be unusual for me, it seemed that Freeman expected her to be there. I followed Freeman and Mario followed me. Wanda? I assumed she followed Moore. If she had, then her actions were consistent with the rest of her night.

Freeman ran into their garage. It was empty. A two-car affair, it held all the stuff of middle-class people who lived in a snow zone. A snow-blower, a pair of skis and snow-shoes hanging together on the wall just inside the door, a ski-doo and several ice chests. Also on the wall were kayaks and several fishing poles and the tackle that accompanied them. All that meant was Freeman was adept in the outdoors.

He looked at the walls, strangled out a cry and then turned and ran into me. I held him, simply kept him from hurting himself and said, "Just say it, Freeman. What did you expect and what did you get?"

"She should be here," he said, his voice sounding strangled.

"Would she take Marcus?" I asked.

"No," he said, thinking. "Maybe there's a message in the kitchen."

The kitchen adjoined the garage and the kitchenette adjoined the kitchen. Still, if Mary Freeman had gone to the doctor or the hospital because Marcus was in trouble, she hadn't left a note that that effect.

Moore came around the corner, Wanda hooked inside his arm. He said, "Can I ask a question?"

"What?" Freeman snapped.

Moore nodded toward the living room. "It's about the pictures hanging on the wall in there."

He turned toward the living room and took Wanda with him. Mario and I followed Freeman as he followed Moore. There was a spread of pictures on other side of the wall from the kitchen. He stood in front of them and said, "First, I need to explain how the transfer happened." Even had we any objections to the way he wanted to do it, he plowed ahead in his normal manner. "The arrangements I had for any specific shipment were always the same. The coordinates were left on the back of the reservation sign back on the rez. They were never the same twice in a row. In fact, the coordinates have never repeated at all. They're always different. After I had the coordinates, I plotted them on a map and figured out where I was supposed to go. Then I went there. The shipment was always buried. Always. The coordinates to receive the envelope were written on the packages that I found buried. I took the package or packages to those coordinates, received an envelope full of money and both of us left wordlessly. That person took the packages and I took the money."

Freeman seemed to know where this was going. He stood in front of Moore and asked simply, "Why?"

Moore turned toward the pictures and pointed to a woman standing next to Freeman. "Is that you wife?"

"Yes."

Moore turned back toward Freeman and said, "That is the person who has been giving me the envelope for the past two years."

Mario seemed to see what was going to happened before I did. He stepped between Moore and Freeman and said, "Sit. Both of you. I've got a gazillion questions and between you I think there are enough answers to go around."

Moore seemed willing, especially with Wanda whispering encouraging things in his ear. Freeman, however, seemed apprehensive, upset and willing to get hurt. I squeezed between him and Mario and said, "Freeman? Please? Let's talk before we do anything stupid. Please? You've come this far."

His eyes burned with the fire of a man for his family. He looked past me at Moore but said nothing. His eyes did all the talking and most of those words were vile and not repeatable by anyone with a family. Still, he turned and headed toward the nearest chair, one in the dining room. He sat at the end of the table, his back to the rest of us, but his thoughts on Moore alone.

I turned to Moore and said, "Please, William?"

Wanda put her hand over his jewels and said, "Or never again, Bill. You hear?"

He slid his hands over her ass, scooped her off the floor and said smiled into her face. "Oh, Fire Dawn. I will give you many red-haired young ones." Then he kissed her nose and said, "But you have no chance." He put her back down, led her to the other end of the table and sat like a Korean War diplomat. Wanda fell into a chair next to him and laid her head on her shoulder. I'd say she was purring, but it was possible she was having an orgasm. Either. Hell, both.

Mario sat to Moore's left; I sat to his right. I had no idea where Mario was going with this, but I was willing to follow him however far he wanted to go. Besides, he had a gazillion questions and I had but a few million. I'd listen to the ones he had that I hadn't thought of before jumping in.

The first one was so obvious that I berated myself for not seeing it. He asked it of Freeman, not Moore. "If he's right, then there were times Mary was away from home with your knowledge. Explain how that is possible?"

Freeman looked hatefully at Moore, but then said to Mario, "She's a nurse, one that travels around the reservation on a schedule that's been fairly constant over the past three years. She gives pre-natal exams to women who can't travel to the hospital in Browning."

"Who regulates her schedule?" Mario asked.

"The Department of Public Health and Human Services," he said. He looked nervous, as though things were beginning to add up. Me? No idea. I was still clueless.

Mario looked directly at Freeman and saw something in his eyes that I couldn't place. You would think that years of marriage would enable me to read him better than this. But I couldn't. We were in uncharted waters and I only hoped he was a better sailor than I gave him credit for being.

"How long has she been on this schedule?"

"Two years," he said.

Mario looked at Moore and said, "I need the truth, Moore. How long has this type of smuggling been ongoing?"

He looked at Freeman and said, "Two years."

And Freeman had been working with Knoll for eighteen months. Suddenly something clicked in my mind and I didn't like where the echoes came from. I looked at Mario and said, "Is it possible?"

"When did Layne get elected?"

"Two years ago," I said numbly. "A bit more now."

Mario looked back at Moore and said, "Who set this up? Who was your contact other than Mary Freeman?"

"There was never a contact, only a suggestion I received."

"A suggestion," Mario said dumbly.

He stared at Freeman again, then returned his gaze to Mario. "A note was left on my steering wheel one night. There was a date, a time and coordinates. Midnight at that place."

"What happened?"

"I went there. I suspected a trap. But there was no one. I waited an hour before committing to anything. I pulled out the GPS unit, walked to the exact coordinates and stood there for maybe five minutes. I still suspected a trap. But no one came and there was no sound anywhere. I dug down about two feet and uncovered a box that had another set of coordinates and a time written on it. The time was for six that morning. The location was right in the middle of Browning in a tavern. The coordinates were at a table where a woman that I now know to be Mary Freeman sat. I sat down opposite her, slid the box to her and she slid an envelope to me. Then she left. Nothing was said. I went outside, opened the envelope and it contained five thousand dollars."

"How often did the pattern repeat?" Mario asked.

"There was no pattern. Sometimes a few weeks. Sometimes a few months. And the amount of money that I received was never the same twice in a row. The pay off locations were always different, too."

"What was the most and what the least at amount of money?"

"The least was twenty-five hundred and the most was seventy-five grand."

Mario folded his hands together, looked down at them and then back at Moore. "This contradicts a lot that you told us earlier. You hinted – strongly hinted – that you knew what you were smuggling. You have also hinted that you did not know. Which is it?"

"Why?" he asked. "Why do you wish to know, Mr. Collins?"

Mario looked at me and said, "Because my wife will not back down and where she is concerned, I will not back down either. If we are involved, then I want to know the truth. You said your rendezvous was in your sister's living room. How can that be if you do not have the package?"

"Who said I didn't have it?" he said. "I do. The coordinates on it correspond to Violet's living room. I know those by heart."

Mario looked at Freeman and said, "Then I think we all know where Mary is."

Yeah. Not even I am that dense. We were going to make a trip to wherever Mary Hatemen lived.

"And my son?" Freeman asked.

"Where would Mary take him whenever she made her rounds?" I asked.

Freeman sighed. "Her mother's house."

Then I knew the next two places I was going to be that night.

But not who I was going to meet there.

Unfortunately.

CHAPTER 30

There was no way we were going to make another three or four hour trip. At least, not that night. Okay, I was willing, but Wanda wanted to sit on Moore's face – or something. The issue became Freeman and how completely unstable he was. Mario was willing to sleep in the house that night – and so were Moore and Wanda. But none of us believed Freeman would be there when we woke the next day. In fact, being a cop of some type, the bets we placed among ourselves said that he'd call the police and have us arrested for breaking and entering. That meant a motel. Wanda was ecstatic.

I was practically hyperventilating when we left Freeman home. It got so bad that I demanded Mario go back and leave me with Freeman. That meant all of us went back and I knew I was never going to hear the end of it from Wanda. I had taken from her a night with Moore, one that she had been looking forward to with nothing but lust. Had Mario wanted to do anything that night, I don't know what I would have done. Fortunately for me, he settled on the couch and was quickly asleep. Wanda and Moore settled for the spare bedroom. Me? I stood outside Freeman's door for at least fifteen minutes before he came out and said, "Okay. I was planning on taking off, but I won't. I know you're worried about me, but please leave me alone for the night."

"How do you feel?" I asked stupidly.

"Like a non-Jewish asshole whose son is probably dying from a disease I gave him. All I want is for him to be okay."

I saw symptoms all over his face and body. If I fast-forwarded through the next year of his life, I saw pain and maybe death, too. Since I was pledged to allay all that, it was almost impossible for me to leave him alone.

"I could lock the door," he said.

"Look, I know. I'm just worried."

He sagged against the doorframe and looked like he wanted to slide all the way to the floor. Instead, he looked at me and said, "You might as well come in."

His bedroom was done in pastels, greens mostly. It's not a room that a cop would decorate. A cop would make a room look hard, as though its pieces were competing against one another. This one tried to be harmonious and soothing. Okay, okay. I think I just showed my prejudice against cops and Freeman was a cop.

"Why did you come to me?" I asked as he sagged onto the bed, lay back and closed his eyes. I watched from the doorway.

With his eyes closed and his arm over his face, he said, "Because of your reputation. I've heard of you despite the fact I've never met you and yet all you will say about yourself is that you're a country doctor. You know where I heard your name?"

"Where? Who?"

"Katy Layne, the first lady," he answered, his arm still over his face. "Mary was pregnant with Marcus and she told me to see you if I ever needed a doctor. She wouldn't say why, just gave me your name and told me not to forget it."

If the timeline was still valid, then Mary Freeman was pregnant when Donald Layne was elected governor.

"Is it normal for her to be gone like this?"

"Yeah," he said. "Didn't expect it this time, though."

"You want to leave, to follow her."

"Yeah."

"But?"

He laughed and it sounded horrible. "You really think Moore is going to tell me where his sister lives?"

It was my turn to sigh. "Freeman? What the hell is going on here?"

He dropped his arm to his side and stared at the ceiling as he answered. "I figure we have a crooked governor being helped by crooked people." Then he struggled to sit up and looked at me as he answered, "I owe your husband for telling me I'm an asshole. He taught me that Layne is a bastard not because he's a Jew, but because he's a crook." His smile looked wan and far away. "I guess you don't have to be Jewish to be a crook."

"No," I said sadly. "History is full of non-Jewish crooks."

"And Layne is one of them. And to think I voted for him."

"Well, I didn't, " I said.

Movement in the doorway behind betrayed Moore. Naturally, Wanda was with him. His arm was draped over her shoulder in a way that spoke, "Mine!" That was another thing I was going to have to talk to her about. She swore no man would ever own her, not after her last marriage. "All I got out of it was Becky and a whole bunch of bruises," she told me once. Now, a man that could easily hurt her had his arm around her in a protective manner that both reassured and scared me.

More spoke over and around me to Freeman. "If you're going to go forward with charges against Layne, you're going to need my cooperation," he said, his voice a low rumble.

"Would you testify against him?" Freeman asked.

Wanda poked him with her knuckles. "Go ahead. Tell him."

"I'd testify but only to the truth – and that is that I have no idea what I was smuggling, or even if it was smuggling. I got money from your wife for uncovering a package and then delivering it to her. You'd have to get her to say who got the package and what was in it." He looked down at Wanda and said, "Happy?"

"Orgasmic," she replied with a wide smile.

I looked at Freeman and asked the only thing that concerned me. "Will you go to the hospital with me? To the nearest one? You need to be tested and so does your son."

"As soon as I find Mary and talk to her. Nothing is as important as her and my son, her first." Then he looked at me and said, "That's the best I can do."

"Then I suggest we all get some sleep," I said.

Wanda pulled Moore down the hall with one hand and sucked one her thumb with the other. Either she had an oral fixation on her thumb or she was planning on having a short night with Moore – and I know she doesn't have an oral fixation on her thumb.

That left me.

Mario was a bundle under the covers. I checked the alarm next to the bed and it was set for six-thirty. Great. *Maybe* six hours of sleep. I rolled over onto my left side and felt an arm snake around my waist.

"I thought you were asleep," I said.

"Was. For a while. Then I started thinking."

"About?" I asked.

His right hand covered my right breast and he said, "Naming rights."

I smiled. But he didn't see it. "So, I'm a stadium? I get naming rights?"

He squeezed. Just enough. I closed my eyes but steadfastly did not moan. His hand ran down my stomach. I couldn't help it. I moaned. "Naming rights to our next baby," he said softly into my ear.

"You'd wind up…"

"Yes," he said. "I'm looking forward to it."

I rolled onto my back and looked up at him. I touched his face and said, "So improbable, so unexpected, so totally unlikely. Where did you come from, my sweet man?"

"You summoned me. I heard your voice and obeyed."

"I was four."

"I was five, yet I heard your voice."

"How could I live without you?"

"You will never know that fear, my love. I will always be here."

He kissed me and time began to coalesce around him, around us.

I still remember our first kiss, the one that we exchanged once we knew we were going to be together. It was easy discount all the juvenile ones, the ones that were little more

Whalebone

than a peck on the lips and then gone. I was fifteen and I was struggling with my virginity. He had no right to it. It was mine to give and mine to exchange. But I wanted to be sure, so I went to California one summer and tried to exchange my virginity with a boy who lived near Aunt Tiffany.

And she held a gun to my forehead. She wasn't apologetic; her voice was firm but regretful. She told me that I wasn't like them, like the rest of the family my grandparents had sculpted from nothing. All of them had been adopted, my mother being the first. She said I was weak and did not deserve the gift my mother had bestowed on me. She shamed me for trying to give the one truly unique gift I had to someone who would not remember me. The best rally I had was, "You want me to marry Mario and I don't know that I love him!" She smiled and said, "Then by your logic, you love that boy. Right?" Then she said, "Say goodnight, Evie," and pulled the trigger six times on empty chambers. "You're dead, kid, and the pity is that you don't even know why."

Well, damn. I spent the next few months trying to figure it out – and then got kidnapped and sodomized by a man that took some sort pity on me by doing it that way. There are any number of reasons why he didn't take my virginity. He could have. I was powerless to stop him and both of us knew it. I told the story to Uncle Alex, told him that I could not tell mother what had happened. I told him that I needed his help and he gave it. Every time I had a bad moment because of that man, I sought him out and he never failed me. But he told me to tell Mario and I did only because I valued his opinion. It was almost too much for him; he almost told Mom, his adopted sister. I asked him the one question that stopped him. "And when it drives her to avenge me and kills her? Will you feel satisfied? She is my mother. She is your sister. We owe this to her."

And we made love.
Since then, there has been no one else.
I gave him naming rights.

CHAPTER 31

We were on the road by seven-thirty. It would likely be noon or close to it by the time we got to Browning on the reservation. Freeman consented to ride with us. That meant we had five people in the Hummer, Wanda driving.

The only person that hadn't popped up at all was Arthur Bridges. If Marianne Dawkins, the office manager from back in Kevin, was right, then Bridges was Beryl and he had his eyes set on something that Moore was smuggling. He'd known about Kevin, about Freeman being there and knew about my involvement with Freeman as his doctor.

"Why would Arthur Bridges, aka Beryl, make an appearance like he did and where he did?" I asked Moore. "And don't tell me you don't know that name."

He was in the front seat. He swiveled and looked back at me. "You want to know why he involved you." It wasn't a question.

"Yes. I'm a doctor, not someone who can lead him to a treasure."

"But you did lead him to me and he knew you would. The same success as a doctor that led Freeman to you, also led him to you. He knew Freeman was after me and by following him, you'd lead him to me. It's all very simple, doctor."

"Then you smuggled something into the country that he both knows about and wants," I replied.

"Yes, but I have no idea what it might be."

I rolled my eyes and said, "Yeada, yada. You never know what you're bringing into the country."

"Yes," he replied settling himself in the front seat again.

Wanda gripped the steering wheel, then re-gripped it and asked, "Then what's Knoll's part in this? What part does his militia have in this?"

I leaned forward to hear Moore's reply. I noted that Freeman did, too.

"Thomas Knoll is an idiot," Moore answered as he watched the road ahead. "He attracts them, too."

"My job was to infiltrate them," Freeman added. "And I agree. Knoll is a fat idiot."

Wanda re-gripped the steering wheel and said, "Well, that neatly doesn't answer the question. What's his role here? Just because he's an idiot doesn't mean anything at all. An idiot with a gun is far more dangerous than one without." She looked at Moore and said, "Answer the goddamn question, Bill."

He looked in the rearview mirror and said, "Just tell them, Fire Dawn."

"You know?" she said.

"Yes. I am aware."

Wanda looked into the rearview mirror, but before she could say anything, Mario said, "We're being followed."

I tried to turn my head and look behind us, but Mario caught me and turned it into a kiss. Then he smiled and said, "It would be better if they thought they were getting away with it."

"I agree," Freeman said.

"So I'm the only one that doesn't know?" I asked.

"Yep," Wanda said. "Clueless as always." Then she asked Moore, "Are we still going to your sister's place?"

"Yes," he said. Then he added, "Well, sort of."

Wanda looked at him and said, "Are you going to tell me or resort to the Vulcan mind meld?"

"We'll stop for lunch in Browning, then I'll drive the rest of the way," Moore said.

"Oh, you will?" she said.

"Yes," he answered. "I will. I think it has something to do with home field advantage."

"You think I'm stupid?" she countered.

It was like watching a tennis match.

"I think I know the terrain better than you."

"You could just tell me where to go," she returned.

"You could simply watch and learn," he countered.

"Maybe you think I'm incapable of learning."

"I would not offer if I thought that was so."

I leaned between them and said, "Wanda? He's right and he's driving. Deal with it."

She turned to me and said, "So, you think I'm stupid, too?"

I frowned, looked at her and said, "Maybe," I said. "But it's probably because you're a redhead. I mean, you started out with a handicap and now you're just swimming as fast as you can. It isn't your fault." I motioned forward and said, "And watch the road. I mean, I don't my tombstone to read, 'Only because Wanda was a redhead'. You know?"

"Funny," she said.

"It is," Moore said not smiling.

"You think I'm weak," Wanda said with a voice that betrayed she was not.

Moore finally smiled. "Right. I think you're weak."

Wanda looked like she's swallowed a bowling ball. "You better never think that of me."

Moore looked at her and said, "I'd touch you but then Doctor Six might have adjust her tombstone."

Wanda sighed and said, "Okay. You can drive when we get there."

"Thank you, Fire Dawn."

We stopped in Browning for lunch. We were quiet and ate in good time. Wanda wanted to take Moore away and have him for herself and didn't need to say anything for me to know that. Still, she maintained her calm and we ate. Mostly, no one talked about where we were going or why.

I thought it was obvious that Moore would be recognized. He was. The waitress smiled and made pleasant small talk with him. He smiled while Wanda fumed silently. Her look got faraway again and I realized his hand was in her lap. *Good for you, girl.* A couple of men nodded at him as they entered. His greeting was little more than a small nod in their direction. It occurred to me that his stoic perception of the world wasn't just one rolled out for us. It looked as though that was how he saw the world and the people in it.

We left at last and I would admit to having butterflies for any number of reasons. The prospect of going into a place where there were guaranteed to be a lot of guns was at the top of my list.

We drove north through town and I avoided rubbernecking only because I've been to Pine Ridge in South Dakota. This place looked like that one. The Pine Ridge Indian Reservation is possibly the poorest place in the country and no one cares. Hard eyes looked at us as we drove through town. Everyone knew we didn't live there, not and drive a Hummer. Moore got a few double-takes, but he ignored them. I saw a pregnant woman sitting outside a house. She looked weary and spent. She was maybe twenty-five.

Moore made a left just north of town. I read the street sign as being Starr School Road. I thought about Aunt Dora for a moment because she runs a school back in Portland. I thought I needed to call her, thought about my entire family just then. Why? What was there about this place that could summon them? I reached blindly for Mario's hand and he took it and held firmly. I felt better.

The road turned almost due west. Moore drove slightly below the speed limit and said nothing. No one else did either. The terrain was growing lumpy as we neared what looked like a river. Pine trees lined its length as it snaked over the ground. Moore pulled off the road and sat on the roadside watching the sky through the windshield and the road via the mirrors. Still, no one talked.

We sat for about fifteen minutes, the heavy Hummer rumbling around us. I watched Wanda intently because she wanted to start screaming. Had Moore not been holding her hand, she would have. I counted it as a good thing that Moore realized it.

"It's going to get bumpy, folks," he said to us. Then he pulled off road and started across the lumpy terrain toward the river. The Hummer was capable of much greater speed than he showed.

"He's keeping down the dust as he drives," Mario whispered to me right on cue.

"Ah," I said with the same voice.

We approached the trees that paced the river. Moore seemed to know where he was going. I only hoped that Wanda understood the need for him to drive. The trees looked like an impenetrable line until Moore found a space between them and drove into the darkness. He turned left inside them and knifed his way through and among the thick trees. I tried to remember if there were any scrapes from tree branches on his pickup but couldn't. It was noteworthy because he avoided the traps those branches might have set for him. *Yes, you've done this before.*

Finally, he stopped and opened his door. "We're on foot for the rest of the way," he said.

We all got out.

Mario stuck with Freeman because Daniel tired easily. I stick with Wanda as Moore led our small group up a slight hill.

"You cool?" I asked Wanda.

"Yep," she said softly. "Evie? What am I going to do when this is over? I live and work in Kalispell. He lives here in Browning."

"Talk usually helps," I said.

She put her palms into her eyes and sobbed. "I need him, Evie."

There was no point in giving her a lecture because I did the same thing in my past concerning Mario. If she said she needed him *that way* I could live with it. If all she needed was a friend to help her through those long nights, that was an easy price to pay for friendship. If she needed a matron of honor, I'd do it easily. She's my best friend and I love her.

Moore stopped. He'd heard her cry and I thought a lecture was coming about silence and secrecy. Instead, he merely held her to himself and ran his hands through her thick red hair. If he spoke, I did not hear it. I don't think he did. Finally, he put his hands on her shoulders and looked at her. Then he kissed her lightly. Then he hugged her to him and she held onto him as though she was drowning. Possibly, she was. Then he looked at me and said, "Take care of her? Please?"

"Sure," I said.

Her eyes were puffy from crying silent tears.

"Are you okay?" I asked.

"Possibly," she said with a choked voice. "Possibly not. I think it depends on what happens to us."

"Let me put it another way. Can you continue with this? Or do I need to take you back to the Hummer?"

"I'll be okay," she said. I wasn't convinced. Still, we continued.

It was no more than five minutes later when Moore climbed a slight rise, trees all around us and said, "Violet lives beyond the crest."

We all lay down on the ground and peered over the ridge line. It was a small house with one car parked next to it. Freeman said, "That's Mary's car."

Moore nodded but said nothing.

He scanned the area, but for what I could not say. Knoll? Cops? Friends? Accomplices? The unknown? He said at last, "I need to talk to Violet."

"I need to talk to Mary," Freeman said.

"Well, I'll be wherever you go," I said to Freeman.

"Can I convince you to stay here?" Moore said to Freeman.

"No. She's my wife."

Moore nodded imperceptibly. Then he returned his gaze to the house.

It wasn't much, just an old mobile home stuck by a river on a poor Indian reservation. A bike leaning against the back of it betrayed a boy, a young Indian. A clothesline that dangled laundry to the wind betrayed no dryer, maybe not even a washing machine.

Moore's words were delivered as bluntly as never.
"I have a bad feeling about this."
He was right. It was about to get bad.
Real bad.

CHAPTER 32

Moore led us down through the trees toward the small home. Wanda walked beside him holding his hand. Mario held mine. Freeman walked between us. I thought Daniel looked weary and might have been pushing himself.

Moore stopped halfway to the small house, his long black hair waving under a slight breeze. He put his face to the sky and looked. I did, too, but saw and heard nothing. Mario squeezed my hand. I wanted to ask him if he saw or heard anything but didn't. I gave myself high marks for discipline. I noted that Freeman did little but watch Moore. If it meant anything other than the anger he'd built up over the man, I didn't see it.

Moore finally dropped his face from the sky and headed toward a small step that led into the back of the trailer. A frail railing bordered the steps. He walked up them, opened the door and called out, "Violet? It's William."

"Back here," a pleasant voice called out.

It must have satisfied Moore because he entered the small trailer. It was a laundry area. There was an old washing machine, but no dryer. Hence, the clothesline. He put his arm out and stopped Wanda from being seen as he stepped into the narrow hallway of the mobile home.

"You okay, Violet?"

"Yeah," the pleasant voice said. "Got company."

"So do I," he said from the hallway. He pulled Wanda with him but held out his arm for the rest of us the wait there. We did even though Freeman looked impatient. Maybe pissed. Me? I was so apprehensive that I wondered how I was going to be able to stand it. Then again, as long as I was with Freeman and could monitor his condition, I was happy.

I squeezed Mario's hand and he wrapped me into him and turned it into a hug. On such things are bliss made.

My bliss became short-lived when the back door opened and Arthur Bridges aka Beryl walked in holding a big gun, a rifle of some type. I frowned and said, "Mario? This is your fault."

He smiled despite the gun. "How so?"

"I know it's a rifle but not what kind."

Bridges leveled it at me and said, "Unless you join the others in the living room, you'll never get an answer to it."

We were herded into the living room where Violet Hatemen was drinking coffee with Mary Freeman. Violet's son, David, was watching the TV, the sound so low that I couldn't hear it.

Mary saw Daniel, put down her cup and rushed to him. "Oh, Danny! I'm, so worried about Marcus!"

Freeman hugged her, but it was of the polite variety. "You've been Moore's contact in whatever he's been smuggling?"

That brought Bridges into the mess. He did something mechanical to the gun that obviously made it ready to fire. Mario? You'd better teach me what this stuff is or we're going to…well…I'm going…and I knew he'd tell me and that I'd forget *since it had nothing to do with medicine.*

Anyway.

Bridges smiled as he trained the gun on Mary Freeman and said, "And that's why I'm here. I know you're smuggling ivory and I want it." Then he smiled at her and said, "Or don't you know the black market price for ivory?"

I thought Bridges was going to shoot Mary right then because her reply was the simplest, "I don't smuggle anything, especially something as stupid as ivory."

Moore was wearing a heavier coat than the weather commanded. While I had no idea that meant he was carrying a gun, everyone else knew better including Wanda. She put her hand on the bulge in his coat and merely shook her head. He looked at her hard but said nothing Wanda's singularly piercing gaze began to penetrate him. Finally he hugged her and said something soft to her, something for her, for them.

Wanda said to Bridges and she hugged Moore, "He's carrying a gun. I'm going to put it on the floor."

Bridges held the rifle to his shoulder and said, "You fuck this up, lady, and I can kill you both with one shot."

"I won't," she said reaching into the small of Moore's back and picking a pistol from it with her index finger and thumb. Holding it gingerly, she knelt and put the gun at Bridges feet.

"Into the living room," Bridges said to us as he held the gun on us from his shoulder. His right eye sighted down the barrel evilly.

We went

It gave me a chance to see Violet Hatemen. While William Moore was a big man, Violet was short and absolutely gorgeous. Her long black hair was pretty in a plain and unstated way in the same manner that William's was plain in a male way. Still, it was easy to see that they were brother and sister when they hugged. Violet smiled at Wanda and said, "It's been a long time since William has shared himself with another."

Wanda extended her hand and said, "I'm Wanda Lansing."

"Violet Hatemen," she answered with her hand outstretched. Wanda took it and then Violet offered it to me. "Violet," she said with a smile.

"Evie," I offered.

If you read this as me not being too intimidated by Bridges, you read it correctly. I've always figured that if a person was going to use a gun, that he'd do it quickly or not at all. Since Bridges seemed willing to threaten us with a gun seemed to indicate that he wasn't going to use it unless pressured beyond his ability to cope. I figured we were safe until Violet did something stupid – and my first impression of her was that she wasn't about to do anything like that.

I looked at Bridges and said, "Hey, Beryl? Why did you tie me to that post? What did you expect to get out of it except a handful of stuff you can get from any girl?"

"It implicated that idiot Knoll," he said with a self-satisfied expression on his face. "That house is his property and anything that happens in it will involve him. I was hoping that him and his stupid militia would have a party with you. I guess he's too stupid to see a pretty girl and the possibilities offered by enough rope."

"Erectile dysfunction," I said calmly. "It happens to men your age."

He lifted the gun to his shoulder and said hotly, "I'm not in this for gratuitous sex! I'm in this for the ivory Moore is smuggling."

I leaned toward him and growled, "Sex with me is *never* gratuitous! I have a great ass!"

Mario nudged Moore and said, "She does, too."

Moore said in his same stoic manner, "Miss Lansing has captured my fancy, so I'll admit that I am not up to speed on the status of your wife's ass."

Mario said, "Wow. I always thought it was kind of obvious."

"Alas," was all Moore said.

I didn't know whether to be insulted or don a cheerleader's outfit and start cheering.

"Um, hello?" Bridges said angrily. "I have a gun here."

That left the madness for someone who was more adept at it. Yep, Knoll and his group literally blew open the front door and six men stormed into it. One of them walked up to Bridges – who had his rifle trained on him by the way – and savagely gun-butted him until Bridges dropped the gun and was out cold.

That left us.

Okay. I'll admit to being a nervous. I immediately began to worry less about Bridges' bloody nose than about my own survival chances.

Knoll said to the guy that put Bridges down, "Unless I get the answer I want, shoot the squaw."

"Yes, sir," the man said training his weapon on Violet.

"The package," Knoll said. "I want it."

"Give it to him," Moore said.

"He'll kill us anyway," Violet said. "And the package is too valuable to give away."

"On three, Harris," Knoll said.

"On three," he agreed, putting the rifle to his shoulder and sighting down the barrel.

"One," Knoll said.

"Give it to him, Violet. It's not more important than you are."

"Yes, it is," she disagreed.

"Two," Knoll said.

Harris flexed his shoulders and rolled his head. Then he smiled at Violet and mouthed, "Three."

Moore said, "Please, Violet. We can always replace the money." Then he stepped in front of his sister and said, "You'll have to kill me, too." He spread his arms wide as though to protect her.

"It isn't the money," she said, and then enigmatically added, "And you know it."

All I knew was that if Knoll counted to the next number, she was dead and so were we. So I added my voice to Moore's. "Please, Violet. Just give it to him. Whatever it is can be replaced."

"My dear?" Knoll said sadistically. "The package or death? It really makes no difference to me because legally you're criminals anyway."

Moore turned to his sister and tears rolled from his eyes as he said, "What is undone can be redone. Please, maybe not by me and maybe not by you, but it can be redone."

I was going to remember that little speech because it was full of portents and intents that I missed as he said it. But I was destined to remember them. But all that was in the future. All my concentration was on surviving the next few moments. I reached blindly for Mario's hand and, like always, he found mine and held it tightly. Then, like always, he rolled me under his arm and held me. The kiss on my cheek felt warm and friendly.

Violet returned her brother's tears with ones of her own. Then she hugged him and said to Knoll, "It's under the porch steps."

Knoll snapped his fingers and said, "Search. Now."

His henchmen, minus Harris, rushed from the room and we heard men tearing apart the stairs up which they had stormed the house. Harris continued to hold his weapon on William Moore, who stood protectively in front of his sister. Wanda stood in front of him, her arms wide as well.

A voice from outside called out, "Got it!"

Violet's voice caught emotionally and it didn't take a genius to know that she was crying. Again, I missed it, totally. But all was going to make sense soon, very soon.

I could not, however, let them take it without knowing what it was. I followed Knoll down the steps and watched him as he torn apart a metal curtain that decoratively hid from sight anything beneath it. A box. That was it, a very long one. Maybe five feet long and one wide, it was as unassuming as anything I could imagine.

Knoll pulled it from beneath the stairs and opened it in order to see it. Had he not, it is possible that the future would have been different only because I would not have seen the contents of the box.

Knoll's voice betrayed some confusion. "This doesn't look like ivory," he said.

Indeed.

As soon as I saw its contents, I smiled.

"Gems and whalebone," I said.

To come this far in my life only to be put in that place at that time was destined. My father did this. No, not Brad Chang. This is something Brian Sixkiller would have done. Brad? Dad? Please don't take this personally because you are a very, very good man, one that Mom deserves. But Brian? Dad? Thank you for this most precious gift. Why? Easy. Knoll was about to prove what a fool he is, was – and it had nothing to do with the gems. That I recognized them and their origin was all arranged by a cosmic stratagem that made me warm all over.

And Knoll? He played his part, the foolish one. "What the hell is this shit?" he said.

"Whalebones and gems," I repeated over his shoulder.

I never saw his smile, but it was there. His voice didn't hide his glee when he thought about it. "Hunting whales is illegal. It doesn't matter that it isn't ivory. This is better than gold." He turned to one of his underlings and barked, "Put this in the truck."

My part was to play the role of the unassuming criminal who only wanted to recant her crime and be graciously allowed to continue her life. I actually put my hands together at my bosom and said, "I'll admit to my part in this when you announce it."

The others were spread behind me as though trying to disappear. I turned to Violet and said, "And I'll be with her when the time comes."

I think Violet knew. Her brother did, but he was ignorant to the details behind his "crime".

When Mario saw my face, he knew better than to ask questions.

That left Freeman.

It was almost done. All that was missing was motive and I was destined to learn it.

Just a few more days.

CHAPTER 33

I had to make certain, so I called my mother. "Mom?" I asked after I explained it to her. "Am I right?"

"I can have it verified, but I think so."

"Would you do it?" I asked.

"Oh, you know better than to ask."

"Thought you might," I smiled into the phone. "Mom? You take care."

"When will it happen?" she asked.

"No idea, but it will."

"I'll be watching," she said.

"Thanks, Mom."

Naturally, everyone wanted to know what I was planning. Wanda was especially insistent. All I could do was hug her and say, "Girlfriend? Do you trust me?"

"It's my life, Evie," she said.

"Mine too," I agreed.

"You don't look worried," she said.

"I'm not."

"So?"

"I'm just waiting for Knoll to make his move."

Oh, lord, but I wanted to say something to someone. I tried to tell Mario but he just smiled and said, "Don't worry. I know what's going to happen and I support you one hundred percent."

Had Knoll done anything intelligent, nothing would have happened. By that I mean, had he said *anything* to *anyone* he would have seen the weakness in his position, but he didn't do anything. He sat on top of his evidence and took great pains to keep it a secret. Not that I knew it, of course. Still, I was grateful for his silence.

The only thing left to do was take Daniel and Mary Freeman to get their son. Oddly, Violet and David came wanted to come with us. But getting seven people into a Hummer proved too difficult, so Moore stayed behind with them. He promised to be there when we returned. Naturally, Wanda stayed with him.

Since Mary was a part of what was happening, she wanted to tell her husband what she had been doing. She was scared, nervous and fearful for their marriage as she talked. You could see it in her eyes, the stark fear she held to herself. Daniel tried to get angry but I looked at him in the rearview mirror and said, "Freeman? Listen to her heart and not her words. She was doing something brave and full of good purposes."

"She could have said something," he countered.

The motive was something that Governor Layne held. I thought that was obvious. If he knew of what had happened, he didn't say anything. That was just as well, I thought. Of course, Layne being a political animal, it was possible that he knew what was going to happen and was prepared for it.

But Freeman.

He took my advice and listened to his wife and her reasons for being a go-between in this. Still, the more I came to know what they were doing, the more I wanted Knoll to play his hand. Mary Freeman put it succinctly. "No one else would do it, so I volunteered. I'd do it again, too."

Mary Freeman saw herself as a criminal. She saw herself taking directions from a man who turned out to be Ted Hentley.

"Do you know what he did with the money once you gave it to Moore?" Freeman asked his wife.

"No. My instructions were to give the envelope to him and he would know what to do with it.

Freeman took that to mean that his wife had agreed to a payoff that involved a known criminal. While I suspected the truth, that lay in the future.

I changed the subject by asking Mary, "What diagnosis have you gotten concerning Marcus's condition?"

"Endless tests that go nowhere," she sighed. "But Danny told me that your preliminary diagnosis was something called Gaucher's Disease. Does that mean Marcus has the same thing? If so, does the disease differ from adult to infant?"

I turned and looked at Mary Freeman over the seat. Like Wanda, she was a nurse and saw a lot of bad stuff. I wondered how she dealt with her son's condition, but was destined to learn all the things she did to figure out what was wrong with him. It started right there and then.

Marcus Freeman was nine months old. His mother suspected something was wrong with him long before she confided her secret to her husband. But even she had no idea what was wrong with her son. The one word that she used to describe little Marcus Freeman was lethargic. He seldom cried and even when he did, it wasn't for very long. Mostly, Mary noted that her son slept a lot and tended to watch his surroundings rather than make any attempt to get involved in them. She kept waiting for little Marc to pitch a fit and he never did, not at least to her expectations.

The issue for her in getting a diagnosis was in testing for it. All that meant was that I was going to talk to Sandy Peterson, the manager of the blood lab back at Kalispell Regional. I needed to ask her the question that I'd missed the last time I saw her. "What made you test for Gaucher's?" That one. She didn't have to test for it but she did. Therefore, she was going to ask Bobby Garrison to take Marcus Freeman's blood and determine his future.

With a long drive back to Helena, I took my time in answering Mary's question. I sat with my back to the door and tried to look upbeat. Still, if little Marcus had type 2, he wouldn't live another year. I smiled, tried out my best upbeat manner and said, "Gaucher's Disease is a condition where a substance called glucocerebroside builds up in the spleen, liver, lungs, bones and sometimes in the brain. Involvement in the brain is fatal. Type 1 does not involve the brain and is the most common type. My guess is that Daniel has that version. If he had type 2, he will not have live past the age of two. Type 2 is the infant variety and is fatal by that age, by the age of two. Type 3 is a combination of types 1 and 2. If Daniel or Marcus has this type of the disease, their survival depends on treatment and how soon it starts." Then I looked as calm as I could and asked, "Has Marcus's condition ever been mistaken for Hodgkin's Disease?"

Mary looked a bit surprised. "Yes. That was the first diagnosis I got on him."

"That's fairly common," I said.

"Why did my symptoms appear so recently while Marcus's condition was apparent at birth?" Daniel asked.

"There are a lot reasons why the diseases progresses as it does. What I'm saying is that there is no easy answer. But both of you need to be ready for Marcus to be diagnosed with type 2 and Daniel to be diagnosed with type 1 or 3. What I'm saying bluntly is that type 1 manifests itself at any time. Type 2 is apparent at birth and that is what you're seeing with Marcus, a disease that manifested itself at birth."

"But?" Mary said, her voice trailing off painfully.

"Anything is possible," I replied.

"What is the treatment?" she asked.

"In the past?" I answered. "The spleen was removed and bone marrow was transplanted. Now? Enzyme replacement therapy is available. It doesn't cure the affected person, but the therapy is given usually every two weeks on an outpatient basis and that allows the person to live a much more normal life."

"But if Marcus has type 2?" she asked fearfully.

"Then there is no treatment available."

It took Mario to change the tone of the conversation. Personally, I believe he knew we needed it. It's like him to know stuff like that. He looked at Mary in the rearview mirror and asked, "What was your purpose in Violet's house?"

I will go to my grave believing that Mary Freeman had no idea what she was doing or providing when she gave a packet-full of money to William Moore in exchange for whatever he uncovered at the coordinates that were provided by Ted Hentley.

She shrugged and said, "Look. I don't know. The package Moore gave me was always left in the same place, a parking lot in Helena."

"The state capital," I said.

"Yes."

"And you don't know what Moore did with the money?"

"I didn't care. Hentley asked me to do this because he said it was important."

"Was it Hentley in person?" I asked.

"No. Hentley is too well known," she replied. "My instruction were to take the package to the parking in Helena and leave it in a certain place. I never saw anyone and never thought about who picked it up. My reward was a good review and a raise."

Actually, it didn't matter who it was. If I understood the operation, then the package came back to the person who first planted it. If it was Hentley then it was as good as Layne himself. The question "Why would Layne go to the trouble of smuggling a package back to himself?" might have been an essential one to someone trying to solve the puzzle, but my focus was still on Daniel Freeman and his son, Marcus.

Trust Mario. He looked at me and smiled. "The gems?" he said to me. "Describe them."

I smiled. "It was a lovely green gem. I'd like to have a ring made of it."

"Or a necklace, or a bracelet or a broach," he added.

"Tell me about whalebones," I asked, his smile still enigmatic, secret."

I did.

He told me about a gem named hiddenite. It's found in just one place in the world.

Between hiddenite and whalebone, I couldn't wait for Knoll to pop up with his stupid press conference.

Again, however, Freeman first.

CHAPTER 34

Mary Freeman's mother was a woman named Adela Hodges. In her middle fifties, she looked much younger. I figured plastic surgery. I have some experience with it. No, not personally, but through my mother. She's had breast reduction surgery and then she had breast enhancement surgery when she realized she was vain and liked the attention having the biggest boobs in town brought her. Oddly, when she ran for office, she had to explain all *those* pictures. No, not nudity, but the ones that showed the ability for her boobs to enter a room several seconds before the rest of her did. Her answer was always a version of, "You mean make excuses for how God made me?" She never bothered to explain her reasons for undoing what God had done and then redoing it. All the public needed to see was her winning smile and the several additional surgeries that erased the crow's feet from her eyes, the wrinkles from around her mouth and the various other surgeries that ensured her butt was still photogenic. No, Adela Hodges had had her share of plastic surgery and I thought it was obvious. In fact, whenever I hear someone say, "God, she's aged well," my usual reply is, "That may be, but thank her plastic surgeon for his work, too."

Looking at Adela, I thought, *boobs, and surgery to keep them pert, liposuction, butt enhancement, facial surgery, botox, collagen injections, a nose job and a good hairdresser.* Her smile was worth every dime she paid her plastic surgeon. "I am very happy to meet you, Doctor Collins," she said.

The effort to correct her was no longer worth the effort. I shook her hand and said, "Thank you. Can I see Marcus?"

She frowned a bit and said, "He's sleeping, but that's fairly common."

There was no Mr. Hodges. Or, more correctly, there had been once upon a time. Edward Hodges had been dead for several years and Adela kept his memory alive by a spread of photographs just inside the hallway that led to her bedroom. That information came from Mary, her daughter. Also, came the information that while there were pictures of old Eddie in the hallway, that there were none in her bedroom because, according to Mary, "Mom likes to entertain men." I guessed what that meant, hence the plastic surgery.

Whatever I might have thought about Adela Hodges, she kept a pretty bedroom ready for her grandson. Painted in shades of blue, Marcus Freeman slept on a light blue sheet with a dark blue blanket and a mobile hanging over his crib.

"Will you need to take him with you?" Adela asked, her surgically enhanced eyes showing concern.

"Technically? No," I answered. "But if we get a diagnosis and treatment is an immediate option, then you might want to make him available."

"True," she answered. "So. Are we going now?"

"Yes," I said smiling.

With the blanket covering him, Marcus Freeman looked every bit as healthy as me or you. It was only after Adela removed the blanket and woke baby Marcus that you could see that something was wrong with him. His slightly curved spine would have been a signal to Mary that her son had something wrong with him. The slight yellow tinge to his skin was another sign, the yellow of his eyes yet a third sign. It made me wonder how many doctors had misread his condition for so long.

Mary picked him up and held her son on her shoulder. She moved slightly and hummed in his ear as she did. It was soft, friendly, loving and protective. It wasn't hard to want to help them, even though I would have anyway. I've seen my share of do-nothing parents who resort to a doctor at the last possible second and then heap scorn on the very people who are trying only to help. Neither Adela nor Mary looked that way. But like I said, even if they had been, I would have helped them anyway. Call it a curse but I'd been chasing them for almost a week now. Time meant nothing until there wasn't any more – and then I'd keep trying anyway.

Adela came with us, but required three changes of outfits before she felt that the public could see her. Mary whispered to me, "Mom is very vain."

"So is mine," I answered with a smile.

"My mother doesn't admit it."

"Neither does mine," I smiled.

That put us on the road back to Kalispell. We had several hours to go and all of us were nervous in one way or another. Mary had the dual worries of her husband and her son. Adela had the worry of a grandmother. Daniel had the twin worry of both his life and the life of his son. As a corollary, he had the worry of a father needing to bury his child. Me? Everything about the past week or so faded away like a bad dream. I had my patients and I was going to get a diagnosis for them and then start treatment.

We got on the road and knew it was going to be late before we got to Kalispell. Mario broached the subject of everyone staying at our home. We had the room, had them built onto our house for just such an eventuality. Adela said yes and so did her daughter and son-in-law. It meant an extra day before I got them to a doctor, but they agreed to do it that way.

Actually, I expected something unexpected. You know? Maybe Knoll to show up. Maybe Bridges. Maybe anyone or anything. But it turned out to be none of those people. The unexpected was put into motion by my husband. More on that later.

However, looking back, I think all of them were fairly transparent. For example, there was no way that Petra and Adela did not know each other. Did that mean they shared a common bond with Thomas Knoll? Well, no as it turned out. How did that little gem come to be excavated? I asked her, "You know Petra Freeman."

"Yes," Adela answered.

I thought it was obvious that she wanted to say more than that and wondered how to make it socially possible. In other words, would Daniel Freeman become upset if Adela Hodges did not like his mother? In order to make the subject socially palatable, I asked Adela, "Do you know or have you ever heard of a man named Thomas Knoll?"

Her lips turned into a sneer. "Oh, the general? Daniel's mother was quite taken by him. Yes, I know of him."

"But you've never met him?"

"No, and that's a thing I am proud to be able to say."

"Does it bother you, Daniel, that your mother-in-law disapproves of your mother and the company she keeps?"

"No," he answered while looking straight down at his lap. "I had no idea she even knew him much less shared her bed with him."

Baby Marcus started to fuss and Mary actually looked encouraged by his small outburst. She took a bottle from the baby bag she brought with her and stuck it to his mouth. He sucked on it hungrily and I, too, took that as a hopeful sign. He didn't feed long and Mary looked disappointed.

"How much did he eat?" I asked.

"Maybe three ounces," she said holding the bottle to the window.

"And when did he last eat?" I asked Adela.

"Lunch," she answered. "About six ounces." Then smiled and said, "And then filled a diaper almost to overflowing."

"And breakfast?" I asked.

"A full bottle. And the same result."

It seemed to indicate that Marcus had a good appetite. In itself, it meant nothing, but it was far better than having an infant with no appetite at all.

"Can we agree that Marcus has a good appetite?" I asked.

"Sure," Mary said putting her son over her shoulder and patting his back lightly. It took only a few moments for the baby to produce an audible burp. We all laughed and hoped that it was a good sign for his future. Me? It was difficult to mask my skepticism. A baby born with Gaucher's has a very slim chance to live to be two. I hoped Marcus beat the heavy odds his life held.

It was dark by the time we got to Kalispell. I asked, "Everyone cool for dinner?"

They were.

"Sonny's," I said to Mario.

He nodded. The bastard was thinking and it pissed me off when he did and then kept it to himself.

He pulled into the lot and I acted like to good host and explained Sonny's fare to them.

My night was about to get interesting – and I had Mario to blame for it.

Damn, I love that man.

CHAPTER 35

Sonny's is a bar/cum restaurant. I made my introduction to it not long after I moved here from Los Angeles. Yes, they thought they'd gotten a doctor who was a Valley Girl from LA. It was cute when I told them that I'd grown up in Portland, Maine, and knew how to cross country ski and ice skate. Since then, I've made quite a few friends and starting noticing them as soon as we entered the place.

The bartender, Doug Stevens and the owner of the place, bellowed, "Six!"

I shouted back, "Tory!"

The hostess, a lady named Elaine, smiled and said, "Follow me, doc. We'll get you a nice quiet booth."

She did, too. The booth in the farthest corner away from the bar was where she put us. It was their biggest booth, sitting at least nine, and we all settled into it. Mary had a small bassinette that she put little Marcus into. He was quiet, too quiet as far as I knew. I looked at his eyes again and saw the faintest bit of yellow in them. While it tended to verify the tentative diagnosis, it also tentatively suggested other conditions.

That was when Mario said, "Long trip. I have to use the bathroom." He kissed me and left.

I paid it no attention. You wouldn't have either. Instead, I settled into conversation with Mary, Daniel and Adela. Mary looked at her mother, teased her and said, "Mom? Settle down. Find a boy, get married and have a family. Mine."

It was cute, but Adela said, "Oh, no. I spent way too much money to look this way and then throw it all on one guy."

We talked for maybe fifteen minutes and only then did I wonder about Mario. I craned my neck toward where he would be if he came from the direction of the bathrooms. I saw lots of people but not him. It took another five minutes before I saw him. Twenty minutes to use the head? Oh, no. Something was up and even someone as obtuse as me knew it.

"What's going on?" I asked him as he slid into the booth. "And don't say 'nothing' because both of us know better."

He craned his own neck but was looking toward the door. Finally, he smiled, waved his arms and said, "Back here!"

I turned and looked and saw Wanda, Violet, David, William Moore and another man I did not recognize. As they say in bad movies, the plot had just thickened.

Wanda was as enthusiastic as ever and led Moore by the hand back to our booth. Her smile was wide, happy and absolutely gorgeous. She slid in next to me and Moore and his friend slid in next to Mario. I didn't realize it, but we were in the home stretch.

"This is Ray Stocker," Wanda said introducing the man sitting opposite me. Then her smile got mysterious and she added, "He's a pilot." Then she looked at Mario and said, "Dude? It's all yours."

I was either going to kill the bastard or give him a son. Maybe, a daughter. All this meant was that *this* is what he'd been thinking about.

"It occurred to me," he said, "that the only flaw in your plan for Knoll was the flight path that package took.

"His," I said nodding toward Moore. "Right?"

"Yeah," he said. "And it occurred to me that someone as careful as Moore has been, would not allow himself to be trapped. So I called him from the bathroom and asked if he knew the pilot who dropped the stuff off." He nodded toward Moore and said, "You finish it."

I never heard Moore get excited, lose control or exhibit anything but the harshest self-control he could place upon himself. If I had to guess, he'd been pressed into that position by people like Knoll, people who saw a criminal and expected crime. I was about to learn a truth about William Moore, not every truth he held to himself, but a basic one. Fortunately, Wanda was first to learn it – and only because she slapped him and screamed in his face, "Do you have any idea the last time I gave myself to a man!" I did only because she told me once. Let's leave it at this: years.

But he was ready to talk to me at the table that night. Wanda made certain of it. Me? My only input was the silent sort, listening. Moore and Stocker had stories to tell me. They would. All I had to do was listen and apply what they told me when Knoll made his move. Had Mario not thought this far ahead, I might have made a fool out of myself when Knoll raised his head. It wasn't that their story was along one, just that it held an important piece of information that became crucial to what happened.

The waitress, Elaine, came to take our drink orders. Mario and Wanda ordered a Coke. Moore and Stocker ordered a beer, Moose Drool. Mary and Adela ordered a glass of red wine. Me? Elaine looked at me and said, "Water. Same as always."

I objected. "What if I want something different?"

"Do you?" she asked, her hand on her hip.

"No," I said.

"Bitch," she said and left.

Elaine is Elaine Edwards. She's married, has three kids and newly laid-off husband named Peter and no medical bills. Her health care is free only because I told her, "If you ever give me less than your honest opinion about me, I'll start sending you a bill." Hence, "Bitch."

That left the ball in Moore's court. Well, Stocker's more directly. Moore knew the story, but wanted Stocker to tell his part in it himself. Stocker, I came to realize, was waiting for someone to figure out what they were doing. Oddly, he thought I knew.

But, no. I did not.

I only knew that William Moore was not guilty of smuggling, that Mary Freeman was not guilty of it either, that Thomas Knoll was a fool, that Petra Freeman was an idiot and that the motives for all of this were irrelevant as far as I was concerned.

Stocker told his story and Moore confirmed it. I shrugged and didn't see why I needed to know these things. But Mario, bless him, made me repeat it until he was certain that I understood their parts and how they operated. Moore was not satisfied and would not be so until the endgame played itself out.

All that started the next day.

CHAPTER 36

Our house is big enough for almost anyone. I thought back to my childhood and the way grandmother's house had all those bedrooms. If I remember, they had thirteen bedrooms spread over three floors, plus a basement. My bedroom was on the second floor until we moved down to The Prom. It was a two-story home until Mom decided, like me, that she liked all that room and added a third floor and four more bedrooms.

Our home in Kalispell was two stories when we bought it, two-stories and four bedrooms. Like Mom, we added a third floor but only three more bedrooms. The space we saved with the fourth bedroom was given over to a play room for whoever was up there. Like me when I was a kid, my own children liked being on the third floor whenever the opportunity presented itself. Well, it did.

They saw David as a new friend. It was Travis that asked, "Mom? Can we?"

"Sure. Have fun, but remember…"

"…don't burn down the house!" he cried as he ran after David, Becky, Maddie and Woody.

Cayn brought them home. Personally, Cayn is the biggest guy I've ever seen next to Uncle Alex. Moore come close, though. While Cayn is taller, Moore is more muscular – if that's possible because Cayn is pretty big. I was afraid they'd start doing Stupid Man Stuff. You know, flexing, posing and annoying the women. But they shook hands and Cayn said to Moore, "You saved Doctor Six and Nurse Wanda. Thanks."

Moore grunted and said, "Looked necessary."

Cayn looked at Wanda neutrally and said, "She looks kind of frail."

Wanda was about to smack him, when Moore said with his same stoic voice, "She's tenacious. That counts for a lot."

Wanda's right arm was raised to smack Cayn. Then she looked at Moore and raised her left arm. "Tenacious? Not gorgeous, beautiful or sexy?" And she smack both of them.

Moore looked at Cayn and said, "Damn, that's sexy."

Wanda wiggled her butt, smacked it and said, "Mr. Moore? You know what you can do with it."

Then she walked into the kitchen, pulling me with her. She broke out in tears and said, "I messed up, huh? They were just playing and I made an ass of myself, huh? Now he hates me and he's going to leave, huh?"

Well, naturally. Moore appeared in the doorway and moved directly toward her. To me while keeping his eyes on Wanda, he said, "You don't need to stay, Mrs. Collins."

"But I will," I said. "She's my friend."

"Very well," he said. Then to Wanda, he lifted an index finger and wiped away her tears. "I was disrespectful, rude and arrogant. Sometimes that is necessary in life, but never toward the one you love. I apologize, Fire Dawn. I was wrong."

She closed her eyes and said, "Evie? If you don't leave right now…"

"Don't worry," I said. "I'll always be around." Then I said to Moore, "She's all yours."

That made our night the task of assigning bedrooms. The kids all took the third floor. Violet was uneasy, but David practically begged to be allowed to stay up there with the other kids. "Well, okay. I'll be right by the stairs if you need me."

And they hugged.

Cayn had no reason to stay, but he did. I think he liked Moore and that was a good omen. As advertised, Violet picked the room closest to the stairs and then slept with her door open. That put Wanda and Moore in the room next to Violet. Cayn stayed in the room across the hall from us because, "I hate the sound of bedsprings." Wanda blushed and I didn't think that was possible. Daniel and Mary picked a room on the third floor that had a crib in it. Yes, I tried to prepare myself for the day when we would have company who would bring a baby. Adela picked a room next to them. Ray Stocker found a room on the second floor. Everyone was set.

We settled in our bedroom, settled in the closed-in balcony and watched the neighborhood. I grew up next to the ocean, Casco Bay in particular. Seldom were there days I could not look out my window and the ocean as it turned and tumbled. Peaks Island was in the near distance and its lights always blinked seductively. I was seventeen before Mario figured it out and we took the ferry out to the island and rode bikes all over it. It was October and a lot of the old homes, the seasonal ones, were closed for the coming winter. But really? It seemed just like another place. The houses looked similar and so did the people and their biology. Yes, I was trying myself out mentally as a doctor. Their homes meant nothing to me, but the bugs and germs that coursed through their bodies, the falls and tumbles they could suffer, the accidents they could have all screamed the same thing: *they're people just like you.* It didn't matter that some of them spoke with the calm disdain of the *Quebecois,* or the nasal twang that screamed, "Boston!" Their biology's were identical and I took that lesson home with me.

But that night, Mario knew my mind was churning with the morrow. "Talk to me."

The stars twinkled overhead and lights in nearby homes spoke of friends and people I knew. Still, I put my chin in my hand, smiled at him and said, "I stopped taking the pill. Wanna mess around? I think Anne is getting impatient."

"You mean, right here on the balcony?"

"We could go back inside and you could fight for me."

"It wouldn't be much of a battle."

"I've heard that my surrenders are classic."

Damn, I tried, tried but I slipped away and started seeing small coffins, ones that fit baby Marcus. I tried to see Daniel and Mary and what they must be feeling right now, but couldn't really imagine it. the death of a child, of a son? How would I spend the night if I knew a doctor might condemn Travis to death the next day?

"It's Marcus, isn't it?" Mario said quietly.

My job isn't about hope and possibilities. My job is about the being as clear-cut as I can be. If a diagnosis of type 2 Gaucher's came down tomorrow, then I'd be as straightforward as I could be. Yes, I'd emphasize the life Marcus had left and hope they could enjoy their son, but I knew that there was nothing I could do in that situation that would ease them, ease Daniel and Mary.

"Yeah," I said sadly.

"You think he has type 2?"

"I won't know until after the tests are run."

Technically, all Daniel needed to do was talk to Sandy Peterson tomorrow morning to get his diagnosis because the lab already had his blood. But the enzyme test was a better arbiter of his condition. Still, I thought he had type 1 but was ready for anything. It was Marcus whose fate was uncertain.

Mario touched my cheek and said, "This is one of your weirder surrenders."

Well, damn. I grabbed his hand and dragged him back into our bedroom. "Like I said, Anne is getting impatient, so we better honor her wishes."

Mario tossed me on the bed and said, "Well, who am I to ignore the wishes of a daughter who could just as easily be a son?"

As he stripped off his clothes, I put my hands behind my head, puffed up my chest and said, "There are no boys named Anne."

Then he crawled into bed and stripped off my clothes. It was fun; it usually is. Still, I knew tomorrow was going to be emotional, so I took all the pleasure I could get from the moment. As people, as humans, it was what we are condemned to do.

But, dang, if that is what condemnation feels like, then all I can say – at the top of my voice – is, "More! More!"

The alarm went off all too early.

CHAPTER 37

Sandy Peterson repeated to Daniel Freeman what she had already told me. "Mr. Freeman? After your enzyme test? I can tell you that you have type 1 Gaucher's Disease. The good news is that it is very treatable. You'll be looking at an implanted IV shunt that you will utilize maybe every other week on an out-patient basis. After the treatment starts, you will start to feel more normal. In fact, I can't see why you're life shouldn't go back to normal." Then she looked at me and said, "Do you agree, Doctor Six?"

Smiles are better, so I gave him one. "Yes. This is very good news. The enzyme treatment will flush the old matter from your body and as long as you keep up treatment, you should do well. It also helps that you were in good physical condition before this started."

Mary breathed a huge sigh of relief. "Oh, Danny!" she rushed. "You have no idea how relieved I am."

But he looked at his son and said gravely, "Now, you need Marcus's blood. Right?"

"Yes," Sandy said.

Bobby Garrison came in, took the sample and said, "I'll need some time to run the test."

"You got it," Daniel said.

I thanked Sandy and said, "We'll be in the waiting room."

Adela was already there. Mary shared Danny's news with her mother and the three of them hugged. I thought it was obvious that Daniel liked his mother-in-law much more than he liked his mother.

You get trained in medical school for times like this. Adela, Mary and Daniel were all nervous about Marcus. Marcus played his part admirably. He slept through it, even through the part that included a needle and a test tube. Personally, I thought Marcus was trying to tell us what to expect. Why? Well, seldom have I seen a baby not fuss when taking blood. Most don't react until the needle pierces their skin. Then the squawking starts. Marcus barely reacted and I thought that was a bad sign. Still, my background is medicine and that is a scientific study, so I decided to remain upbeat until the test came back.

I think Mary was already burying her son. She looked awful, looked as though her life was going to end if Marcus's did. Daniel tool her out into the hallway while Adela watched the baby.

Quietly, she asked as she stroked his hair, "Honestly, doctor. What are the odds? His?"

"It's better if you remain optimistic until the results come back. Otherwise? You wind up betting on the wrong horse. Just be upbeat, optimistic and don't overreact until you have a reason. So far? Marcus is just ill, not dead." I said it all with a smile and hoped that my message got across.

"God…" she said as her voice failed.

Daniel and Mary came back inside with Mary crying. Adela sat with her daughter and said, "Marcus is here and that isn't going to change today, Mary. No matter what, let's enjoy him. Okay?"

But before the diagnosis came back, I had to know one thing. "Daniel?" I said. "You might not be Jewish through your heritage but you're Jewish through this disease. You got it from your father just like Marcus did. You have to come to terms with it before they tell you what is going to happen to your son. No matter what, you gave this to him and only a trick of human rules marks your son as anything but Jewish. Jews didn't do this, genetics did. Or would you rather him have a disease common to Arabs and Turks? That's what Mediterranean Fever is, a disease common to people of that area. Would that make you happier? Or Sickle Cell Anemia? That's common to African-Americans. You can blame anyone you like, but it won't change your basic humanity."

Mary took his hands and said, "She's right, Danny! It isn't the fault of the Jews that you got this disease. It could be anything, any of them! Listen to her!"

Shedding prejudice is hard, perhaps as hard as anything you will ever do. I already knew he was second-guessing his past choices, but this was his family and his life before him. If Marcus managed to beat this, and Daniel reverted to form, then I could see a disaster forming the ashes of his family. He needed to see that the disease, their condition, was one of humanity and not segregated groups. If he could do that, then they might reasonably be able to survive whatever happened to Marcus. A genetic test before their next child might help them to decide.

He put his hands on Mary's arms and said, "I know, Mary. I know. The doctor already gave me this speech and I've thought it. She's right. We need to be more focused on who we are than in blaming others on how we got here." And he hugged her. She cried, but then I would have, too.

That put us in waiting mode. I knew that it was taking longer than a test required. The most logical reason was Bobby Garrison was rerunning the test, maybe more than once. That was fine. Being accurate at a time like this was crucial. So we waited.

Mary basically broached the subject of future children. "If we have more, we won't know until it's conceived if the child has Gaucher's. Do you have any suggestions, doctor?"

"Two," I said. "One? Abort the child if it has Gaucher's. If you have scruples that would prevent that, then adopt healthy children. Most of my mother's entire family was adopted. It works, or can if you allow it. Still, it's your choice."

There are women who like being pregnant, who prefer it over raising the resulting child. If Mary was that way, then their choices would be harder. Of course, she was already on record as asking her husband to drop a prejudice – and he was trying. Could she if the ball fell in her court?

She looked at Daniel and said, "Adopt? How do you feel about that?"

He took her hands and said, "You know I wanted a big family. But enduring something like this again? No. I can't imagine either of us ever sitting in a hospital waiting room wondering if our baby was going to live or die. We can adopt if you want to go that way."

Adela leaned into them and said, "Mary? Not bearing them is not a crime or a fault of yours. Children should be wanted. If you adopt them and tell them later on that they were, then you can tell that they were wanted so badly that you went out looking for them."

Mary nodded but did not reply. Maybe she was fighting the issue of pregnancy. There are a lot of women who put the issue of pregnancy as the primary reason for having a family. The longer she thought about it, the more likely I thought that it was her issue.

I said, "Your mother is right, Mary. Adopted children are usually more wanted than many naturally born ones. You can skip this agony – and I know it is – and adopt future children. I assume abortion is out?"

She nodded, then said, "Yes. I couldn't, just couldn't."

"A lot of women can't," I agreed. "I'm not sure what if I could have done if the issue presented itself to me with either of my kids."

She looked at her husband and said, "Can I think about it? I mean, I'm so worried about Marcus that I'm afraid I might make a bad or hasty decision."

"Yeah," he answered. "You don't need to decide right now."

Another ten minutes passed before Bobby Garrison appeared in the hallway with Sandy Peterson. They had an answer.

Daniel said, "I want Doctor Six to tell me. Only her."

"No problem," I said and went to Sandy. She held the report.

Sandy held out the report to me and pointed to the relevant area. "You see it?"

"Yes," I said with relief. It was type 1.

"You can do this?"

"Yes," I said hugging them both. I gave the report back to Sandy and they left.

I turned to Mary, Daniel and Adela and said, "Type 1. He'll be fine. Both of you will."

The relief I felt from them was palpable. Mary began to cry and took her mother with her. Daniel hugged both of them and then turned to me and said, "You see why I found you?"

Okay, he won. I saved their lives and they were grateful, all of them. But that was when they real fun started. Why? Well, my phone rang.

It was Mario. He said, "Knoll has a press conference scheduled for tomorrow at noon, the capital steps."

Oh, goody. It was the endgame.

Time to put *that* crap to bed.

CHAPTER 38

Mom called when we were en route to Helena.
"Evie?"
"Yes, Mom."
"I had a staffer do some research on that law and you are exactly right. How did you know that?"
"It was in *A Beauty That Transforms*." I waited.
"Oh, no."
I smiled. "Oh, yes. Dad wrote a most beautiful love story about an Eskimo girl and had to research that law and their culture before he could do what he wanted to do with the story. I take that you didn't read it?"

Brad Chang, my nominal stepfather, is a writer of some renown. He totally credits Grandma Nikki with his success, a thing I hope he will explain to me someday. But I read that book when I was sixteen, just after my kidnapping ordeal and it helped me to survive the madness that tried to swamp me. I needed those warm and friendly images that he sketched about the harsh climate, the easy death that awaited people in it and how two young Yu'piks survived it and grew together in one love. But the law that outlined their survival was real and he said so in an addendum he added to the book.

"Well, I am now," she said.
"But I'm okay with it?" I asked.
"Yes, you are."
"Thanks, Mom."
"Hey, what are mothers that are US Senators for unless you can get them to do your homework and send you to class on time?"
I laughed. "Yeah, what are mothers worth otherwise?"
"You be good," she said.
"I'll be in touch."

We arrived in Helena in good time. With me were Mario, Daniel Freeman, William Moore and Ray Stocker. No one else was necessary and I asked everyone to stay home, at ours. Wanda went ballistic. "There are women in short skirts there! And heels! And blonds! You can't ask me to…"

Moore stroked her cheek, hugged her and said, "I see only you, Fire Dawn. You need not worry. I will come back to you."

"I'll miss you." she wailed.

"No more than I will miss you."

We rehearsed en route. I insisted. Everyone knew their role and everyone was prepared to do them. We rehearsed right up until we saw the crowd around the capitol.

It was intense. Knoll had advertised his speech as "Catching Layne Red-handed". His handout to the local press indicated that he had evidence that Layne was smuggling illegal whalebones from Alaska and jade from China. I knew both charges were bogus, but my motive for being here had nothing to do with justice, personal or otherwise. It had everything to do with Daniel Freeman and his journey to the light. Such are the things I will do for my patients.

Helena, Montana, doesn't attract much attention on the national stage. Still, a governor accused of smuggling *anything* from China was news. Yes, the media was there. All the news vans, all the cameras, all the recording devices, all the fools, all the charlatans and all the people who thought, "Aha! Another politician with his hand in the bag." We stood at the back of the crowd that numbered in the thousands and waited our turn. I was certain it was going to come.

Knoll appeared about fifteen minutes later. I felt bad for Freeman because his mother, Petra, stood shoulder-to-shoulder with Knoll. Maybe it was a sign, but no one else from the militia group appeared with him. Maybe the rest of the troops weren't as stupid as I feared.

It was only after Knoll started that I thought a gemstone expert might be handy. *Don't worry about it, girl. Just do what you came to do. Right a wrong and make sure it stands up.* Anyway, Knoll said as the cameras rolled and the listening devices listened, "I have proof that Governor Donald Layne is illegally smuggling both whalebone artifacts from Alaska and jade from China. I am going to name names and hope that the authorities of Montana will do the right thing here."

I don't think anyone would begrudge Layne from smuggling jade from China. No, not because they're chinks, but because they're communists. But whalebones? Whales have a protected status in our culture and I don't mean that legally. Whales are thought to be noble creatures that cannot withstand the technological superiority of humans. They are thought to be intelligent and reactive to their environment. It was here that Knoll was going to make his inroads on public thought. He was going to downplay the jade and hammer away at the helpless creatures Layne was exploiting. He did.

With his face bristling with cameras, recording devices of all kinds and microphones, he began. He held up samples of the gems. "Jade from China. It entered this country a week ago on the Blackfoot Reservation just northwest of Browning at the airstrip there." Then he held up the long whalebones and said, "Bones from a sperm whale! Butchered for his bones and what potions can be made from them! Sperm whales, people!" he said holding them high. Then he named his first name.

"William Moore, a known criminal from the Blackfoot Reservation, took the package that contained these things and exchanged them for money. That person was Mary Freeman, wife of Daniel, who until eighteen months ago served as a bodyguard for Governor Layne. He received fifty thousand dollars each time he performed this exchange and he did it at least eighteen times in the last eighteen months. Fifty thousand dollars a month for smugglings things for the governor of the state is a good living." Then he screamed, "But sometimes, it was more than that! Sometimes he got as much as a hundred thousand dollars for the things Layne smuggled into the country!" Then he screamed, "Impeach Governor Layne!"

The inevitable questions began.

Curiously, not one of them asked for proof that the items came from either Moore and Layne. It dawned on me that Knoll could have held up anything and made that accusation. It was a moment of insight that was not lost on me.

"Folks?" I said as the questions became monotonous and repetitive. "Get ready and follow me if you have the stomach for it."

I edged my way through the crowd until I was near enough the front where Knoll would easily see me when I started to talk. I did. "Hey, Tom!" I called out from the crowd. "Are you going to let me talk or do I have to tell them how you know me?"

Every digital and recording device in the crowd pointed at me. Some of the reporters started shouting questions. Most of them were of the, "How do you know him?" type. Still, I waited for an answer.

"She'll lie to you," he said.

"Let her speak!" a few people shouted in disjointed calls that soon became more organized.

Petra looked like she wanted an hour alone with me in a closed room. Still, both of them stepped aside. I walked to the podium, Freeman, Moore and Stocker behind me.

The array of cameras and recording devices in front of me made me wonder what Mom got out of this. Anyway, I was here because a patient's life demanded me to be. I started by introducing myself. "I am Doctor Evangeline Monica Sixkiller-Collins Collins. Doctor Six for short. My practice is in Kalispell." Then I smiled because Mom always said that smiles help. "For those of you who don't know, that's in northwestern Montana. I'm a GP there."

I turned and motioned for Freeman to stand next to me. He did. He did not smile. "This is Daniel Freeman, the man Thomas Knoll referred to in his speech. I met him not quite a week ago when he sought me out for medical attention. He

Whalebone

has a condition that is under control." Then I added, "As an aside, our fear was that his young son a fatal version of that condition. He does not. Both should survive the illness and live more-or-less normal lives, depending of course what you folks do to them."

Snickers.

"But without going into all that tedium about how I met Mr. Freeman and Mr. Knoll," I said turning to Knoll, "can I have one of the pieces of jade?"

He gave me one. Reluctantly.

Then I tossed it to the first person in front of the podium, a guy in a suit holding a recording device in his outstretched hand. He caught it and Is aid, "Sir? That is not jade. Trust me here. I know what jade looks like. That gem is called hiddenite. While I could be wrong, that gem is mined in only one place in the world – North Carolina. That gem did not come from China." Then I reached into my purse and extracted my first document. I handed it to the same guy and said, "That's a copy of a shipping manifest from UPS. Please note that the place from where the gems were shipped was from a place called Hiddenite, North Carolina. I'll let you figure out where that is." Then I called out to the crowd, "Can we rest on that score? Governor Layne imported a gem from North Carolina. Okay, his manner of getting it here was a bit out of the ordinary, but unless using UPS to ship a package from North Carolina is illegal, the governor is off the hook on that one."

The guy in front of me asked, "That's all well and good but trading in whale products is illegal."

Aha.

I smiled at him and said, "Actually, no it isn't." And held my smile until he bit.

"How so?"

"By a law passed in 1972 and amended in 1981, the Yu'pik Eskimos of Alaska have the legal right to trade and sell items that they catch and/or acquire. The only catch is that the shipments can only be domestic. If the package containing those bones came through Canada or any other country, then the governor would be guilty of what Mr. Knoll accused him of being." I rummaged in my purse again and produced another golden UPS shipping manifest. I read from it, "The original package shipped from a place called Bethel, Alaska, about two weeks ago. It arrived in Anchorage and was shipped to Helena, Montana where it was delivered to a man named Theodore Hentley. From there, it wound up in Browning at a place Mr. Freeman can describe better than I can." I turned to Daniel and said, "The floor is all yours, Danny."

Daniel did not want Mary involved in this. Rather than argue about it, she agreed that by staying with their son and arranging the proper medical care for him was a better utilization of her time. He had her story and started with it.

"The money my wife gave to Moore came from Ted Hentley. That much is true. Why would he pay William Moore for a shipment he already paid for? I have no idea. You can ask him. Lastly? Yes, it is true that I worked on Governor Layne's bodyguard detail. That much is true also. The rest of the story?" Well, *he* smiled and said, "Is none of your business." Then he added as he agreed to, "My wife received the money from Hentley. Yes. She agreed to give it to Moore, a man she recognized because she was shown his picture by Hentley. Her instructions were to give it to him and no one else." Then he turned to Moore and said, "I think that takes us Mr. William Moore."

Moore stood like Rushmore at the podium. Finally, he spoke. "I have a record," he said in the same stoic voice I'd long since gotten used to. "I was arrested and convicted of breaking and entering ten years ago. I did not serve time; I received a probationary sentence. While I have never been caught or convicted of smuggling I have done it, but not since I started working for the government. I believe the technical term for my services is 'informant'." Then he curled his right hand into a fist and said emphatically, "And for the record: I have never informed on anyone. Period. They simply needed a way to describe my services. Also for the record: I was paid ten percent of whatever package I moved. Also for the record: I did my own investigation of what they were asking me to do and I have always known that I was doing nothing more illegal than taking a white man's money. In this case, the governor's."

If it was possible, he stood a bit straighter and said, "Until recently, I thought all white people were a bit crazy. Now? There is at least one that I will take very, very seriously. Fire Dawn? I know you're watching. This is for you." Then he said, "I agree with Mr. Freeman. I have no idea why Layne would ask Hentley to hire my services in delivering a package that he'd already paid for." His smile was small and enigmatic. "You'd have to ask him." He uncurled his hand and placed both of them flat on the podium. Then he finished with, "The money I was given was delivered back to Hentley on a road just outside of town. He gave me ten percent of it and then asked in every single transaction if that was enough. Ten percent of easy money? It was always enough. My only regret is that it is probably over." Then he looked at Ray Stocker and said, "And my friend, Ray Stocker, will finish this."

Stocker is shorter than either Freeman or Moore. His features are dark like Moore's but slender like Freeman. He wears his black hair shorter than Moore's but longer then Freeman's. I didn't know him and wondered if he was trustworthy. I was about to find out.

His voice was heavy and firm. "My job was to take the packages that came here to Helena back to Browning and take them to various places and bury them. Then I was tell Mary Freeman where they were buried and she was to dig them up and make sure Moore got them. I received twenty-five hundred dollars each time I did these things. Are they illegal?" He laughed. "I knew the packages came from the United States because I paid the shipping charges in every case. Who am I? Am I am Governor Layne's personal pilot. I know where each of those packages came from, what they contained and that there was nothing illegal in any of the transactions. The governor paid for them out of his funds and then paid Moore the same way. Like Mr. Freeman and Mr.

Moore before me, I have no idea why Governor Layne would do these things. But he did and spent a lot of his own money in the process." Then he looked at me and said, "I think this is where Doctor Six wraps it up."

The three men stood directly behind me. "Folks?" I said with my mother's smile. "The only reason I'm here is for truth and fair play. Mr. Knoll cannot have known these things and cannot be faulted for thinking Governor Layne was guilty of something. If it becomes necessary to stand before a judge and swear to these things, I will do it most eagerly. I think that ends what I and we came to say. Thank you."

Well, every reporter and person there began shouting questions. I had no intention of answering them, however. But just as I began to walk away from the podium and all the various microphones, the capital doors above and behind me opened and Governor Donald Layne came down the steps accompanied by Ted Hentley.

It was *really* time to put this crap to bed.

Really.

CHAPTER 39

Layne's face was neutral as he descended the long steps, and so was Hentley's. When he preached the podium, he reached out his right hand and said quizzically, "Doctor Collins?"

"Yes," I answered with a smile. "But before you do anything? I have to admit that I didn't vote for you." Left unsaid was that I didn't vote for anyone. I'd admit to being too busy being a doctor to make time, but that sounds stupid even to me – and I did it.

"Well, the information I got was that you live in Montana so that makes you a constituent," he said with a winning smile.

"I do. Kalispell."

Then he said it. "Let's finish this."

"Sure," I answered. "Whatever 'this' is."

"No time like the present to find out."

And he took the podium.

Hentley guided all of us – Freeman, Moore, Stocker and myself – to a point just behind and to the left of the governor and in line with all the cameras.

Layne started with a deep and commanding voice. I could see him on horse crossing the prairie with others like him. He had that effect. "Ladies, gentlemen, the press and anyone else I missed," he started. "I think Doctor Collins and her friends deserve a thank you in several respects." He held up one finger and said, "As near as I can tell, her only reason to be doing this was her patient, Daniel Freeman." Then he held up a second finger and said, "But what pains me is that she had no reason to track down this mystery. I expected one of you to do it. I expected a member of the press, a journalist to find the motive behind this, yet none of you did. She did.

Doctor Collins did and I think that's a shame." Then he held up a third finger and said, "Did it escape anyone's notice that the program Mary Freeman was working under was written out of the budget two years ago, just when I took office? If so, how did she continue to work under the provisions of her department? Does anyone know?"

The crowd murmured, but it was of a silent sort, of a sort that held shame. He was about to tell them how deep their shame went.

"Legally, Mary Freeman's job was eliminated by an act of the legislature two years ago. By law, she should not be working on the reservation in the capacity of nurse or any other. Yet she continued. How and why? You have no idea how much this pains me to say it because someone of you should have figured this out long before now. I pay her to do her job. That much is public record. I started a private foundation that funds her job through the state. The money that Mr. Moore receives? His ten percent is written into the charter of the foundation. The rest funds Mrs. Freeman and her staff in the capital. Mr. Moore gives the money to Mr. Hentley who puts the funds in the proper places. It is all very legal and a thing I will continue to do because the Blackfoot need her services, need someone to make house calls up there."

Then he looked down the steps to where Knoll stood with Freeman's mother and said, "Yes, Daniel Freeman was one of my bodyguards, one of my best. And, yes, we have been getting regular reports from him regarding Mr. Knoll and the activities of his militia." His gaze riveted on him and he added, "And it is in one of his reports that I received notification of what Thomas Knoll was doing to Doctor Six. That is my next target."

Well, no.

I walked to the podium and said, "A moment of your time, governor. Please?"

"Pertaining to what?" he asked.

"Me," I said with my best firm face attached. "And what happened to me out there."

Knoll came running up the steps, Petra close hind him. Knoll started to berate me and I'm sure there were cameras that caught everything he said. Me? I just looked up at Layne and said, "Anything Mr. Freeman said about me is hearsay because he wasn't there when anything happened. Mr. Knoll is entitled to his opinion and I know what those are. Everything else is between him and me."

Layne looked at Knoll and said, "What Mr. Freeman described to me was a crime, a most serious one."

"And what happened is past and I prefer to forget it," I said insistently.

"Why?" he said. "Knoll and his ilk can be put away for a long time. You'd sleep easier."

"The way I sleep is none of your business," I said with a bit more venom than I intended. "If you press charges against him, you will need my cooperation and I can guarantee that I will have an attack of amnesia in this matter. Knoll is not guilty of anything you are not guilty of yourself. He has an opinion, just like you do. Maybe his methods are out of the middle ages but you aren't going to change them. Maybe you should make that speech about constituents to him and not to me. I think he needs it more than I do."

Hentley was there, just behind him and listening to everything we said to each other. Finally, he said lowly so that the cameras wouldn't hear, "Don? Leave it." Then he nodded toward Petra and said, "And ask her how she feels."

Layne did. He looked at Freeman's mother and said, "I know you to be Petra Freeman, ma'am. And you're with Mr. Knoll. How do you feel about this?"

Actually, I didn't care how she felt. But listen? Okay. I would and did. Still, knowing that she was in this for herself and no one else, I expected nothing from her but self-serving nonsense. What I got was something else.

She turned to me and said, "I apologize to you, Doctor Collins. My mistake was in listening to Tom's bullshit. I wish there were more people like you in the world, more people willing to reach across the table with an open hand rather than a clenched fist."

Considering she, too, tried to kill me, that was quite a statement.

Then she turned to Knoll and said, "And you're going to ask me to marry you and I'm going to say yes. I am going to ask Mary if she'll be my matron of honor and I suggest that you ask Danny to be your best man. Understand?"

He looked like a shell shock victim, or as the current generation calls, a victim of Post-Traumatic Stress Disorder. I think they describe the same condition. In either case, Knoll had the spacey-eyed look of a victim. Then he stammered, "Okay."

She spat back, "And your stupid militia? Where are they? Or am I the only person that noticed they aren't here?"

Daniel nodded toward the crowd, "Well, there's one of them."

I looked in the direction he had indicated and saw John Donor out of uniform. Dressed in a khaki t-shirt and Levi's, he was toward the back of the crowd. I waved at him and called out, "John! Come on up!"

He smiled, waved back and began weaving his way through the dense crowd. Once up the steps to where we stood talking, I hugged him and said, "Thank you for delivering the blood sample."

"Well, I knew it belonged to Freeman. He was always decent to us and I came to respect him. Is he okay?"

"He will be. He has a condition that is treatable and he will start soon."

"That's great," Donor said. Then to Knoll, he said, "And I quit. You're an…"

I just smiled and filled in the blank. "equally qualified person to give an opinion on a subject no one else agrees with."

"Yeah, that," he said without a smile.

Well, all this was fine, but it still left unanswered the basic question of: why whalebones and hiddenite? And why all the other shipments? And what were they? Okay, tweaking the press is probably warranted in this country, but besides funding a canceled government program personally,

Whalebone

what was reason for those particular items? I wanted to know but wanted to keep Layne's options to himself. So I asked, "Can I ask you a question in private?"

"Here?" he asked with a politician's smile.

I nodded toward the top of the steps and said, "Up there?"

"Sure."

It was just us at the top of the capitol steps. We had our backs to the crowd, me because that was how he was standing and him because he knew the power of microphones. "So, Doctor Collins? Ask your question."

I was curious, that's all. I said, "I can understand the hiddenite, the gems. You can use them for anything. A necklace, a bracelet, or charm. Anything. But whalebones? What use were they?"

His answer was a curious mixture of love and intrigue. "You're right. Katy fell in love with the gem when she saw someone wearing a necklace with the stones in it. I might be a politician, but I also love my wife, so I determined to find the gems and then have them put into several pieces of jewelry. Our anniversary is soon and they will be made into a matching set of necklace, bracelet and rings." Then he smiled and said, "I'll have Katy call on your in your office. I'll let her explain the whalebones."

And he wouldn't discuss it further.

I was going to have to wait for Katy Layne to pay me a visit in order to discover why I had endured such personal hatred from so many of Thomas Knoll's henchmen.

It was two weeks later. I was so mad at Layne for cold-shouldering me that I decided not to vote for him again. Then I added, *well, if I vote at all, I'm not voting for you.*

Uh huh.

Two weeks later…

CHAPTER 40

I was with Savory Wright, a teenager who believed in vampires, witchcraft and all that implies. Yeah, she had *a lot* of tattoos and most of them were unintelligible to me. She was there because she was *convinced* she'd been bitten a vampire. She turned her head to the left and said, "See? I was bitten by a vampire. This proves they're real."

Her mother, a piece of work named Noreen, beamed triumphantly. I understand both genetics and the impact of the environment, so it didn't necessarily follow that the daughter was as stupid as the mother because of their genetics. It could easily be that their lifestyle had kicked in and that genetics played no part in this.

The bite was red, but did not look as though there was any venom in it. Had there been, she could easily be exhibiting signs other than teenage stupidity. There was one wound and it appeared to have been several days old. "I thought vampires left two wounds. There is only one."

Her mother, a daughter of the American entertainment industry, said as though she had a special insight on vampires, "He probably lost a fang in a fight."

"Ah," I said. "While that might be, this isn't a vampire bite. You've been bitten by a hobo spider. It's oozing from the center and it will most likely leave a scar, but you're in luck. You're neither in danger of becoming a vampire nor falling ill to a bite. I don't think you will have any complications." But then I looked at her mother and said, "But Noreen? If she starts getting headaches, you bring her here immediately. That is a complication you don't want to assign to a vampire. All a vampire will do is turn her into one of them. This bite? This could lead to trouble you don't want to risk. Other signs including nausea, vomiting and signs she might have the flu. If any of that happens, you call me. Do you understand?"

"A hobo spider?" she asked *stupidly*. She was outside her expertise – and that was vampires and the occult. Living in *this* world is much too complicated for her.

"Yes. They're common in gardens and I know you have a big one and that Savory helps you in it. How are the dahlia's doing?"

"Oh, good," she said rallying. "So, Savory wasn't bitten by a vampire."

"Um, no. Vampire bites don't look like that. They're deep puncture wounds that go all the way to the jugular and this one was made by a creature with fangs much shorter than the ones your average vampire has."

Well, Savory started whining, but that was all I could so for her. The last thing I heard was Noreen saying to Savory, "She's right. Vampire bites are deeper and they come in pairs. You tell me if you start to feel nauseous."

They left and I readied myself for my next patient. That was a guy named Sidney Long. He'd developed a cough and I suspected the lingering effects of a flu bug. I didn't think he was in serious jeopardy.

When I stepped into the outer office, Daniel Freeman was standing at the counter in front of Flo. Flo turned and looked at me. "This young man, Mr. Freeman, is accompanied by a woman who wants to see you. He says it's an emergency." Then she said, "I think Mr. Long can wait."

I looked at Danny and said, "And her problem is?"

He smiled and said, "I'll let her explain it."

The door opened and Katy Layne, Montana's First Lady, stepped into the office. Freeman turned to her and said, "And that's the last time I leave you outside, Mrs. Layne. My job is to keep you safe."

She hugged Daniel and said, "Well, thank you for playing along, Mr. Freeman."

He rolled his eyes and said, "Protect her from harm and what do you get? Mr. Freeman."

"Down, Danny," she teased. Then she looked at me and said, "You must be Doctor Six."

"Guilty," I said bowing.

"Well, Donald suggested that I come here, so here I am. Can we be alone?"

"Sure," I said thinking of the room Savory and Noreen just exited. "Follow me."

The weather in Montana in September is iffy. It rained today, so I wore a black turtleneck that matched my umbrella. Katy wore a plum–colored one that was baggy and looked comfortable.

"Donald asked me to give you an answer about the whalebones," she said once we were in the room. She has beautiful shoulder-length auburn hair and the cheekbones of a model. Maybe she was a model once. I mean, I'm not a political junkie, so I don't follow all the latest news. In fact, the only thing I knew about Katy Layne was that her name was Katy and not Kathryn. Maybe I knew subliminally that she had auburn hair, but it certainly wasn't conscious knowledge. It came as a pleasant surprise.

"Oh," I said as though I'd forgotten. I was still fuming over his brush-off of me. "Okay, what was so special about those whalebones?"

God, she *blushed* and it looked better on her than on Wanda. "Well," she said hesitantly. "In order to show you, I have to remove my sweater. Is that okay?"

I laughed. "Sure. I'm a medical professional. I doubt you have any new pieces of anatomy."

She sighed and said, "This is so embarrassing."

"Let me be the judge of that."

"Okay," she said and slowly lifted her sweater over her head. I saw where the whalebones had gone before she had the sweater off.

A corset.

And, damn, it was beautiful. Black and red vertical stripes and a bodice that even my mother would envy.

"Donald asked me to tell you not to say anything about it. There are activists that would cause him lots of grief. The bones that made this corset are over a hundred years old and the seller verified it before Donald bought them." Then she grimaced and said, "Okay? Please?"

I smiled and said, "Oh, hell, no. I'm going to tell everyone I know starting with my receptionist."

"Doctor…" she started to beg.

"Unless…" I countered.

"Anything."

"I saw that shipment and there were a lot more bones that are in that corset. You tell whoever made this that he needs to make another one for me." Then I smiled and said, "That's my price."

She extended her hand, smiled and said, "Oh, doctor. You drive a hard bargain."

I took her hand, shook it and said, "So, it's agreed?"

"My corsetiere will call you as soon as I get home."

Well, you'd think that it ended there. Right? I had answers, patients and felt rested for the first time in months.

But, no.

There was one, no there were three more pieces of information ahead of me.

And then it was done.

CHAPTER 41

"We need a poker game," I said to Mario about two weeks later.

"Anything to show off your new corset, huh?"

"Damn right," I said. "Set it up."

That was a Wednesday. By Friday night we had *seventeen* people who wanted to come to our poker game. I told Mario to invite all of them and we could fight over who actually got to play cards and who got to gawk. My biggest fear was: *what if no one does, gawk, I mean?* Well, that was the chance I was going to take. I was going to wear it and try to look *svelte*.

The seventeen invitees turned into thirty-one people. It was the biggest crowd we'd ever had at our home. Had anyone else showed up in a corset, I might have cried. Wanda showed up in her red Playboy bunny suit and actually cried real tears when she saw me in my corset. "It's not fair," she cried on Moore's shoulder. Oh, *he* showed up first. A knock came at the door and it was him. He was dressed as a Kalispell police officer, long hair and all. He said in his usual grave voice, "We have reports of a disturbance at this address."

I stared up at him with my best Popeye look and growled, "The only disturbance that is going to happen is if you start it, *William*." His job was real, a gift from the governor.

Anyway, Wanda muscled past him and growled, "Oh, stuff it, Collins.." and then she saw me and started crying.

Moore lifted her at least a foot off the ground and kissed her in a way that made me want to find both Mario and a bedroom. He said to her calmly and passionately, "No one is as beautiful as you, Fire dawn."

Her eyes bulged and she cried, "You *have* seen her, haven't you?"

"Yes, She doesn't compare."

All that meant was that she pestered me all night long for where I got it. Finally, out of exasperation, I said, "I'll make a call and we'll get you fitted."

Mine was pure white. She wanted a red one.

"And shoes!" she barked. "I want the same shoes you have!"

Black five-inch heels. Nothing special. I know she has at least three pairs of heels, and a few with taller heels.

"Sure."

Her best news was their engagement. They were planning a January wedding, four months away. We squealed like school kids on the playground and jumped up and down to boot. I was so happy that I didn't mind that *everyone* stopped and watched me jiggle.

Well, the game wound up in three places because so many people wanted to play. Flo Pillow has been to all of our games and she's the best poker player I've ever seen. Unflappable, thy name is Flo Pillow. She comes to play and win and she usually does. Cayn is pretty good, too. He claims he wins a lot because he's gay and our outfits don't distract him. Well, maybe. Norma Young, my PA, was there with Kris Tice, a doctor who works in the ER at Kalispell Regional. They're gay and have been a couple for about eighteen months. Kris came in a Playboy bunny outfit but it was Norma who grumped when she saw me. "That should be illegal," she said indicating my corset. Kris giggled and the night continued.

Danny and Mary Freeman showed up. Danny had had his first enzyme therapy session, had the IV shunt installed and even looked better. Adela had Marcus and their report on him was very upbeat.

The biggest surprise of the night were Thomas and Petra Knoll. Yep, they married. They found a justice of the peace, got Daniel and Mary to help them and showed up looking happy. Well, Knoll looked nervous around me until I got him alone and hugged him. "Don't be nervous, Tom. I'm cool."

"Um, I'm not nervous because of those nights, but because you are the most beautiful woman I've ever seen and Petra is the jealous type. Please. Don't do this." Well, that meant I had to find Petra and calm her. She just laughed and said, "Oh, don't worry. That's my way of making sure he doesn't stare at you all night."

Well, it was a good night by everyone. I got enough stares and gawks to satisfy my vanity quotient. Mario even won a pot and his winnings totaled thirty-seven cents. Yeah, we play for pennies. I had to learn how to dip in my corset because I couldn't bend. At all. My job is usually to keep the drinks and goodies flowing. I make certain that no one gets stinking drunk – or he sleeps upstairs. But try as I might, I couldn't stop Wanda from dropping pennies down my bodice. Each time she did, she stuck out her tongue and said, "You deserve quarters and barb wire."

The first of the two things that happened to end this came when the doorbell sounded. I went to it because it was late and I didn't expect more partiers. I had no idea who to expect and was surprised when it was Violet and David Hatemen.

"Well, hi," I said with clear surprise in my voice.

She had *a lot* of luggage behind her and was holding David's hand.

"Oh, god," she said putting her hand to her face. "I get to work for crazy white people."

Travis saw David through the doorway and came running. He pulled him into the house and they disappeared to the third floor.

I wanted to ask what she meant by "working for" when Mario skirted past me and said, "Oh, cool. You're here! Let me get Cayn to help with your luggage."

Mario kissed me and said, "Meet the newest member of the family. I promised not to call her a maid. But she's going to be here from now on and she gets whichever room she wants."

Violet waved her hand at me and said, "And how often does this happen? If I have to stare at this all day long, I don't think my pride could stand it."

"Whenever we have poker night," I said. "And that doesn't happen nearly as often as I'd like."

She looked at Mario, "I have another condition."

He smiled. Babe?" he said to me. "Take her with you when you get Wanda's fitted."

"About a week?" I said.

She extended her hand. "Deal."

"Welcome to the family," I said.

And that's how Violet – Vee – came to live with us. Mario paid her and told her *never* to tell me how much she was earning. That was their arrangement and I lived it because it didn't matter how much she got from us. She was smart, energetic and a wonder with the kids. It was later the next afternoon when the idea hit me. I was watching Violet and the kids. Travis and Maddy already loved her and David looked at home.

"Hey, Vee?" I asked.

"Deep red, almost burgundy," she said. "And I want the laces to tighten all the way down."

"Well, okay," I laughed, "but that's not what I wanted to ask you."

"Strapless."

"Okay."

She finally smiled and said, "Okay, what?"

"Do people on the reservation need medical help beyond what Mary Freeman provides?"

"Yes," she answered immediately. "While there is a nice medical center in Browning, there are hundreds of people living miles from town that almost never see a doctor until it's too late. Why?"

And I told. "I'm going to arrange it with Mary, but I want to donate a weekend a month traveling to people on the reservation that don't see doctors. It would better if Mary accompanied me, but that's not necessary."

In the end, Mary was ecstatic and became my nurse when I traveled around the Blackfoot Reservation. I don't know who started it, but most of the people I met already knew of me and they called me, "The crazy corset doctor." I had one old Blackfoot who steadfastly refused to cooperate until he saw why I was called that. Well, damn. I had to donate a second weekend that month and that's when I made the discovery that doctors and corsets don't agree very well. But the old Blackfoot grunted and extended his arm, palm up. "Take your blood." But he smiled and never once looked me in the eye.

And that left the third thing that had been left undone.

Well, not undone actually because it was already done. I just had to tell someone

CHAPTER 42

Mario *really* liked the corset. He got to be the best person at getting me into it. Wanda tried but I don't think she wanted mine to look better than hers. Oh, look,. She's absolutely frigging gorgeous and doesn't need a corset like I do. Well, no one agrees with me, but I know a fat ass when I see it. Anyway. A corset looks second-rate when the laces aren't all the way tight. When it gets that way, I feign not being able to breathe and that leads to sex. Between Mario and I, I mean. Vee had the same issue as Wanda. I think they conspired to make my corset look like I was too fat to get all the way into it. At least I think that's what their high-fives meant.

I actually cried one night after the three of us had our pictures taken wearing our corsets. Wanda and Vee got theirs all the way closed but I had two inches of skin showing up my back. Wanda looked crushed. "It's the best I could do, Evie," she said and then high-fived Vee behind my back.

Well, Mario to the rescue.

He saw how upset I was that night and brought it out. He laced me up as tight as it would go and then said, "I think your friends are just jealous."

Well, to men, gratitude sex counts as much as any. We even did it while I still was wearing it. Lord, that was weird.

But that's not what the third thing was.

That happened about six weeks later.

I suspected it, but needed a test first. I could have gone to the hospital, gotten one done in my office, but then everyone would have known the results before the one person that needed to know more than anyone.

Yep. I got a home pregnancy test.

Mario got home from the school late that night, Vee had the kids at a movie and I was alone when he got home. Giddy? You have no idea. I was so happy that Mario saw the change in me as soon as he opened the door.

"What's wrong?"

With my right index finger in my mouth, I said, "Nothing."

"Well, then, let me ask it another way. What's up?"

"Oh, nothing." I said. I felt more alive than I had in a very long time. And happy? Well, my face was probably next to that word in the dictionary.

"Evie," he said. "Please. Just tell me. If it's something bad, I can handle it."

"Oh, seriously," I said. "It's nothing. Don't worry about it."

Well, that was a planned response. If I knew anything about my husband, it was that all I had to do was use the word "worry" in a sentence and he would. Well, worry about me. He's been that way since I was four.

He sat down next to me, took my hand and said, "Please, Evie. Tell me. What's wrong?"

I cannot hold secrets from him. I mean, period. I try and he finds out just by touching me. He took my hand and looked at me tenderly and asked one more time. "Evie? What is it?"

And all those feelings for him came rushing back like they always did. He completes me, makes my life better than it would be, makes me a better person just for knowing him, makes me a better mother by being his wife. I see him in our children and only hope that they got more of him than they got of me. He's patient with me, tender and giving. There are times when I wonder if my meager efforts at being his wife is equal to his efforts to be his husband. Sometimes, I am cruel to him in little ways. I discount him, ignore him and assume he will take care of things that I have no right to ask. And he does. He is always there and never with an ulterior motive. He never expects anything but what I have to offer. Could he get more from someone else? Probably. But he loves me and I only that he takes my news and happily as I did.

"Mario? I'm pregnant."

Then I held my breath.

And he shouted with delirious joy.

And hugged me.

And danced with me.

And held me as my heart overflowed with happiness.

Then he kissed me and I grew into him, melted with him and didn't want to let go. I think they call it love. If so, I can live in it forever.

And ever.

www.ingramcontent.com/pod-product-compliance
Lightning Source LLC
LaVergne TN
LVHW021809060526
838201LV00058B/3300